The Darkest Corner

LILIANA HART

The
Darkest
Corner

POCKET BOOKS

New York   London   Toronto   Sydney   New Delhi

Pocket Books
An Imprint of Simon & Schuster, Inc.
1230 Avenue of the Americas
New York, NY 10020

This book is a work of fiction. Any references to historical events, real people, or real places are used fictitiously. Other names, characters, places, and events are products of the author's imagination, and any resemblance to actual events or places or persons, living or dead, is entirely coincidental.

First Pocket Books paperback edition June 2017

POCKET and colophon are registered trademarks of Simon & Schuster, Inc.

For information about special discounts for bulk purchases, please contact Simon & Schuster Special Sales at 1-866-506-1949 or business@simonandschuster.com.

The Simon & Schuster Speakers Bureau can bring authors to your live event. For more information or to book an event, contact the Simon & Schuster Speakers Bureau at 1-866-248-3049 or visit our website at www.simonspeakers.com.

Interior design by Bryden Spevak

Manufactured in the United States of America

10 9 8 7 6 5 4 3 2 1

ISBN 978-1-5011-5003-6
ISBN 978-1-5011-5004-3 (ebook)

*To Scott—Because I can't think of a
better love story than our own*

PROLOGUE

The summer sun beat down with a vengeance on the day thousands would die.

Sweat glistened on pinkened skin, but the discomfort was easily forgotten with every crack of the bat. The air was stagnant—thick with humidity—and the scents of popcorn and beer mixed nauseatingly with the steam from the hot dog carts. Unforgiving metal benches blistered the thighs of those who were unfortunate enough to be seated on the east side of the stadium. The announcer said it was one of the hottest days on record for the month of June, like it was something to be excited about.

Ten-year-old Carrie Anne Fitzgibbon swatted at a horsefly as big as her thumb and shot her mother a scathing look. She didn't see why they had to drive all the way from San Antonio to stupid Omaha, Nebraska, just to watch her brother play baseball. Brothers were the *worst*.

Curt had ruined everything. Julie was her best friend in the whole world and Julie would never ever have another tenth birthday party, even though Julie's parents had promised her she could have post-birthday cupcakes with Carrie once they returned. It wasn't the same. Her life was ruined.

"Stop pouting, Carrie," her father said. "Look, Curt is up to bat next."

She sat between her parents, her arms crossed over her chest, and tried not to show interest in her brother, who was currently taking practice swings inside the stupid little circle. She hoped he struck out.

"This is a once-in-a-lifetime opportunity," her mother said. "The Bulldogs have never made it to the College World Series before. This is history in the making."

"Julie's birthday party would've been history in the making," she muttered under her breath.

Her mother reached into the small cooler at her feet and pulled out one of the icy washrags to lay on the back of her neck. Her blond hair was the same color as Julie's, pulled back into a ponytail.

"Can you imagine getting to play in front of twenty thousand people?" her mother went on excitedly. "It'll be something he can tell his grandkids one day. And there are pro scouts here. This could be his chance to get into the majors."

Carrie's denim shorts and royal-blue Bulldogs shirt clung damply to her skin, and she wished she'd listened to her mother's suggestion to wear a baseball cap. The top of her head felt like it was on fire from the heat.

"Whoop-de-do," Carrie said sarcastically.

"I've had enough of your attitude, young lady," her

father said. "You'll straighten up right now if you want to see Julie when we get back home. Otherwise, you can be grounded for the rest of the summer."

She kicked the back of the seat in front of her, but knew not to push it. Her dad had his angry face on, and the last thing she wanted was to be cooped up inside the house for the rest of the summer.

"Can I get some popcorn?" she asked, deciding to switch tactics.

"Good idea," her dad said, whistling between his teeth as Curt was announced to bat. He took his wallet out of his back pocket and pulled out a twenty without taking his eyes off of home plate. Her mother had her iPhone out and was busy recording.

They don't even care about me, Carrie thought angrily. All they've ever cared about was stupid Curt and his stupid baseball. She'd heard her grandma say once that Carrie had been their accident baby. Her mom, her dad, and Curt had probably been perfectly happy before she came along.

They probably wished she'd never been born.

She shoved the money in her pocket and made her way to the aisle, apologizing to an old man for stepping on his foot in the process. And then she ran up the concrete steps all the way to the top, tears stinging her eyes.

It wasn't much cooler in the shade under the covered area where the concession stands were, but at least she was out of the sun. The stadium was huge, and the covered area went the entire way around the ballpark.

Dad hadn't told her to stay close or come back quick

like he usually did, so she decided maybe she'd get her snacks from the other side. Maybe they had different choices. As she set off, her stomach felt squishy because she knew she'd get in trouble if they found out how far she was going. But she tilted her pointed chin and walked off defiantly. It's not like they would notice she was gone anyway. They were too busy with *Curt*.

She heard the crack of the bat and the crowd go wild with cheers. Curt must have done something good, but she didn't stop to try and see what was happening with the game.

It wasn't until she'd been walking awhile that she realized she couldn't remember what the number was for the section where their seats were. The butterflies in her stomach were fluttering harder and she really had to go to the bathroom, but she stood in line at the concession stand on the opposite side of the park, one that served the exact same food as the one she'd seen just by their seats.

Carrie ordered a hot dog with chili and cheese and a Coke, because she wasn't supposed to have soft drinks. She figured she might as well break all the rules she could at one time. Once she had paid and shoved the change back into her pocket, she took her dog and her drink and started back the way she'd come.

A glimpse of the field caught her eye. She liked how green the grass was and that they'd cut it to look like a checkerboard. The sand was reddish, and she'd watched in fascination as they'd wet it down before the game started. Her dad always said there was nothing in the world like baseball—the people, the energy, the loyalty to the team whether they won or lost.

Carrie stood in the arched opening that led to a section of seats and looked at the crowd, swallowing hard at the thought of finding her parents again among so many people. She took a deep breath and tried to think about what she'd been told to do if she was ever lost. There was no policeman she could ask for help, at least not that she could see, and there was no way she was staying put and waiting for someone to find her. It would be hours.

She tried to remember what their section looked like, and then it hit her. They'd been sitting just behind home plate. And from where she was standing now she could see the front of the batter, and she had an even better view of the outfielders. All she had to do was make it back to home plate.

Carrie breathed a sigh of relief and took a sip of Coke, wetting her dry throat. And then something curious caught her eye. A huge puff of smoke went into the air just behind the dugout. Players and people sitting in the stands scattered, climbing over each other as they tried to get onto the field. It looked like they were having trouble breathing and many of them were crawling on the ground.

The concrete beneath her feet trembled, and her shoulder bumped the wall as she lost her balance. And then there was a giant boom in the air that was louder than any of the fireworks she'd ever watched. Her Coke and hot dog dropped to the ground. Chaos erupted, and the people around her were screaming and pushing as they tried to run. Her bladder released, and urine ran down her legs as fear overtook her. She didn't know what was happening, but she stood in the middle of the fray alone, wishing for her mom and dad. She tried to run, but it felt like the ground was moving beneath her feet.

A man bumped her as he ran by, and she fell, landing inside the door to one of the restrooms. She huddled in a ball on the ground and screamed for her daddy as the earth fell apart around her. The people who'd been running seemed to fall away as the floor disappeared and the ceiling caved in.

A man leapt toward her and the opening of the bathroom, but she was too afraid to scream. She didn't want to die. She wanted her mommy and daddy. And she wanted Curt.

The man crawled in next to her, blood trickling from his head. Something huge crashed behind her, and the man screamed as the ceiling in the bathroom caved in. The entire lower half of his body was buried in the rubble, and Carrie just made herself as small as possible, her whimpers going unheard as everything crashed around her. The space in the doorway was getting smaller and smaller, and she couldn't see as clouds of dust filled the air.

"I'm sorry, I'm sorry," she sobbed. "I'm sorry, Daddy. I want to watch Curt play baseball. I'm sorry."

Carrie felt the hand of the man lying next to her as it reached for her, and she put her hand in his. She held on for dear life. And kept holding. Even as he took his last breath.

CHAPTER ONE

There was something about the time between three and four o'clock in the morning. When people with good intentions were tucked safely into their beds. When those without them crept into the alleyways like rats. And when warriors got shit done.

For Deacon Tucker, that meant it was time to get dirty.

The rain slapped against Deacon's face like tiny daggers. Lightning flashed—followed by sharp cracks of thunder—and the smell of ozone, wet dirt, and urgency lay heavy.

Deacon pushed his shovel deeper into the soggy ground, the muscles in his back straining as he lifted a mound of dirt and tossed it onto a pile over his shoulder. The four other members of his team did the same, each one stripped down to nothing but black cargo pants and combat boots, covered in a thick layer of mud. They worked in silence, an unspoken communication and familiarity between them.

The cemetery was old. It was a place where the oldest headstones told stories and the newer ones told a person's worth. It was where generations of those who shared blood now rested—a place for the elderly who had lived long and full lives and the young who had been taken too soon.

Heavy iron gates closed it off from the public after dark, and towering oaks had been planted in rows some hundred years earlier. Gnarled roots made the ground uneven, cracking the drive that snaked between the rows of headstones.

They worked by flashes of lightning and the sliver of moon that peeked around thunderheads. Everything was cast in shades of gray—from the pale marble of the headstones to the silver shimmer of water droplets as they collected on leaves and rained down on them. Black trunks speared menacingly from the ground—the branches creeping over them like bony arms.

The clank of metal on something solid made Deacon stop and look up at his brother in arms.

"I've got something," Axel said, letting his native Australian accent slip through. He pounded the tip of his shovel a couple of times against the top of the coffin.

Deacon nodded. "Let's get him uncovered. He's been here two days already. He doesn't have much longer. Grab the chains," he instructed Colin.

Deacon returned to the task at hand, doubling his efforts to clear the mud and water rapidly filling the hole. It was fortunate the casket was waterproof and had a rubberized seal around the lid. The rain had come steady for more than twenty-four hours, and changed their original timeline of removing Levi Wolffe from the ground the night before.

A man's life was at stake, and Wolffe had already been through more than most. It was going to be traumatic enough for him to wake up in a different country, surrounded by faces he'd never seen before, and unsure whether he'd been captured by the enemy. Fishing through the lies to get to the truth would take time.

Deacon knew *exactly* how Levi Wolffe was going to feel.

"Fuck me, this is a never-ending battle," Axel complained. "There's no way we're digging this thing all the way out of the muck."

"All we've got to do is uncover the handles on the sides," Deacon said. "We'll let the Bobcat do the rest."

"Got it, mate." Axel tossed his shovel out of the hole. "Give me a boost, will you?"

Deacon steepled his fingers together to make a sling and braced himself against the casket so he wouldn't slip. They were close to four feet down into the hole, but with the rain and mud, getting out wasn't going to be easy. Axel put his hand on Deacon's shoulder and his foot in the sling, and then grabbed for Dante's hand as he was boosted up.

The casket was an upper-end model—they had to be, for what they were used for—made of glossy oak and brass. Colin tossed Axel the chains, and he looped them through the handles on each side, using a carabiner to hold them together.

"Elias is ready to roll with the Bobcat," Axel called out, extending his arm to help Deacon out of the hole.

Deacon was two hundred and thirty pounds of solid muscle and a couple of inches over six feet. His boots and knees couldn't find purchase in the mud, and his grasp of Axel's hand was slipping. He finally grasped Axel's arm with both hands, hoisted his feet onto the coffin, and used his legs to push off, launching himself out of the grave.

Axel moved out of the way at the last second, and Deacon flew right into the pile of mud they'd dug up. He heard the snickers from Dante and Colin and took a fistful of mud in each hand as he got to his feet, launching it at them in quick succession. Elias's howls of laughter could be heard from inside the Bobcat.

"They'll both be out for vengeance now," Axel said, lips twitching in as close to a smile as he ever gave.

"I hope so," Deacon said. "I'd hate for things to get boring around the office."

The rain was coming down hard enough to rinse some of the mud from his torso, and he lifted his face to the sky to wash it from his cheeks. The thong tying his hair back had come loose and dark strands clung to his face. Thoughts of a hot shower and a beer were becoming a priority. Right after getting Levi Wolffe out of the ground.

"It was my understanding that Winter wasn't bringing any more of us in," Dante said as they hooked up the chains to the Bobcat and moved back out of the way. His accent was English, but he had the Italian genetics of his namesake. Dante was as refined and suave as any man Deacon had ever known. His clothes were always tailored, his haircuts expensive, and his knowledge of the finer things in life unparalleled. Standing in the pouring rain, covered in mud, was probably grating on him immensely.

"That's what she said, but who the hell knows what her plans are." Deacon had been wondering the same thing. "She only tells us what she thinks we need to know."

"Which isn't a bloody thing," Dante said.

It was a sore spot for certain. Deacon had served his country for most of his life. He'd been recruited by the CIA during his third year of college, the high scores on his aptitude tests and his skills for languages having alerted interested parties. His course in life had been clear from the moment that recruiter had left him. He'd gone on to get a master's degree and the necessary field training, which he'd also shown an exceptional aptitude for. In twelve years of covert ops, he'd never had a sleepless night after completing a mission. He'd gotten the job done. Until Eve Winter had gotten ahold of him, and everything he'd thought he'd been fighting for was turned on its head.

He didn't like being kept in the dark. He understood the hierarchy of a rank structure and the necessity of secrets. You couldn't survive in the CIA without that understanding. But his handler had once told him, *"Rules are for the obedience of fools and the guidance of wise men."* Deacon had never been a fool.

Eve Winter had saved him, and for that he was grateful. He'd never be anyone's pawn again. But here he stood, in a cemetery in the middle of the night, digging up a man who was about to have his entire life turned upside down.

Elias reversed the Bobcat, and mud spewed beneath the wheels as the chains drew taut. Inch by inch the casket was dragged out of the grave. The rain was relentless, the thunder a continuous rumbling growl. And the men stood in the middle of it, like marionettes on a string, doing the bidding of people who sat warm and comfortable and safe in their homes.

Once the casket was free and the chains unhooked, Deacon, Axel, Colin, and Dante got two to each side and lifted. Their boots slurped and sludged as they made their way to the black panel van that was owned by the Last Stop Funeral Home. A magnetic cling with the funeral home logo was attached to each side of the van.

The whole setup was bizarre, and Deacon had wondered more than once if he really was dead, only to be caught in limbo between one world and the next. But several years had passed since his own revival, so he guessed he was here to stay.

Until The Directors decided he wasn't.

They slid the casket in the back of the van and slammed the doors shut.

"Poor bastard," Colin lamented, shaking his head hard enough that water droplets flew into the air. "He has no clue what he's about to get into. That the life he knew is over."

"Dead men don't talk," Deacon said.

"Yet here we are." The anger in Colin's face was palpable. His eyes blazed with hatred for the government machine that had confined him.

"Save your anger, Col," Axel said. "What's done is done. It'll get easier over time."

"Is that what you tell yourself as you watch your wife from afar? As you wait for her to find someone new to take your place?"

"Enough, Colin," Deacon said. "We all do what we have to do to cope. Our only focus right now should be getting this poor bastard back to headquarters."

Elias used the Bobcat to push dirt back into the hole, and the others tossed their shovels and other equipment into the back of the van. The burial site for The Gravediggers was at the far corner of the cemetery, next to a thick copse of trees and two plots of unmarked headstones where paupers had been buried more than a century before.

The Shadow crew would send a team to make the area look untouched. By the time they were finished, sod would have been laid and all traces of mud tracks would be gone. They specialized in cleanup. The Shadow was never seen. They did the work and provided the resources for The Gravediggers. The Gravediggers couldn't do their jobs without The Shadow.

Colin and Dante climbed in back with the casket and closed the doors from the inside. Deacon took his place behind the wheel and Axel got in beside him. Elias drove ahead of them in the Bobcat, returning it to the storage shed where they kept the lawnmowers and other cemetery equipment.

Deacon backed the van around the curve and then put it in gear, navigating his way out of the twisting turns of the cemetery. He idled behind the menacing, black iron gate, waiting for Elias to open it once he parked the Bobcat.

"As soon as we drop the new guy, I'm heading home for eight hours of uninterrupted sleep," Colin said.

"We've got a ten o'clock briefing," Axel told him.

"This is how many fucks I give," Colin said, his hand popping between the space of the driver and passenger seats, his thumb and forefinger pressed together. "What's she going to do? Kill me? Oh, wait. I'm already dead."

Deacon exchanged a concerned look with Axel. Colin was the newest recruit, but he wasn't adjusting like the rest of them had. His anger was manifesting, and his attitude was deteriorating. Not qualities Deacon wanted to see in a man who was supposed to watch his back.

"I can't be the only one who's tired of being dicked around by that frigid bitch," Colin pressed on. "Does Eve Winter have your balls in such a stronghold that you'll listen to her lip service without question?"

Axel's eyes hardened. "There's a chain of command, mate. We've all been in the game long enough to know it. We're here for a purpose."

"Except it's not my country I'm fighting for," Colin said. "Just like you're not fighting for yours. We're all goddamned traitors."

"Bullshit," Deacon snapped, his temper finally pushed

too far. "We're fighting for every country. There are times to ask questions, once you know the right questions to ask. But foaming at the mouth because shit isn't the way it always was doesn't do a damned bit of good for anyone. Be smart, Col. If you think Winter won't cut you off at the knees and bury you alive, you're mistaken."

"Easy for you to say. You're the golden boy. The first that was handpicked. And you know The Directors personally. You have a voice."

Deacon rolled his eyes inwardly. That was an illusion, but one that he had no intention of disputing, for the innate sense of power and authority it gave him among the other men. The Directors thought he was as dead as the president and the director of the CIA did. Eve Winter might report to The Directors, but that didn't mean she didn't have her own cards up her sleeve. Deacon also knew the fact that everyone but Eve Winter thought he was dead made him very, very expendable.

Elias hopped in the back and slammed the door, and Deacon took off. The tension in the van was thick enough to choke on, and it seemed everyone would be better off with a little bit of sleep and space.

The cemetery they used as an extraction point was a good twenty-minute drive from Last Stop, where their headquarters were located. The location was strategic, just as everything else about their existence—or lack thereof—was. The Gravediggers might be the heart and soul of the operation—the men who did the dirty work—but dozens more worked in The Shadow, making sure the billions of dollars that never showed up in any government expense report were well spent. It wasn't cheap faking the deaths of elite agents all over the world and transporting them to the United States under cover.

They'd been driving down side streets, staying off the main road, for a few minutes before Axel let out a low whistle. "Shit. You seeing what I'm seeing?"

Deacon let out a slow breath. They were almost to the county line. And just on the other side of it was the town that had become his prison, ironically named Last Stop.

Truth be told they all enjoyed playing the good Samaritan. It broke up the monotony of training and typical missions—and by typical he meant dangerous as fuck, because Eve didn't send them on jobs that other agencies could do. And every once in a while, jumping into the fray and being the hero reminded them of the men they'd been once upon a time. Before their armor had been tarnished.

It wasn't the wisest move interfering in a job so close to home, but they all shared one thing in common—the need for risk in their day-to-day lives. Some would call them adrenaline junkies, but it was more than that. It was a trait all those in special ops had in common. It was the difference between turning down the dark alley just for the hell of it and moving past it safely.

They looked for risk in all things. Even sex. The rush of fucking in a crowded room and wondering if someone would see, or taking sex to its limits with the tightening of a belt around a slender neck. Risk was risk. And tonight the risk was an armed robbery.

Deacon grinned. "Yeah, I see them."

He lifted his foot off the accelerator, but didn't hit the brakes. He didn't want to scare them off.

"What's going on?" Elias asked, sticking his head between the seats.

"Burglary in progress," Deacon answered.

"Oh, good. We're cutting it close as it is. It's almost five o'clock. Sun will be up in another hour."

"Are you suggesting we let them go?" Axel asked, his voice even, as if he didn't care one way or the other. But Deacon knew Axel was the one who'd been left with the most humanity—the most compassion—of all of them. Only a man who felt deeply would still cling to his wife, after all, even though she thought he was dead.

"Of course not, mate," Elias said, mimicking Axel's accent. "But you know Winter will be pissed if she finds out. The mission comes first. Always. No distractions. And right now, our only mission is getting Levi Wolffe back to headquarters."

"In or out?" Axel said, his voice hardening.

Elias sighed. "You know I'm in. But she'll find out. She always does."

"Fuck her," Colin said dismissively.

"Very mature," Deacon said. "I'm telling you, brother, one day she's going to hand your ass to you on a platter."

"I'm French," Colin said. "I've never met a woman I can't handle."

The others hooted, and Deacon just shook his head. The French had never met a woman like Eve Winter. He wasn't really a hundred percent sure she was even human.

"Let's make it quick," Elias said. "We've still got to send the van off to be detailed. The sexy Miss Sherman is bound to notice all the mud inside one of her transport vans."

"Stop calling her that," Deacon growled. "It embarrasses her."

"Hey, it's not my fault she can't see what a package she is. I wouldn't mind helping her discover it, though. All that freakin' red hair. Drives me crazy when she sticks those pencils in it to get it out of her face."

Deacon gritted his teeth and shot Elias a look that told him he'd better shut up or he'd end up with a fist in his face, but Elias's crooked grin mocked him in the rearview mirror.

"I can't imagine how she's managed to keep her distance from you as long as she has," Dante said smoothly. "You're so charming."

"You're in America now," Elias told him. "Women like straightforward men. I'm amazed the British have managed to populate the country as long as it takes you to make your move."

"There's nothing wrong with romance," Dante said. "Besides, I haven't had any problems with an empty bed since I've been here."

"It's that accent," Elias said. "Puts the rest of us at a disadvantage."

"Or maybe it's just that I have manners."

"If you blokes don't mind," Axel said, interrupting their argument, "our new friends are armed. And since we've already agreed to deviate from the mission, maybe we can take care of business and get the hell out of here."

"Visual on two suspects," Deacon said before things could escalate. "Weapon visible."

"Thanks, Grandpa," Elias said. "Lord, the two of you need to loosen up. It's like we're in that movie with all the retired spies."

"I liked that movie," Axel said. "I could still kick your ass when I'm in my fifties."

Elias snorted. "In your dreams, *mate*. I was a SEAL."

"In other news," Deacon broke in, "the homeowners are either contained inside or they're dead." Sometimes he felt like he was the only adult in the room. An unusual feeling considering the level of expertise the five of them had.

"Let's hope everyone is still alive," Elias said. "Dead bodies are a pain in the ass to deal with."

"There you go. Always looking on the bright side." Deacon pressed his foot on the accelerator. "Picking up speed. In and out, boys. Clean and easy."

"I'd rather just kill them," Colin said. "It's not like we're going to wait around for the police one way or the other. The world doesn't need any more scum."

"Maybe you'll get lucky, bro, and one of them will shoot at you first," Elias said. "Maybe it'll knock that stick out of your ass."

Deacon heard the familiar sound of magazines being checked and loaded from the back, along with a lot of smart-ass comments he blocked out. The two males loading the big-screen TV into the maroon minivan were barely older than teenagers. Hell, they were probably using one of their mother's vans to transport the stolen goods.

"Hang on," he called out and made a hard left into the driveway of the house that was being robbed. He flicked on his brights at the last second, and it came as enough of a surprise to the amateur burglars for both the boys to drop the TV and put their hands up to shield their eyes. He turned the wheel hard, mud spewing up and hitting the windshield, and then the back doors flew open and all hell broke loose.

"Down on the ground!"

"Drop your weapons!"

Deacon and Axel pushed open their doors to join in the fray. Two rounds were fired off in rapid succession, one hitting the open back door just a few inches from Deacon's head, the other burying itself in the mahogany casket.

Elias didn't hesitate to return fire, hitting the shooter in the thigh. Deacon breathed a sigh of relief. They *really* didn't want to deal with the mess of a dead body. And it wouldn't put anyone in Winter's good graces.

The shooter tossed the gun to the ground and went down, pressing his hands down on the wound. He was crying and making a racket, so Elias chopped him in the back of the neck to get him to shut up.

"What the hell kind of person shoots a casket?" Elias asked the other boy, who stared back at him wide-eyed, his hands raised.

"I . . . I don't know," the boy answered.

"I think that was a rhetorical question," Deacon said, binding the boy's hands behind his back with a zip-tie he'd pulled out of his pocket, and then making sure the other one wasn't in danger of bleeding to death before tying him up too. It didn't look like the bullet had hit anything major, so he left him where he was and pulled out his phone to call the local cops.

Axel and Colin had gone inside to check on the homeowners, and they were back out within a couple of minutes.

"They're alive," Axel said. "Tied up and sitting in the bathtub."

"Bloody lucky," Dante said.

"For us or them?" Elias asked.

"Both."

Deacon disconnected the phone. "Cops are on the way."

"Anyone want to look inside the casket and see if our new teammate is still among the living?" Elias said it jokingly, like he did most things, but they all knew if anything happened to The Gravediggers' newest recruit, Eve Winter would make them wish they were all dead.

Axel hopped into the back of the van. "I don't suppose anyone has a casket key?"

"There's one in the toolbox behind the driver's seat," Deacon said. "Tess keeps an extra there in case of an emergency."

"I can't imagine many people understand the true meaning of a casket emergency," Elias said.

"Yet, here we are," Deacon responded dryly, checking his watch. They might have another five minutes before the cops showed up. They needed to move quickly.

Axel found the key and shone his flashlight at the tiny hole at the other end of the casket, where the key was supposed to be inserted. It worked like a crank, and he spun it several times to loosen the lid.

They all gathered around and used their flashlights. And then Axel very carefully opened the top half of the casket where the bullet had gone in, and they all peered inside.

"This never stops being creepy as shit," Elias said. "Pale motherfucker. He looks dead to me."

"He's supposed to look dead," Deacon said. "He'll get some color back once the serum starts to work. Speaking of the serum, go ahead and administer it to him. I don't like how long he's been underground."

"I don't see where the bullet entered the casket," Dante said.

"Thank God for hardwood," Axel said, using the casket key to push inside the tiny bullet hole from the outside. "It didn't go through."

Metal hit metal. Deacon really hadn't wanted to have a confrontation with Eve over the death of one of her men. It had become hard enough lately to hold his tongue. She was a stone-cold bitch, and was entirely unapologetic about it. The job—the mission—always came first. Over her men and certainly over the life of everyone else. Anyone was expendable. The only thing that kept him from going rogue was the fact that she did have to answer to The Directors, so someone was holding her in check.

Who the hell knew? Maybe if he had to answer to The Directors, he'd be a stone-cold son of a bitch too. What he did know was that the lines blurred a little more every day. Sometimes he wondered if they really were the good guys.

"Let's move," he said. "I hear sirens."

Deacon got behind the wheel once again. The others closed the back doors, and he was reversing out of the driveway and heading toward the funeral home before Axel got back into the passenger seat.

"You know," Axel said. "Our first worry was what Winter would've done if that bullet had hit her new recruit."

"And?" Deacon asked.

"What we need to be worried about now is what Tess is going to do when she sees that bullet hole in her van. That redhead's got a hell of a temper she keeps repressed."

For the first time that night, Deacon smiled. Maybe he was as bad as Elias, because suddenly all he could think about was seeing the sexy Miss Sherman in a full temper, and he wouldn't mind it one bit.

CHAPTER TWO

There were those who said Last Stop, Texas, should've been named Pass On Through.

The town had been founded back in 1850, at the height of the Wild West, as men on horseback made an impressive picture driving cattle straight through the middle of town to much fanfare. They'd let the animals stop and drink out of the watering hole on the Larson property, and sleep in the grassy fields under the stars. It was their last stop until the Oklahoma border.

It was a short-lived claim to fame, as the railroads came to Fort Worth in 1876, changing the way cattle drives were done. It was just as well, as Mr. Larson's watering hole had all but dried up about the same time.

From that point on, prosperity had overlooked Last Stop. It was so close to Dallas a person could all but stand in the center of town and throw a nickel at it. And in a cruel twist of fate back in the eighties, when they'd gone to put in the bypass, it had bypassed right by Last Stop.

That had been the last straw for a lot of folks, but

the die-hards had stayed—those with the last names of Webb, Coward, Hawkins, Larson, and Jessup—whose ancestors had been the first to be buried in the tiny cemetery. Those five families owned most of everything in Last Stop, including any viable farming land. Others, whose blood didn't run quite so pure as the town founders', had also chosen to stay for one reason or another, but they made the commute into the city each day and prayed for cheaper gas prices.

Last Stop wasn't the prettiest town, and it had never gotten its picture in a magazine for being one of the "cutest small towns in America." Not like Rose Hill, which was only a half-hour drive on the other side of the Trinity River. In Last Stop, the streets were cobbled and the buildings that lined Main Street were two-stories of plain brown brick that looked like cardboard boxes. The city council had tried to come up with some money to put striped awnings over the walkways, but the taxpayers decided they'd rather save their pennies and just get wet when it rained.

Those who lived in Texas understood how the seasons worked—that summer lasted a minimum of nine months throughout the year, and winter usually visited in the month of January, just long enough for everyone to buy boots and winter gear before having to shove it back in the recesses of their closets come February. Drought was a serious problem from May to September, and playgrounds sat empty as one-hundred-degree days and a sweltering humidity made the outdoors a miserable existence.

It was an endless cycle that kept on year after year, without changing—but Last Stop wasn't big on change. When it came down to it, people would still spend their Friday nights watching high school football, their Saturday mornings mowing lawns and washing cars, their Sunday mornings at church, and the rest of the days of the week looking for somebody else's sins to pray about the following Sunday. Last Stop was caught in the past and had no plans of moving toward the future.

Tess Sherman took her life in Last Stop in stride. The name Sherman didn't mean much around town. In fact, most people raised their brows when the name was mentioned. She wasn't deaf. She'd heard rumblings about how she thought she was too good for anyone. They said she liked spending more time with the dead than with the living, and she guessed that was at least partially true. There was no need to worry about the dead running off with ten thousand dollars from her savings account or stealing her car. At least not that she'd encountered.

Of course, it was her own mother who kept the gossip mill going. People got their hair cut at the Clip n' Curl because Theodora was better than Channel 8 when it came to reporting the news. Whether the news was true or not didn't seem to matter so much. Theodora Sherman wasn't known for her honesty.

Or for her scruples. After all, it was also Tess's mother who'd run off with her savings and her car.

She'd flitted in and out of her daughter's life since she was a child, leaving her with her grandmother when it suited her and popping back into town when she needed money or a new man. Her grandmother liked to say that Theodora would steal anything that wasn't nailed down. Tess hated to break it to her, but a few nails wouldn't stop Theodora if she had her mind set on having it.

When Tess had moved back home to Last Stop after college, she'd had a mountain of student loan debt, and she couldn't impose on her grandmother by staying with her. Her grandmother had sacrificed enough over the years, and it was time she got to live her own life without having to worry about anyone else.

So for the past seven years, Tess had lived at the funeral home because she didn't have to pay rent, and because the funeral home had given her exactly what she'd needed: privacy. After growing up in a house where her mother riffled through her drawers looking for cash or mementos to pawn, it was a relief to know she could buy nice things and not worry about keeping them in a box buried in the rosebushes.

Living at the funeral home should've been the perfect solution for her "life plan." Once she'd paid off her student loans, she'd started setting aside money for a home of her own and for the day when she could either buy the funeral home from George Jessup or move on and open her own place. She wanted something that would last. Something that would be only hers.

About two years ago, Theodora had pretty much sent her life plan spiraling down the toilet. Tess had made the mistake of leaving her online bank account open when someone buzzed at the door. Theodora had been doing hair and makeup on Cleo Clancy in the embalming room, but she must've gotten curious when the buzzer had rung and wandered out to see if she could pick up any new gossip.

The open office door and bank information had stopped her in her tracks. Theodora could smell money a mile away, and it hadn't taken long for her to transfer funds out of Tess's savings account and into her own. By the time Tess had consoled Cleo's grieving husband and made it back to her office, her computer was closed and she'd forgotten all about paying her bills, which was why it had been open in the first place.

Theodora hadn't finished Cleo's makeover. She'd hightailed it out of Last Stop, straight across the Oklahoma border, until she saw the flashing lights of the casino beckoning her. It had taken just a smidgen longer to lose the ten thousand dollars than it had to steal it. She'd come home three days later without a by-your-leave, asking if Tess had managed to do anything with Cleo's hair.

That had been the norm in Tess's life for as long as she could remember. Her irresponsible, scatterbrained, childlike mother was what she was. There'd been no point in filing a police report or sending her mother to jail. Even if her conscience had allowed it, seeing the heartbreak in her grandmother's eyes would've changed her mind. There'd been nothing more she could do than to start over and take more care with hiding her money.

Theodora had a sickness. The thrill of flashing lights and the clang of the machine as dollar signs lined up had always had more of an appeal than choosing to do what was right. Or her only daughter.

Now Tess was finally at a place where she could financially stand on her own, and her savings was growing little by little every month. But her "life plan" had certainly veered off course. And though she hated to admit it, because she took pride in the fact that she was a planner, she was starting to think that Last Stop might not be in her plans after all.

She was the director of the funeral home, but she wasn't the owner. And as much time and personal investment as she'd given to the place, it would likely *never* be hers. Even if the new owner wanted to sell, she couldn't afford to buy her out. The last two years had been the strangest of her life. And it had all started when Eve Winter had purchased the funeral home.

What Tess needed was to pick up and start over—maybe—she thought, biting her lip. The only time she'd lived away from Last Stop was the five years she'd spent at the University of Texas—three for her mortuary science degree and another two for her MBA. Her plan had been to run a funeral home after all, so she figured she needed to know as much about the business side of things as she did about the death side of things. She could go anywhere or do anything, but she didn't want to be someone's employee forever. That she knew for certain.

She wasn't even a hundred percent sure how she'd ended up in the mortuary science program. She'd gone to college with most of her basics already taken, so she'd had a semester to experiment and try to figure out what she wanted to do with her life. Because she'd had *no clue* what she wanted to do with her life.

The pottery class had been an utter failure since she had zero artistic talent, and her accounting professor had gotten arrested by the FBI and had his computers confiscated the week before finals, so she figured the life of a CPA probably wasn't for her either. She loved to read, so she thought an English degree might work out, but then she realized she'd eventually need to be able to find a job, so she discarded that idea.

The class that had stuck with her had been intro to pathology. Maybe it was because the professor had looked like he'd come off the set of *Grey's Anatomy*. Or maybe it was because she'd found a quiet peace in that class she'd never experienced before. Lord knows her mother had never given her much peace.

Tess found the dead fascinating. What had happened to them? Were they young or old? What kind of life had they lived? Did anyone miss them? She'd almost gone pre-med to become a medical examiner, but she realized that would only answer some of the questions she had about the people who would end up on a slab in front of her.

The other questions could only be answered by the living—by a spouse or parent or child. Tess wanted to know what made the person worth remembering in death. It seemed a question that was more important than it should've been. Maybe because she constantly wondered who would remember her when it was her time to lie on someone's slab.

A crack of thunder shook the panes in the windows on the third floor of the old Queen Anne house. Rain pelted against the roof as Tess lay on top of the covers in nothing but her underwear. But it didn't do much to help cool her off. She propped her hands behind her head and stared at the cracks in the plaster on the ornamental ceiling. The fan in the corner was working overtime, and she'd opened the two windows as wide as she dared. The edges of the white curtains were damp, and she'd put a towel on the floor in front of each window to keep the wood from getting wet.

She glanced at the big red numbers on the clock sitting on the bedside table, just like she had for the last two hours. It was five-thirty, which in her mind was at least a somewhat acceptable time to be up and about, and she did have work to do.

Delores Schriever was in the cooler and ready to be dressed and made up, so she could be laid out in slumber room one. Delores had been the first customer she'd had in weeks. Business wasn't exactly booming at the Last Stop Funeral Home. Which was a good thing for the citizens of Last Stop. Not so great for her.

Tess knew the funeral home should have been operating in the red. But her paycheck showed up like clockwork every two weeks in her bank account—and it was more than a decent paycheck—almost double what George had paid her. And when she went to pay the home's bills, there was always money in the checking account. Eve Winter had no interest in running a funeral home, but she had a lot of interest in keeping it afloat.

Tess had no idea what those reasons were, but for the time being she had a paycheck and health insurance, so she couldn't complain too much.

The Last Stop Funeral Home had been in the Jessup family for three generations. And since George's son Jesse was a no-good son of a bitch, there'd been no chance of it being passed on to the fourth generation of Jessups. Which was why George had hired Tess when she'd moved back home after college. He'd shown her the ropes and she'd learned under his tutelage. The funeral home was supposed to be hers, and in another ten years or so, when George was ready to retire, it would've been.

Except Eve Winter had ridden into town like one of the four horsemen of the Apocalypse, with her floor-length white coat and cherry-red Porsche Carrera, and made George an offer he couldn't refuse. George had no chance against a woman like Eve. Apparently George had ignored weeks of phone calls from the woman and wouldn't entertain the offer of selling the funeral home over the phone. So she'd made the trip personally and brought cash. A lot of cash.

Fortunately, George had the wits about him to remember that he'd promised Tess the funeral home. And though he could no longer keep that promise, he at least had the wherewithal to put it in the contract that she'd be in charge of the funeral home until she chose to leave or until Eve decided to sell, in which case she had to give the first option to Tess to buy her out.

George had signed the papers, taken the exorbitant

amount of money, and packed up his wife of thirty years so they could live on a Carnival Cruise ship. They'd left their no-good, son-of-a-bitch son behind.

The people in Last Stop weren't fond of change, so word spread like wildfire about the fancy city woman who'd bought out George Jessup lock, stock, and barrel. But since no one but George, Tess, and the attorneys had actually seen Eve Winter, the exaggerations of her physical appearance had grown by leaps and bounds.

They'd gossiped for months about the rich woman and the extensive renovations on the funeral home and outbuildings. Tess had been living there on the third floor the entire time, and even *she* wasn't quite sure what was happening with all the construction work. They'd set up partitions and giant drop cloths to keep the curious from seeing what was being done. In a place like Last Stop, hiding the progress only made people more curious, so there'd been a few late-night instances of people sneaking onto the grounds and peeking between the partitions.

The work had been completed in record time. Tess had woken up in the middle of the night more than once, hearing the distant sound of some kind of heavy piece of machinery. She'd worked around the chaos and clutter, but in reality, the construction crew had done a great job staying out of her way.

The unveiling hadn't been a big to-do. There'd been no ribbon cutting from the Chamber of Commerce or open house. One morning Tess had woken up and gone down to the kitchen to start her morning coffee. It had taken her a moment to realize that something was different. There were no partitions. No drapes or curtains covering certain areas. Everything was finished and looked as if it had been there forever.

She'd stared in shock out the back windows of the kitchen. A full-fledged English rose garden had been planted at some point. And the carriage house, which the Jessups had originally used to park the hearses in the bays on the first floor and storage on the second floor, had been gutted completely and doubled in size.

It now looked like a miniature version of the main house, which wasn't all that miniature if she thought about it. The carriage house had been painted solid white, and the bottom story still had the original carriage bays where buggies had once been stowed. The three bays were no longer used for parking, and large glass windows had been installed into each of them. The carriage house had been turned into a home gym of sorts, though she'd seen gyms that required a paying membership not have equipment as nice as that in the carriage house.

She didn't know how much square footage had been added to the carriage house, she just knew that when she looked at it from the side, it took up twice as much space as it previously had. And then there was the casket warehouse. She also knew there had to be a hidden passageway somewhere on the property. She'd never seen a group of large men able to move in and out of space so quietly. One minute she was alone, and then the next . . . *pffft* . . . they just appeared out of nowhere and scared the ever-living hell out of her.

All funeral homes were required by law to have an area designated as a casket showroom and to provide caskets at different ends of the price spectrum. Mr. Jessup and his family had run a successful business for generations, but they also knew the scope of the clientele and the infrequency. Nothing was wasted and everything possible conserved.

The old casket warehouse had been not much more than a shed with metal siding. It was large enough to fit the six different caskets people could choose from and that was about it. The small metal building was no longer there. In its place was a warehouse that looked like it had been made out of concrete. There were several large windows with casket displays in them, and there was a large garage door on the opposite side to get the caskets in and out.

Tess had wondered if maybe she should have a talk with Eve. They weren't the kind of funeral home to do the volume of business that the woman seemed to be preparing for. Half the people in town would have to drop dead for them to do that much business. But maybe Eve didn't realize how inconvenient Last Stop was to get to from the city and that the only candidates who might use the funeral home were the 3,047 people who lived there.

Ultimately, Tess had decided it wasn't her business. She wasn't the owner, and it wasn't her problem. Only, it kind of was her problem because if they went bankrupt it would mean she was out of a job.

While people had certainly talked, taken pictures,

and gawked from Main Street at the Last Stop Funeral Home, it wasn't the only thing getting attention.

What *really* had tongues wagging was the men. Five men, to be exact.

Eve had chosen Tess's staff for her. Tess had been appreciative, but considering there was barely enough work to keep *her* occupied each day, she couldn't imagine what she was supposed to do with the five men—the overbearing, larger-than-life, sexy-as-hell men. But Eve had told her they'd be busy enough, and she'd left it at that.

They certainly didn't fit in with Last Stop, and there was something about each of them that made her a little bit wary and a whole lot cautious. Maybe it was the way they were always watching their surroundings, as if they expected the worst to happen. Or maybe it was the way they seemed to distrust everyone on sight. Tess couldn't really blame them for that one. She always figured just about everyone had an ulterior motive when they showed interest in a person. But maybe she was just cynical.

What she didn't like was all the talk around town about her and her merry band of death men, which was the name her friend Miller was passing around town, the traitor. Over at the Clip n' Curl, they apparently filled hours of conversation with whether or not Tess knew the men intimately. And if she didn't, would she be willing to make an introduction? Since her mother was the owner of the Clip n' Curl, she liked gossip almost as much as money and men, so she didn't bother trying to defend her only daughter's reputation.

All of the ladies at the Clip n' Curl were in unanimous agreement that Tess's men were about as close to male perfection as they'd ever seen. There was Deacon Tucker and Axel Tate. They'd been her first two employees to show up out of the blue. One look at Deacon had made her briefly wish she was the kind of woman to grab the attention of a man like that, but looks were fleeting and she'd always have a brain, so she didn't let it faze her too much.

No, Deacon had definitely given her a few of those breathless moments. The ones she remembered from her youth where her heart fluttered and her words stumbled over themselves every time she tried to speak to a guy. It had been a long time since she'd had feelings like that. She'd certainly never had them with Henry, the man she'd been engaged to. But she'd always assumed that flutter and anticipation would fade with age.

There was a reason there was a saying about people who made assumptions, because boy, had she been wrong. The flutters were more like jackhammers in her belly, and her fantasies were a lot more explicit than they'd been when she was fifteen. She'd once seen Deacon mowing the yard without his shirt on and the primal urge to pounce on him and stake her claim had been so strong she'd called her friend Miller for an emergency wine intervention.

She hadn't had the same reaction to Axel. There was something about him that reminded her of a wounded lion. He had a great deal of pride, but he'd been flayed open by the enemy. He didn't want to show weakness.

And then there was the wedding ring he wore, even though he appeared to be flying solo. She'd never seen him without it, and he never looked twice at any other woman.

Less than a month after Deacon and Axel arrived in Last Stop, Elias Cole had joined them. He was different from the other two. He was more relaxed and even prone to making jokes from time to time. Of all of them, he was the one who'd stop and talk with her or see if she needed anything if he was going to the store. He was also the only one who'd ever shared anything personal about himself. She knew he was from Texas originally, and that he'd been in the military, though he'd never mentioned what branch of the service.

It had taken another six months for Dante Malcolm to join the group. She'd liked him immediately, though Miller said he was a little "too" suave for her liking, and that she thought his English accent might be fake. But he had manners and at least acknowledged that Tess was in charge of running the funeral home, whereas the others pretty much did as they pleased and showed up only when needed.

It had been a few months after Dante came that Colin Moreau had appeared, seemingly out of nowhere, just like Elias and Dante before him. There was an anger to Colin that made her steer clear of the Frenchman. He was handsome enough, and he was always very polite. But she could see the rage bubbling just below the surface, and she wanted to be nowhere in the vicinity if he ever blew.

Eve had made it clear that the men's employment was nonnegotiable, so there was no point in Tess complaining about them. They mostly stayed out of her way. Deacon, Axel, and Colin all lived in the carriage house. She had no idea where Dante lived, though she didn't think it was anywhere in Last Stop. Everyone in town would know if he did. He seemed like a city boy to her with his fancy shoes and expensive suits, so her best guess was he had a place in Dallas.

Elias was a different story. He lived a few blocks away, in Last Stop's one and only apartment complex. The reason she knew that was because Stella Longbow had followed him home one afternoon and then tried to tell everyone at the Clip n' Curl he'd invited her inside but she'd turned him down since she was a happily married woman. What she'd failed to mention was that Elias had called the sheriff about a Peeping Tom, and when the deputy had shown up he found Stella crouched in the bushes.

But Eve had been right. The five of them always found ways to occupy themselves. If she didn't need help with anything funeral home–related, they kept the grass mowed and the flowerbeds weeded, maintained the upkeep on the old Queen Anne house, kept all the vehicles maintenanced, and generally did the things she never could've done herself. She especially appreciated it when they did those things without their shirts on.

They'd started a pool at the Clip n' Curl to see who would be the first to get one of the men into bed, though they'd told Tess she wasn't allowed to enter since she had the unfair advantage of practically living with them. Since Tess had no intention of sleeping with any of them, and even less intention of telling everyone at the Clip n' Curl if she did, she was fine with the banishment. So far, no one had claimed the $347 pot.

If Tess had a choice, she would never step foot in the viper's nest that was the Clip n' Curl, but every Friday like clockwork her grandmother had an appointment to get her hair done, and Tess was her only mode of transportation, so she was a firsthand witness to the conversations held between the sacred walls of Last Stop's only beauty salon.

Tess had tried to explain to the women that Axel seemed devoted to his wife, but Jo Beth Schriever—great-grandniece of Delores from slumber room one—said that if Axel had a wife she was either dead or long gone, which meant he was fair game. Tess had never heard that rule before, but she'd conceded to Jo Beth's explanation because the young woman had a gleam in her eyes that could only be attributed to baby fever or mad cow disease.

Carol Dewberry, who'd been happily married for forty-seven years, had offered to be the treasurer of the pool money since no one in their right mind would let Theodora be in charge. And anyone who had a lick of sense would know Carol would be holding on to that money for eternity, because men like the ones living in the carriage house weren't looking for women like what Last Stop had to offer. They probably looked for women with edges and attitudes as rough as theirs. Someone as dominant as they were.

Tess had much better things to do than waste time chasing men. When she'd been engaged to Henry, she had barely dodged the marriage bullet. She was an educated and independent woman with her whole life ahead of her. She'd watched her mother do nothing but chase men and money, and she'd be damned if she ever did the same.

That wasn't to say she didn't want to settle down someday. She did. And she wanted a family. The kind of family she'd missed out on growing up. But she also wanted to be picky. She didn't want to settle for someone like Henry, and she almost had. She wanted to be an equal partner. And she wanted excitement and passion at least once in her life. There was nothing wrong with that.

She was thirty years old, so she figured she had a few more years before she really needed to panic. Besides, her social calendar was about as full as it could get. She worked (granted, the dead weren't exactly considered social), she took yoga three mornings a week (though sometimes she walked right by the studio to the donut shop next door), she was a member of a book/wine club (albeit, she and her best friend Miller were the only members), and she'd almost worked all the way through her expert-level crossword puzzle book.

Busy. As. Hell.

She'd never been the type of woman to be able to attract a man like Deacon Tucker, but there was something about him that . . . clicked. Sure, he was sexy as hell. He had those dark, brooding good looks that reminded her of the heroes she liked to read about. And his hands . . . they were large and rough—working man's hands. Then there was that hint of a dimple in his cheek that peeked out during one of his rare smiles, and the slight misalignment in the bridge of his nose that made her curious to know how he'd broken it.

And then there was the fact that he was just a good guy. He was a man who liked to keep busy, and more often than not if things were slow, he'd fix something around the funeral home or work in the yard. The harder the work, the more he seemed to like it, as if he were punishing himself by working himself to the bone.

He wasn't amusing or boisterous like Elias, or smooth and charming like Dante. But there was an air about him that stood out from the others. He commanded without having to say a word. She was drawn to him, and there were moments when they spoke or stood close that the space around them was so electrically charged she didn't know how others couldn't feel it.

His eyes were an intense blue she could get lost in for hours. There'd been a moment not too long ago when she thought he might lean down and kiss her. When they'd been lost in conversation, their words softening to whispers and their breath mingling as they stood close together. A spell had been cast, and she'd leaned in, only to be interrupted when the back door opened.

He hadn't seemed to mind that afternoon that she

wasn't a bombshell and didn't have the same raw sex appeal he did. He'd wanted to kiss her anyway. She hadn't imagined the desire in his eyes. But she wasn't going to change a darned thing about herself to try and get his attention. She was who she was, and what she *wasn't* was the kind of woman to make heads turn when she walked into a room. Except the time she'd gone to a wedding reception with the back of her skirt tucked into her underwear.

She was done trying to please men. She'd learned that very difficult lesson with Henry. She wanted a man to please her for once, and if Deacon Tucker couldn't look at her and see how great she was, then he just didn't deserve her.

"Gah," Tess said, grabbing one of her pillows and whacking herself in the face a couple of times with it.

Her internal monologue sounded dangerously close to the pep talks her grandmother used to give her as a kid. There was no dwelling on things that couldn't be changed. What she needed to do was to make a choice for her future. Whether or not that future included the Last Stop Funeral Home was still up in the air. She'd never fit in in Last Stop. But it was the only home she'd ever known.

The biggest question was, if not Last Stop, then where?

"I'm a grown woman," she muttered, tossing the pillow aside in frustration. "I'm not going to fear change. I'm going to take life by the balls . . . and . . . and . . . never mind. Life doesn't have balls. It's a ridiculous saying. I'm going to make an adult decision about my future and be happy about it. Dammit."

Having made up her mind, she nodded defiantly and threw her legs over the side of the bed. She had no idea what that future held, but she couldn't see herself living forever on the third floor of a funeral home she didn't own. She should be settled by this point in her life—with long-term job security and at least the possibility of a home and family on the horizon. What kind of quality of life was it to spend each day behind her desk, wondering when someone would die? That was weird, even for her.

Another crack of thunder shook the room, and this time the red numbers on her clock went blank as the electricity went out.

"Well, shit." It looked like she'd be showering in the dark. And she definitely needed a shower, considering the fine sheen of sweat that covered her body. Even with modern conveniences like AC, it was still an old house and heat rose to the third floor.

She moved to the window and stood to the side, slightly behind the curtain. She didn't figure anyone who had to get up this early needed to be greeted with the sight of her naked body. She had the pale skin of a true redhead, to the extent that Henry had once shielded his eyes because he'd said her paleness was like staring into the sun. He'd been kidding—she was almost positive—but there was no need to be a glowing beacon in the window to anyone who glanced up.

The view from the top of the funeral home was

something she'd miss if she left. It was the best view in town, not because downtown was especially nice to look at, but because it was interesting to watch the comings and goings of people in their daily lives. Watching from above sure as heck was more fun than being down there in the middle of them all.

The Queen Anne Victorian mansion, which had once been a combination of the Jessups' family home and the funeral parlor, sat at one end of Main Street. At the other end was a Gothic-style courthouse, complete with ugly gargoyles and creepy statues of Justice and Mercy.

When the funeral home had started encroaching on their living space, the Jessups had built a new mansion outside of the city limits. The funeral business had boomed in the twenties, when prohibition and public hangings were all the rage. It had been convenient to put the bodies in a wagon and wheel them down the street in a public procession to the funeral home.

Nowadays, the most exciting thing she'd seen from her window was Ernastine Forster get into a tussle with Earl Twitty over the last handicapped parking space. Ernastine had used her battle tank of a Buick to push him right out of the spot. And then she'd popped him in the nose when he got out of the car to confront her.

Headlights glared through droplets of water as a vehicle turned onto Main Street, coming straight toward the funeral home. The closer the vehicle got, the closer she moved to the window, squinting so she could see better. If she wasn't mistaken, that was her body transport van.

Her skin flushed with annoyance and she could feel the blood rush to her face. She'd always cursed her redhead's complexion, but at least people could tell in advance when she was irritated or angry.

"What the hell are they up to?" Tess fumed.

The last time she checked, she was the one in charge of the funeral home, and she wanted an explanation as to why they'd taken company property out for a joyride in the middle of the night. Good grief, she didn't really know *anything* about the men other than their names and a few things she'd picked up from conversation here and there. What if they'd been out drinking? What if they were using her van to sell drugs? She could get in a whole heap of trouble and never even know what hit her until it was too late.

She decided not having hot water was the least of her worries, so she hopped in a tepid shower, soaped, rinsed, and brushed her teeth to save time, and then hopped back out again just a few minutes later. Since she'd be working on Mrs. Schriever for most of the day, she pulled on jeans and an old button-down oxford shirt in a blue pinstripe. It was soft and a little frayed around the collar and cuffs, but she'd keep the sleeves rolled up. It wasn't like Mrs. Schriever was going to complain about her sartorial choices.

Tess had never been one for makeup, but she slathered on moisturizer and piled her wet hair on top of her head, pinning it with a couple of bobby pins. It probably wouldn't stay, as her hair had a mind of its own, but trying was half the battle.

She grabbed a flashlight from her nightstand drawer and headed into the darkness of the house. When Eve had done renovations, she hadn't touched the top two floors. Tess wasn't sure if she was trying to save money, or if it was her way of showing her irritation that George Jessup had made sure Tess was there to stay. Either way, the old and new didn't mix all that well, and it was probably a good thing no one but her ever ventured past the first floor.

The floors and wallpaper were original to the house, and the hallways were cramped and narrow. And when it was raining, like it was now, it smelled like a hundred-plus years of moldy, wet house. The only rooms on the third floor were the large bedroom she used, which had once been the nursery, an attached sitting area, and a bathroom that had knocking pipes and low water pressure.

She stifled a sneeze at the small landing on the second floor, and then squeaked as something nipped her ankle.

"Dammit, Lucifer," she hissed, letting out a shaky breath. She shone the light on the cat and he hissed back and ran upstairs. She wasn't sure how he'd do it since she'd closed her door, but he always managed to find a way into her room. When he was in an extra special mood he'd leave a mouse on her pillow for her.

The black cat had come with the house, and according to Mr. Jessup, Lucifer's ancestry went back as far as his own family. Tess was more inclined to believe that Lucifer was actually the devil incarnate and had been the *only* cat ever on the premises, since no one could remember kittens being born or a female cat in the general vicinity to make the mating dance possible.

Tess kept him fed, but he was just as unpredictable as the men who'd taken her van, coming and going at all hours of the day and night and generally being rude and surly. Though none of the men had bitten her on the ankle yet.

The beam of the flashlight didn't hide the disrepair of the upper floors. The red-and-gold floral wallpaper had faded to orange and was peeling in places, and the carpet runner was thin and worn. The second floor wasn't in use. The doors were always kept closed and most of the rooms were vacant. The rooms that did have furniture had white sheets draped over it. There was a full second-story balcony that went the entire way around the house, and there were white rocking chairs placed in pairs every so often. Green ferns hung from hooks and the glass gleamed. But the exterior was a façade that only pretended to welcome guests. Who'd want to be a guest at a funeral home anyway?

Once she got to the landing between the first and second floors, it was like walking into another house. The curved staircase and bannister were a focal point from the front of the funeral home. The carpet became thick and lush beneath her feet, and the bannister gleamed with polish. The original chandelier, which had once held tapered candles that some poor soul had to light every night, hung from the foyer, only with the candles replaced with candelabra lights.

Flashes of lightning lit the interior ominously as she

crept down the stairs. She hadn't heard the rumble of the garage door open, but the thunder had been pretty vigorous, and with the electricity out they probably couldn't get the door open anyway.

It was an old house that creaked and moaned from time to time, but tonight, as the storm raged around it, it was silent. If there was anyone in the house, she should've heard them.

Unless they didn't want to be heard.

She shivered, her flesh pebbling despite the heavy heat. The beam of her flashlight seemed insignificant against the big and drafty house. The front door was locked up tight, and she shone her light into the room to the left of the door—slumber room one. It was empty. At least for the next few hours.

Across the foyer was slumber room two, the wooden double doors wide open. Tables were set up with dark blue cloths for refreshments, which reminded her that she needed to put in a call to Piper Prewitt to see what time she could deliver the cookies for the viewing the next night. Piper made cakes and other bakery items out of her house because rent was too high in the strip down Main Street. But there wasn't a person in a fifty-mile radius that could bake better than Piper.

Toward the back of slumber room two was a small formal parlor that had been beautifully decorated in shades of ivory and cream. The furniture was antique and uncomfortable, and the room was only used to meet with grieving, and sometimes not grieving, families as they picked out burial plans. She hated the room. It seemed cold and distant, whereas the rest of the rooms were done up in warm, tasteful colors.

Her office was under the stairs directly across from the parlor. Her door was also closed, which was just how she'd left it. She turned the knob to see if it was still locked. It was. The house opened up toward the back, where the kitchen was, and a wall of bay windows looked out over the rose garden. They were taking a beating out there, thanks to the storm.

She crept into the kitchen next, her favorite room in the whole house. It was open and airy, and there were pale yellow padded benches with pillows beneath each of the bay windows. She'd often grab a book and read there for hours, occasionally looking out into the gardens and daydreaming. Or when her grandmother came to visit, she'd make a pot of tea and wheel it over on the little tea cart, and they'd sit and talk about everything from the weather to politics. And they'd do it in Russian, because her grandmother was always afraid that the harsh, heavy language that was a part of their family heritage would someday be lost if not used.

Tess spent most of their time together promising her grandmother that she'd teach her children the language and tell them stories of the old lands. Though Tess wasn't going to tell too many stories, because her grandmother had led a pretty colorful life. As the daughter of a Russian mobster she'd picked up a lot of things that most children shouldn't.

The talk of heritage and children often led to her grandmother asking if she was any closer to giving her great-grandchildren, and if not, she knew of a nice young man or two who could probably get the job done. Russians were hardcore. And Russian women were worse than hardcore. Tess would rather face an alley full of maniacs than cross a Russian woman during the wrong week of the month. Or her grandmother any day of the month. So the suggestion of her having children wasn't really a suggestion, but more of an order. And Tess wouldn't put it past her grandmother to hire a man to show up on her doorstep one day ready to get the job done.

The longer she searched the house the more uneasy she felt. There were no beams from flashlights or headlights that she could see. It was nothing but darkness, the raging storm, and the occasional flash of lightning. It was moments like these when she wished she had a dog to keep her company instead of a satanic cat.

"Oh, for Pete's sake," she whispered. And then she wondered why she was whispering. "Because I'm losing my mind."

She'd seen the van coming straight toward her with her own eyes. They were around here somewhere, and they couldn't hide from her forever. She wanted explanations.

Tess moved quickly through the kitchen and into the long hallway that led to the embalming room and attached garage. Those rooms hadn't been part of the original structure and had a much more modern and clinical feel to them.

The hall floors were tile, and she'd once had hall runners put down, but the gurneys got snagged on them when she tried to wheel a body from the garage to the embalming room. It had only taken once for a body to almost tip over before she'd rolled the rugs back up and shoved them in a closet.

If people knew some of the things that happened behind closed doors at a funeral home, they'd more than likely opt to give their loved one a Viking funeral complete with flaming arrows. She'd heard some doozies of stories when she'd gone to a mortician's convention, and she prayed she never had to explain to a family why their loved one had accidentally been cremated or why the wrong body was in the coffin.

The embalming room always stayed locked since there were thousands of dollars' worth of equipment inside—not to mention a body—but she checked the doorknob anyway just to make sure.

Locked.

She wiped her sweaty palm on her jeans and moved across to the door that led into the garage. She fully expected to find the transport van inside, along with whoever had taken it out for a spin. But when she opened the door, the space where the van should've been was empty.

The garage was oversized so they could maneuver bodies between the vehicles, and her voice echoed as she shone the flashlight into the cavernous space and said, "Hello?"

Nothing but silence answered her back.

The black Suburban she used for funerals was parked in the middle space, and the twelve-year-old Corolla that only started if she put a screwdriver in the ignition was in the far space. But the transport van was gone.

She pointed the flashlight over the concrete and noticed the floor was wet with shoe prints, tire tracks, and mud.

"See, Tess? Not crazy," she said, feeling vindicated.

So now what? She'd proven they'd been out with the van. And obviously they'd come back, at least for a short time. But why would they leave again? She looked at the time on her cell phone and saw it was just after six in the morning. None of it made any sense.

Eve Winter might own the place, but Eve wasn't here, and Tess had only seen her the one time in two years. Tess was the funeral home director. Everything that happened within those walls was her responsibility, including the employees. And employees didn't have carte blanche to use the funeral home's equipment at their whim.

The hum of electricity filled the room just before the lights flickered back on. She blinked a couple of times and then turned off the flashlight. When she looked at the shoe prints a little closer, she realized they led right to where she was standing. At least a couple of the guys had come inside. But she hadn't seen any sign of them.

Tess turned back inside the house to follow the prints, but the tile floor had been wiped clean. She could practically feel the electricity crackling around her. She wasn't sure if it was because of the storm or her temper. Either way, her hair felt as if it were standing on end, and every time she touched something she got a quick jolt.

She closed the door to the garage and dug her keys out of her jeans pocket as she went to the embalming room door. Since no one was in the house, and she didn't feel like going out in the rain to bang on their door to ask about the missing transport van, she decided to get to work. They'd have to bring it back at some point, and when they did, she'd be ready to pounce.

Mrs. Schriever needed to be bathed and made as presentable as a ninety-year-old woman could be made before Theodora showed up to do her hair. That's *if* she remembered to show up. Theodora played bingo on Wednesday nights, so she wasn't always in top form on Thursday mornings.

"Don't worry about things you can't control," she whispered, feeling the familiar knot form in her stomach like it did whenever she thought of her mother and responsibilities in the same sentence.

A cold blast of air hit her as she opened the embalming room door. It was temperature-controlled to make working with the bodies easier when they were pulled from the refrigeration unit. The pungent smell of chemicals greeted her, and she knew the smell would permeate her clothes in the next couple of hours. In all honesty, she wondered if she ever really got rid of the smell or if she was just so used to it she no longer noticed.

Her hand fumbled for the light switch, and then she stood blinking as the fluorescent lights came on one by one. There was nothing old or antique about this room. It was white and sterile, and the light was painfully bright. It helped when mixing the embalming chemicals and getting just the right amount of color under the skin to make the person look alive. The fluorescent light was unforgiving, so it helped when reconstructive work needed to be done—from skin problems to autopsy sutures—a lot could be done with makeup and putty.

People wanted to remember their loved ones as they were when they were living, so she worked from photographs and anything else she could find to help make it easier on the families. It was easy enough to add the dye to the embalming solution so the skin took on a lifelike glow instead of the gray pallor of death.

The room was a large rectangle. The wall closest to the door on the right had cabinets and a granite countertop with a large farmhouse sink in the center. The wall directly across from the door was floor-to-ceiling sturdy metal shelves that held every piece of equipment imaginable. Sometimes mortuary work required being creative, depending on how a person had died.

The far wall was where the walk-in refrigeration unit was. The industrial door was large and stainless steel, and it locked from the outside with a lever. It could hold several bodies comfortably, though she'd never had occasion to use it that way. The wall to her left had more shelves and hanging racks, for the deceased's personal belongings. But it was the center of the room that held her attention.

There were moments in time when what the eye saw didn't necessarily compute with the brain. She'd taken three steps into the room before she really grasped what the body on the embalming table meant. Especially since it wasn't Delores Schriever, who was supposed to be the only body in the room.

It looked like she'd solved the mystery of why they'd taken her transport van.

But who was the man laying on her table?

CHAPTER THREE

Tess had worked with the dead for a lot of years, so nothing much surprised her. She'd once had a man's hand jerk up and hit her in the side of the face just as she was about to embalm him. It had certainly gotten her blood pumping a little faster, but dead bodies did weird things sometimes.

What they didn't do was appear out of nowhere and end up on her embalming table.

"Think this through, Tess," she said out loud, creeping closer to the body.

Her grandmother had always told her she needed to be more Russian. Logic always trumped emotion.

"Obviously they took the van to make a pickup. The question is, why didn't they tell me? And where did the body come from?"

There was no paperwork that she could see. And paperwork was absolutely a necessity. There had been more than one occasion when the hospital had tried to give her the wrong body. And without paperwork, she couldn't legally take the body into possession.

"Idiots," she muttered.

There was still no sign of anyone else—at least anyone living—in the house. Maybe they'd just crossed paths while she was looking through the house. It was a *big* house. Maybe right at this very moment one of them was knocking on her bedroom door—preferably Deacon, because good God those shoulders—letting her know they'd picked up a dead body and he had all the correctly signed paperwork right in his hand.

"Because they're super-thoughtful like that," she said, blowing out a breath.

And now she was thinking of Deacon's shoulders. And the rest of him. Which was about the most horrible thing she could do because on a scale of one to ten, he was a twenty-two, and she had the feeling he had the ability to make all her Russian logic fly right out the window.

She sighed and put Deacon out of her mind, and then she peeked out the door and down the hallway again to make sure she was alone. What if they hadn't brought the dead guy into the house at all? What if it was just a terrible coincidence and she'd been caught in the middle of some kind of horrible crime?

Her palms were damp with nerves and she again wiped them on her jeans, debating whether or not to close the door. Of course, then she wouldn't have an escape if the body turned out to be a zombie and tried to eat her face off.

"I should probably cut back on the caffeine," she muttered. "Though I haven't had any coffee this morning, so maybe I need to increase the caffeine."

She left the door open and headed back to the body, determined not to let her imagination get the best of her.

"No need to complicate matters. I'm sure I'm completely safe and that there's a reasonable explanation for this."

The body on the table didn't seem to have an opinion one way or the other, but she liked to think he'd agree with her.

"This is what I do," she explained to the corpse apologetically. "I reason things out. I'm all about the logic. Why can't I fantasize about Deacon without wondering if he is a criminal? Why won't my subconscious let me be wild and crazy? It's damned irritating if you ask me. Being responsible is for the birds."

She sighed and then pursed her lips together. "And I don't need your silent judgment either. I know that one of the reasons Henry broke up with me is because I talk to dead people." She bit her lip and moved closer to the table. "Of course, Henry was the type of man who made lists of my faults, so Henry can suck it. There's nothing wrong with talking to the dead. Unless they start talking back. Don't do that, okay?"

The silver necklace around the man's neck immediately caught her attention. Not because the Star of David was unusual, but because the hospital always removed all personal belongings from the body and gave them to the immediate family. And if there was no immediate family to sign the paperwork for the body, they sent personal items along with the body in a labeled plastic bag.

It wasn't just the jewelry—where the hospital normally removed the corpse's clothing, this one was wearing what looked like a flight suit in dark gray. One of the sleeves had been rolled up and the front zipper had been pulled down to his navel, showing a patch of dark chest hair. There was a needle mark in the arm with the rolled-up sleeve.

"So weird," she whispered.

He didn't look like the normal bodies she worked on. This man was massive in size, but not with fat. The flight suit strained over muscular thighs and broad shoulders. He barely fit on the metal embalming table. He looked like one of . . . them. Except dead. His skin was cold to the touch, and though he looked to be Hispanic or Middle Eastern, he had the grayish hue of the recently deceased.

He had a puckered scar on his chest that was no doubt from a bullet, and she pressed her lips together tightly, thinking this was a man who'd cheated death on more than one occasion and now it had caught up with him. He was too young to be on her table. That was for damned sure. He looked to be in his mid- to late thirties, though death often made people look older than they were.

She spread the flight suit a little farther apart to get a better look at the scar on his chest, and maybe see whether cause of death was visible. The unease in the pit of her stomach had only intensified. Dead men without paperwork were nothing but trouble. She didn't know that from experience, but common sense told her that was the case. She bent over to get a closer look, but there were no recent wounds that she could see.

Tess rose again and moved to zip the flight suit back up, but as soon as she tugged at the zipper the man on the table gave a great gasping wheeze and his hand clamped around her wrist. The force of his grip brought her to her knees, and terror clawed at her as his body went into a seizure, his legs jerking uncontrollably as his grip on her wrist grew tighter. It wouldn't take much more to break it.

And then he did the unthinkable. Something none of her dead bodies had ever done before.

He sat up and stared at her out of eyes that were very much alive and very, very angry, his grip so strong she bit her lip to keep from crying out.

"You ever heard the saying about curiosity killing the cat?" a graveled voice asked from the doorway.

Her eyes wheeled around and she stared incredulously at Deacon from her crouched position on the floor. "Seriously? That's what you're going to say?"

"It seemed like a good idea at the time." He came toward her, and she felt the space close in with every step he took. Maybe she was the one who was dead and she'd been transported to Valhalla. It would certainly explain why she was surrounded by giant men who looked like gods.

"A good idea?" she repeated. "Maybe next time try 'Hey, Tess, let me help you with the giant dead man trying to kill you.'"

"I'm not sure if you've noticed, but he's not dead.

Thank God," Deacon said calmly. "We thought he was, which is why we put him here. And he's not trying to kill you. He doesn't know what he's doing. It's just the body's natural reaction."

He'd said more to her in the last thirty seconds than he had in the last couple of years, and the closer he came the more worried she got. He didn't look like her savior. He looked more like the Angel of Death. His dark hair was pulled back into a stubby tail at the base of his neck and his eyes were the iciest of blues. His skin was bronzed due to the fact he spent a great deal of time outdoors. He was built like a laborer instead of someone who spent all his time in a gym, though she knew he did that too. But when she looked at him, all she saw was . . . *man*. His jaw was angular and his lips—sweet Jesus—his lips were the kind that could tempt anyone to stray from well-laid plans.

She wasn't sure which man she should be dodging, but it seemed like a good sign that Deacon was removing the hand from her wrist instead of trying to strangle her. She cradled her wrist as soon as it was free, and flexed her fingers. Nothing was broken, but she was going to be sore and bruised for a few days.

"Thanks," she said and watched as Deacon pushed the man back down on the table. He took a syringe from his pocket and tossed the cap aside before sliding it beneath the man's skin and pressing down the plunger.

"Umm . . . what the hell is going on here? Do you always carry syringes in your pocket? That seems dangerous."

She was babbling, but that's what she did when she was nervous. It didn't seem to matter though, because Deacon's full attention was on the man on her table. Almost immediately, the seizure stopped and the man's body went slack. He no longer had the grayish hue of the dead.

Deacon put two fingers at the man's neck and felt for a pulse. Tess was guessing he must've found one, because he dropped his hand and nodded with satisfaction.

"Now that you know your boy is alive, can you answer my questions?" she asked.

He looked at her, his eyes piercing, but he didn't answer.

"Hello?" she said. "I'm talking to you, Valhalla," she said, cradling her wrist as she rose slowly to her feet.

"You need to get some ice on that," he said.

"No shit. A dead guy just latched onto me like I was his last meal."

"You're being dramatic. It's not like he was trying to eat you. It was just an automatic reflex. It happens."

"No, it doesn't," she said incredulously. "And I should know because I see some pretty strange stuff." She took a couple of steps toward him and his eyes widened the closer she got. "Do dead guys in your world normally sit up and start breathing again too?"

He shrugged and looked down at his watch, as if he'd already given her too much of his time. "It can happen."

"No!" She seethed. "When someone dies, they usually stay dead. I've had it with you people. I want to know what the hell is going on around here. You guys swoop in like Satan's army and make camp in Last Stop like it makes sense, when it doesn't make any sense at all. A funeral home of this size doesn't need five full-time employees. It's ridiculous. You'd be of better use figuring out why the pipes rattle in my bathroom or whether or not the floor is rotting in front of my fireplace." She paused to take a breath, but not for long. "I have nightmares about falling straight through to the bottom floor."

"I can fix your floor," he offered. "And the pipes."

"Really?" she asked, losing her train of thought. "Because that would be great. I didn't get upgraded like the rest of the place. I'm in steerage."

His lips quirked and she felt a small victory. She could count the number of times she'd seen him smile on one hand.

"Anyway, thanks for the flooring offer. I'll take you up on it. But that's not my point. My point is random dead guys don't just show up out of the middle of nowhere. And people don't just bring them back to life."

"Isn't that what doctors do?" he asked.

She narrowed her eyes and put fists at her hips. "Don't be deliberately obtuse. And you're not a doctor."

"How do you know?" he asked. "You don't know anything about me."

She stared at him blankly for a second and realized he was right. "Are you a doctor?"

"No, but I could be."

She growled and he full-out grinned this time. Apparently her temper was entertaining.

"I'm in charge here. What I know is that you or one

of the others took the transport van out in the middle of the night, without letting me know I might add, and you came back with a body and no paperwork."

"If you'd woken up at your usual time, you wouldn't have seen him at all. We just needed a quick place to put him while we tended to some other things. I'm really glad Eve put that tile floor in. It makes cleanup a lot easier."

"So what you're saying is if I hadn't had insomnia I'd have never known the difference."

"Pretty much. You're a creature of habit. We can set our clocks by you for the most part. We had a small setback while we were out, and time wasn't on our side. It was a simple race against the clock."

"So y'all frequently use company equipment to joyride and pick up random bodies while I'm sleeping?" Her temper was on the edge of the boiling point.

"Not random," he said.

"If you hadn't showed up when you did, he could've killed me."

"If you'd stayed asleep until seven, you'd have never been in danger."

"So this is *my* fault?" she asked incredulously.

"More or less."

"You must be out of your damned mind."

"I wouldn't have let him hurt you," he said, shrugging.

"How would you have stopped him? It was just chance that you happened to walk by."

"I never do anything by chance."

"You are the most maddening man I've ever met in my whole life."

"Thank you," he said, nodding.

"It wasn't a compliment!" She paced back and forth along the side of the body. "I'm the person responsible for anything that happens with the funeral home. Did you kidnap this man? Are the police going to be banging down the door looking for him? I deserve an explanation."

He stared at her a few seconds, his face set in determined lines. She wouldn't be intimidated by his size, and she wouldn't back down.

"No," he said after a moment of silence, and turned around and walked out of the embalming room.

Her mouth hung open in a surprised O, and then her brain processed his rudeness and she ran after him.

"What do you mean, no? You can't just say no. That's ridiculous." He was already to the other end of the hall. "Good grief," she muttered under her breath and sprinted after him. "He's like a damned gazelle."

"My hearing is excellent," he said.

"What the hell am I supposed to do with that guy?" she asked. "I've got a body to prep today."

"He'll be out of your way in the next couple of hours. Don't worry about it."

"Oh, sure. No problem. I'll completely ignore the hulking guy on my table. I'll just put Mrs. Schriever right on top of him while I get the liver spots off her face. My mother is going to have a cow."

He stopped in his tracks at that, and she ran right

smack into his back with an *mmmph*. "Your mother is coming today?" he asked.

"She's doing Mrs. Schriever's hair. Why?"

"No reason. I'll warn Dante. She bit him once."

Tess pursed her lips tightly. "She has a fondness for British men. I guess she couldn't help herself."

Deacon's lips twitched and he moved forward, but she rushed in front of him. "I'm serious, Deacon. I need to know what's going on here. I'm not stupid. I've got eyes and ears. This was supposed to be my funeral home. I've put blood, sweat, and tears into this place for a long time. But then you guys move in and all of a sudden there's a room I can't access inside the casket showroom and the carriage house is protected like Fort Knox." He shook his head like he was going to deny it, but she cut him off before he could speak. "Do me a favor and don't lie to me. I'd rather you ignore my questions than lie."

His lips pinched together, but he eventually nodded. He didn't deny or confirm her accusation of the hidden room.

"My grandmother's ring got stuck in one of the memory compartments on one of the caskets, and I was on the floor trying to get it unstuck. Axel didn't notice me when he came in and went to the back wall with the three stacked caskets. I couldn't see what he did to open it, but the wall slid open. I've known about it almost since the beginning."

"Interesting," Deacon said. "I'd really love to talk, but I need to get a couple hours of sleep before our new friend wakes up. He's going to take a lot of energy to deal with. Just let him sleep it off and stay out of his way."

"*Yebat', chto*," she said.

In loose translation, it meant something along the lines of "Fuck that." Her grandmother had taught her all the really important sayings before she'd started school. She'd been the only kid in kindergarten who could call her teacher a Commie bastard and get away with it.

"*Nerazumnym zemleroyka*," he popped back.

Her mouth dropped open as he answered in the language of her childhood.

"An unreasonable shrew?" she asked, her voice pitching higher on the last word. "An unreasonable shrew?"

She spat back in a tirade of back-alley Russian that would have made her grandmother proud. Her body was hot all over, and she figured she probably looked like a teakettle ready to blow, complete with steam coming out of her ears.

His brows rose high and he said, "Pretty talk."

"I haven't even gotten started," she said, blocking his attempts to get around her. "And since we're on the subject—"

"No we're not," he said, picking her up by the elbows and lifting her to the side.

She wasn't deterred. "I was told you all were experienced employees and mortuary assistants. You've always helped when help was needed, but none of you know Jack squat about digging graves or your way around an embalming table. Or even what to do with the fluids for cleanup. The first time Axel assisted with an embalming

I thought he was going to vomit. I've never seen a man gag like that."

A definite twinkle came into his eyes at that bit of information.

Tess crossed her arms. "I'm not stupid, so I know there's a specific reason she put you here. I don't know what it is, and I don't care. Okay, maybe I care a little, but only because I'm curious. What I *really* care about is my reputation and whether or not it gets damaged. Whatever the real scenario is with the body in the embalming room, it doesn't play out well. You were surprised he was alive. Which begs the question, did you try to kill him or try to save him? And when did you learn to speak Russian? I feel like I'm in the Twilight Zone."

"I'm never surprised by anything," Deacon said, expertly ducking all her questions. "Being surprised usually leads to being dead."

"That's very philosophical. But it still doesn't explain the very alive man on the embalming table."

"Like I said, he'll be out of your hair in a couple of hours. You'll be seeing him around once he gets used to this place. We've all gotten along just fine. Don't start sticking your nose places it might get cut off."

"Like *I* said, I'm tired of being kept in the dark. I'm not even sure what I'm still doing here, other than it's the only thing I've ever done. I'm about this close to walking out of here for good and letting you explain to the nosey people in this town why you can't bury their loved ones because you don't know a vein expander from a hole in the ground."

"You think you're irreplaceable?" he asked, narrowing his eyes.

"Of course not." It was the first time she'd voiced her thoughts of leaving out loud, and it felt powerful. Or maybe that was her temper. Either way, she was bound to say something she'd regret later once her good sense returned. "Everyone's replaceable. But I won't be bullied into doing things I don't agree with. And I won't be steamrolled by the five of you because you're taking orders from Eve Winter instead of me. I'll do my job the right way or I won't do it at all.

"So if this is the way you plan to do things, you can relay my resignation to your boss. Don't ever underestimate the people in this town. They're nosey as hell, and if I leave here they're going to invade your personal space like you've never imagined. They're going to ask questions, no matter how personal. And then they're going to take their business into the city, because they're not going to let an outsider they don't trust handle the bodies of their loved ones. Only there's just one problem with that."

"And what would that be?"

She moved in a step closer, so her chin almost touched his chest. "It's going to be pretty difficult to explain to the feds why enough income for ten funerals a month comes in consistently when we're lucky to do one. The money has to come from somewhere, right? Maybe they can find out whatever scam it is you're running and using the funeral home to do so. Maybe I should go wake the John Doe on the table in there and ask him what he knows before you get your hands on him."

"That would be a mistake," he said gravely. "A big one."

"I don't appreciate being used to take the fall for whatever kind of fraud you're involved in. I don't know what scheme you're running, and I don't care. But I'll be damned if I'll have the IRS or FBI looking at me as the responsible party because my name is on the account and I write all the checks."

His eyes went frigid and she hoped to God he couldn't smell her fear. Because once she'd started talking she hadn't been able to shut up. It was like the pseudo-dead guy on her embalming table was the last straw, and something in her had cracked. Up until this point it had just been her gut telling her something was off with her sexy and secretive employees. It hadn't stopped her imagination from picturing them as part of a prostitution ring or black-market baby scheme, but she figured most of that had to do with the fact that she read a lot of romance novels. The body on her table was a different story. She deserved some answers.

All five-foot-six of her faced off against a man who looked like he'd have no problem snapping her neck.

"You're playing a dangerous game, Tessera."

She narrowed her eyes and said, "Don't call me by my full name. And how in the world do you even know that name anyway?"

"It's beautiful," he told her.

She backed up a step and crossed her arms over her chest. She was never very comfortable with compliments, so she ignored him. "Besides, we wouldn't have to play any games if you just told me the truth. This is my life you're messing with."

He took a step forward, until their bodies were almost touching and his gaze bore into hers. Her breathing was ragged and her heart pounded in her chest, and she felt the electricity from their tempers and the storm crackling between them.

He leaned a little closer, and then he said, "Has anyone ever told you you look a little bit like a hedgehog when you're angry? It's terrifying."

Tess didn't recognize the sound that escaped her lips, but she thought the synapses in her brain must've been exploding one by one, because all she saw was red. And then he leaned the rest of the way down and kissed her right on the lips.

The heat that was already infusing her body went molten as his lips pressed hard against hers. He didn't touch her anywhere else, and her arms dropped to her side as she went boneless. He tasted of mint and man, and her tongue stroked against his. She felt as if she were falling, and she brought her hands up to grasp hold, but he pulled away from her mouth and took a moment to nuzzle her neck before taking a step back.

There was a loud buzzing in her ears, and it had been going on awhile before she realized someone was at the door. It was followed by three loud knocks.

"Tess, open up. It's Cal."

Cal Dougherty was the sheriff in Last Stop. Her eyes widened and she looked up at Deacon, but he'd already taken a step back. The teasing glint that had been in his eyes was gone, and in its place was the same unreadable mask she'd seen for the last two years. She wanted to kick him in the shin, but she figured it was probably best to refrain. Deacon was a bit of a wild card.

"Sounds like you've got business to tend to," he said, stepping around her. "I'll let you get back to work."

Her emotions were wreaking havoc inside her body. All she'd wanted was a few answers. Instead she'd had the rug pulled out from under her. What the heck had been with that kiss? She'd imagined kissing him for two years, though in her fantasies it had transpired a little differently. There hadn't been the arguing. And he hadn't called her a hedgehog. Other than that it was as spectacular as she'd imagined.

"Why did you kiss me?" she asked him hotly.

"Because I wanted to."

"Seems awfully coincidental that you'd pick now of all times."

"You're very cynical." His voice was calm and his breathing even, as if he hadn't just had his tongue in her mouth.

"I've got reason to be."

"Not really. You dodged a bullet with that jackass you were engaged to. I can't believe you were even engaged. He wasn't your type at all. You'd railroad a man like that in no time."

She huffed indignantly. "I would not," she said. "I'm not some overbearing nag. I'm a very nice person. Dammit."

Bang, bang, bang. "Tess, are you in there?" Cal called out again.

"You are a very nice person," he agreed, pacifying her a little. "But putting your personality with his would be like letting a hurricane loose on a trailer park. You'd mop the floor with him and come to resent him. And you wouldn't be able to pretend to be the meek and subservient wife forever, which was how you ended up engaged in the first place."

Her hands went back to her hips and she scowled. "I'm sorry, but I didn't realize you'd been such an active part of my relationship. No wonder you have such insight. Maybe you could've told me all this a couple of years ago instead of letting me make an ass of myself in front of the entire town."

"Sometimes you've got to learn lessons the hard way. Besides, it was pretty entertaining the way you threw that ring into that Dumpster. And it was more entertaining to watch him go in after it. What'd you do with it? I know you didn't actually throw it in that Dumpster."

She narrowed her eyes. "How do you know that?"

"I'm observant. It's part of the job."

"Which job would that be?"

Buzz. Buzz.

He just smiled.

"You know, I don't think I'm cut out for whatever is happening here," she said. "I'd already been considering a change, but I'm feeling pretty strongly about it now. I'm resigning."

"No, you're not." And with that, he moved around her and headed out the kitchen door and into the rain.

"I'm really getting tired of you telling me no," she yelled after him, and then went to let in the sheriff.

In her experience, it usually wasn't good news when the cops showed up at the door before the sun had risen.

CHAPTER FOUR

Cal Dougherty was a couple of years older than Tess, and they'd gone to school together. He'd become sheriff during the last election cycle when he'd beat out Sheriff Brown by a landslide.

That was mostly because Sheriff Brown had gotten caught with his duty belt around his ankles and the mayor's wife sitting on his face—at least according to Georgia Ambrose, who'd walked in on them doing the deed. Of course, no one had bothered to ask Georgia what she was doing at the Bluebonnet Motel on a Tuesday afternoon or why the key she'd used unlocked Sheriff Brown's room. But rumor was that Sheriff Brown had cuffed a lot of women in room 202.

Tess and Cal had grown up with the same circle of friends, so they knew each other well, but it had never been her favorite thing to deal with the police, so she'd kept her distance the last several years. Mostly because she'd spent her fair share of time trying to explain to the cops why they shouldn't toss her mother in jail and throw away the key. If Theodora was in a financial fix and the slot machines were calling, there was no limit to what she'd do to feed her habit.

Tess had gone to school with Cal's first wife. She was a nice girl from a nice family, but she and Cal hadn't been married more than a year when Victoria decided she wasn't meant for small-town life and moved down to Austin. Cal hadn't seemed too bent out of shape about the whole thing, so everyone figured it was probably for the best.

Cal didn't really get too bent out of shape about anything, unless it was the Dallas Cowboys or that time a group of teenage boys changed his election signs to read "Erect" instead of "Elect."

He was handsome, with dark brown eyes and black hair threaded with the occasional strand of silver, which he kept cut short in a military style. He was dressed in jeans, and his neon-yellow police slicker was snapped all the way to the collar. He'd spent his rookie years plus a few more working patrol for the Dallas PD, and he'd taken a couple of bullets in his vest during a routine traffic stop.

"Sorry to bother you so early, Tess," he said. "Whew, it's bad out here."

"No problem. I'm just getting up and started for the day. Come on in out of the wet." Tess stood back so he could get past her. It was then she really got a good look at the front yard. "Good grief, we're all going to be under water before too much longer. I've never seen it so high." The grass and sidewalk were completely covered with several inches of water.

Cal lowered the hood of his slicker and unsnapped it, shrugging out of it before laying it across one of the rocking chairs on the front porch. He wiped his feet on the mat before stepping inside.

"And doesn't look like it's going to stop anytime soon. Never seen rain like this in July."

"I hear it's El Niño," she said.

Cal gave her an odd look, and it was then she realized they were standing mostly in the dark. The downstairs lights were still off since she hadn't opened for business yet, and only the wall sconces were lit. She reached over to flip on the main light switches, and the foyer was instantly flooded with light.

"Why don't you come into the kitchen?" she said. "I haven't had a chance to make coffee yet."

"Sounds good. I haven't been home yet. There's some flooding on the south side. Worst thing was getting Jed Larson's cattle out of the muck. Cows are the stupidest animals I've ever seen. It's a good thing they taste so good."

She snorted out a laugh and felt herself relax a little. If someone was hurt or in trouble, Cal wouldn't have been making small talk. She motioned for him to follow her to the kitchen, flipping on more light switches as she went, and made her way to the coffeemaker. Tess pretty much lived on coffee, and she almost always had a pot ready for visitors.

"You take cream and sugar?" she asked.

"Nah, just black. I've got time to go home and put on dry clothes, but I've got to be back at the office in an hour or so. I need something that'll keep me awake."

She got out the cream and sugar for herself and then grabbed two mugs from the cupboard.

"This place sure looks different from when George owned it," Cal said, looking around.

"Yeah, it's probably a good thing he's sailing the Pacific. George hated change."

"He also hated spending money. George was tight as a tick, and it must've taken a ton to get this place looking like it does. It must be nice to have it to yourself."

Tess looked up at him and arched a brow. Like the rest of town, he must know about the men who lived out back. "Sometimes I get a roommate who passes through, but for the most part they're nice and quiet." Unless they came back from the dead and tried to grab her, she said to herself.

Cal smiled and then said, "I don't suppose you have a piece of toast or a biscuit you could spare. I missed dinner last night and my stomach is trying to eat itself."

"Sure." She pulled a loaf of bread from the pantry and put a couple of slices in the toaster. She could make toast. Barely. Then she grabbed butter and grape jelly from the refrigerator and placed it all in front of Cal, who nodded appreciatively.

"Okay, I can't stand it anymore," she finally said. She'd spent the last several minutes getting herself worked up. "I'm guessing you're here because of Mama. I'm not bailing her out of jail again, do you hear me?" She wagged the butter knife at him and then set it down in front of him and grabbed him a plate. "She's just going to have to do the thirty days this time and maybe she'll learn her lesson."

Cal's lips twitched and he said, "I doubt thirty days in jail will make a blip on her radar. She'd have all the cells picked clean and the items sold on eBay before we noticed, and then she'd be halfway to Oklahoma and the nearest casino before we noticed she was gone. Last time I saw her she told me to take all my savings and put it on lucky number thirty-one, because thirty-one was how old she was when she won that forty thousand dollars."

Tess smiled, but it was bittersweet. "Yep, the best year of her life was watching all those sevens line up in a perfect row. She never talks about how all that money was gone two days later."

"I've got to tell you. I've never met anyone in the world like your mama. She's a beautiful woman, and she's clever and persuasive. She always seems to land on her feet."

Tess sighed. "You're not the first person to tell me that."

Theodora *was* beautiful. Her hair was a vivid red and her eyes emerald green. She wasn't shades of pastels, as Tess tended to think of herself. Theodora was Technicolor in every way. A slightly older version of Rita Hayworth, with a little more va-va in her va-va-voom.

"I know it's hard," Cal said sympathetically. "But you're doing the best you can for her. She's got a sickness, that's all. Unfortunately, she's independent and her mind is sound. The state would never intervene at this point. The best you could hope is to get her into rehab for gamblers."

"She won't go to extended rehab," she said with a sigh. "It's a sickness that there's no cure for. She has to want to get better. And she likes where she is just fine. There's always someone there to bail her out. She's somehow miraculously never managed to hit rock bottom. The judge said she just needs to keep going to therapy and she'll get better."

"Does she go to therapy?" he asked.

"Yes, but only because she's sleeping with her therapist. I don't know many people who can deny Theodora when she sets her mind to something."

Tess poured the coffee into mugs and then passed the blue one to Cal. She doctored hers with a liberal helping of cream and sugar.

Cal winced. "You might as well be having dessert with all that sugar in there."

"Everything should taste like dessert," she said. "Only way I'll even touch a brussels sprout is if it's wrapped in maple bacon. Whoever invented that was a genius."

Cal took his first sip of coffee, and it wasn't until she saw the relief on his face from the hot drink that she realized how tired and overworked he looked. The toaster popped and she put the two pieces on his plate. They were only slightly burned around the edges, which was an improvement over the last time she'd made toast and had to use the handheld fire extinguisher under the sink.

Cal didn't complain. He slathered the toast in butter and jam and swallowed it down in three bites, along with the rest of his coffee. She refilled his mug for him.

"That hits the spot," he said, pushing back his plate. "Thank you. And I can promise you I'm not here because of Theodora. She's been off the radar for the most part. Maybe the therapy really is working."

The relief that overcame Tess surprised her a bit, and she braced her hands on the counter to keep her balance. She'd been mentally preparing herself to go down to the jail and see who Theodora had stolen from so she could pay for her habit. It was a lot easier to lose other people's money than her own. Cal's words had taken the wind right out of her sails.

"Well, that's a relief," she said at last. "That's good enough news that I'll offer to make you a full-fledged breakfast if you'd like."

His eyes widened comically, and she couldn't say she blamed him. If she screwed up toast, she couldn't imagine the kind of damage she could do to an actual meal.

"I'm good, thanks," he said after a pause, and Tess had to hold back a laugh. "I'm actually here because I got a call from the sheriff's office in Dallas County. They had a home robbery that took place a couple of hours ago. The police recovered two armed suspects who'd been tied up and left out in the rain until the authorities arrived. But one of the suspects had been shot and lost a fair amount of blood. He was mostly incoherent when the police got to him, but he kept babbling about the devils from the funeral home. The detective pieced together enough to understand that the robbers had allegedly been subdued by several men with guns and driving a black van."

Tess felt the color leach out of her face. "Wow."

"You don't happen to know anything about that, do you?" he asked. "I'd like to take a look at your van if you don't mind."

She wasn't sure why his request irked her so much. Maybe because of the way he'd phrased the question. He'd been buttering her up and was now asking questions like she was hiding some deep dark secret. And technically, maybe she was harboring a secret, since she knew they'd taken the van out and there was a dead/ not dead body on her table. All she knew for sure was that she had a lot more questions than she was getting answers for.

"Of course I don't know anything about it," she said, sounding properly insulted. "I told you I was just getting up for the day."

"You haven't been out in the rain?" he asked.

"No," she said, perplexed now. "People generally don't go out in the rain in the middle of the night."

"I just noticed your hair was wet, that's all."

She arched a brow and felt her cheeks heat with anger. "The electricity went out, so I wasn't able to dry my hair after my shower this morning. I didn't realize having wet hair was a punishable offense."

"Now, there's no need to get that temper of yours riled up," he said, holding up his hands. "I wouldn't be doing my job if I didn't ask."

"You've known me my whole life, and unless I'm remembering wrong, not once have I ever been accused of taking my van out for a joyride and shooting a couple of robbers. I'm not G.I. Jane or Annie Oakley."

"Then you won't mind if I see the van?" he asked.

"I'm more than happy to show you the van when it gets back from being cleaned. They took it yesterday after Mrs. Schriever was dropped off from the hospital. The inside was a mess after all the rain we've been having."

The lie flew off her tongue before she even knew what hit her. Good grief, what in the world was wrong with her? She was lying to a man of the law. And by the way he was looking at her, she wondered if he knew it. But she'd be darned if he was going to come into her house and accuse her of a crime she didn't commit.

She had no reason in the world to cover up for Deacon Tucker or any of the others, but that's exactly what she was doing. One stupid kiss and her sense had gone right out the window.

"When was the last time you saw your employees?"

She shrugged and went back for a second cup of coffee. She could already tell it was going to be one of *those* days.

"I brought Mrs. Schriever back about two thirty yesterday. Deacon and Colin were both here to help me unload. I didn't see anyone after that because I was embalming Mrs. Schriever. I didn't get finished until close to six."

"What about after?"

"Well, golly gee, Cal," she said, her eyes wide with

sarcasm, "I washed the scent of formaldehyde from my body and then we had a giant orgy."

He scowled and stared into his cup. "There's no need to be snippy, Tess. I'm just doing my job."

"Chush' sobach'ya."

"I've heard your granny say that before," he said. "So I know it's not very nice." Cal finished off his coffee and then took his mug to the sink to rinse it out.

He was right, but she didn't figure it was in her best interest to tell him he was full of shit. At least in English.

"I noticed you're favoring your wrist," he said, changing the subject. "You made the coffee and got the mugs out with your left hand. I thought you were always right-handed in school."

"I had a run-in with a heavy piece of equipment," she answered automatically, drawing the aforementioned wrist in tighter to her body. "The equipment won."

"If it's bothering you that much, you might ought to swing by Doc Carlisle's before things get too busy around here. Might be broken. Your fingers are looking a little swollen."

Since Doc Carlisle was the biggest quack in a hundred-mile radius, she wouldn't be paying him a visit if her wrist was dangling by no more than a thread of skin.

"It's fine. Just a sprain. I've got a brace I can put on it upstairs."

"You remind me a lot of your granny," he said with a sigh. "She's got a head hard as a rock too."

"Thank you." And she sincerely meant it. Her grandmother was a hell of a woman. Being compared to her was a million times better than the alternative of being likened to her mother.

"Let me know when that van gets back. I'd still like to take a look at it."

Damned man was tenacious as a bulldog. She tried to hide her scowl behind her cup.

His lips quirked in half a smile before he said, "Anyone ever tell you you don't hide your feelings very well?"

"It's my stupid red-headed complexion," she said, rolling her eyes.

"And probably the fact that everything you're thinking appears right across your face. You probably shouldn't ever play poker."

"I'll keep that in mind."

"Since cards are out, how about dinner?"

She'd just taken a sip of coffee, so when the question finally penetrated her brain, she tried to suck in a breath at the same time she was swallowing. It didn't work out all that well and sent her into a fit of coughing.

Tess pounded on her chest and prayed coffee didn't come out of her nose. It was sixth grade all over again.

"That wasn't really the reaction I was hoping for," Cal said, his voice amused.

Her eyes were watering and she knew her face was probably blotchy. She wasn't a pretty crier. "No," *cough, cough*. "Sorry," *cough*. "You just took me by surprise."

It's like she'd started the day in an alternate universe. She hadn't been on a date since Henry left. Now all of a sudden it was raining men, and the sun had barely risen.

"I guess I've been out of the game too long," he said. "I think people text stuff like that these days."

"And they probably don't treat the person like a suspect first," she said. "You might want to work on your timing."

"Right," he said. "Perks of the job. It always comes first."

"Also probably not something you want to tell a woman before you ask her out. They tend to not want to be second in a man's life."

"Huh," he said thoughtfully. "Never did understand women."

"Good luck with that. The good news is you've still got lots of time to learn. You're still in your prime. And Clarice Grabel says you're real good in bed, so there's that too."

Cal sighed and pushed up from the table. "I knew that one was a mistake."

She nodded sagely. "We all make them. But at least the gossip is positive instead of negative. I'm sure your street cred has gone up tremendously since you made your mistake with her."

"You're a nice woman, Tess Sherman. Try to stay out of trouble, and make sure you're not making any mistakes of your own. I'll show myself out." He paused on his way out of the room. "No hard feelings, right, Tess?"

"We're good."

"I'll be back to check the van later."

She scowled and heard the front door close softly. "I

guess that could've gone a lot worse," she said, freshening her cup. "Of course, it could've gone a lot better too."

And now she was afraid things would be awkward between them from now on. Cal had never once shown an inkling of interest toward her, and she'd never seen him as anything but an authority figure. She couldn't even figure out if she could have those kinds of feelings for him. He was attractive, sure, but he'd always just kind of . . . been there.

At least he hadn't said anything about a missing body. She wasn't sure she could've lied her way out of that one, even knowing the body wasn't really dead.

Now all she had to do was wait until the mystery man woke up, so she could get to work. Or she could hunt down Deacon and demand answers, especially since she'd just lied to a cop for him.

And maybe he would kiss her again.

"No," she said. "No, no, no."

Her mama wasn't right about much, but she was right about one thing. Men made women do stupid things.

CHAPTER FIVE

Deacon ran the three miles through the tunnel, ignoring how the walls closed in on him. How his lungs tightened and fear crept in like a shroud of blackness, making him light-headed. He focused on his breathing—in and out—in and out—and not on how his legs felt like jelly or how his heart pounded painfully in his chest.

He tortured himself the same way every day. Three miles underground until he reached the end and used the ladder to climb out, and then lie flat on his back as he gulped in breaths of fresh air. The cool mud seeped into his clothes and the rain chilled his overheated flesh. His eyes were sensitive to the daylight, so he kept his eyes closed.

They owned the abandoned lake property, and there was no danger of others seeing him there. So he lay there and let the seconds tick down in his head while his heartbeat slowed and the blackness ebbed away.

He allowed himself exactly four minutes to lie there before dropping back into the tunnel and starting the three-mile trek back to the house. Maybe someday he'd be able to make it in each direction without having to stop and remind himself he wasn't dying. He'd made a lot of progress in two years. But there were some things— some horrors—that stuck with a man forever. And the day he died and rose again was his perpetual nightmare.

The last mile was always the hardest, when he was so close to the end but the urge to quit rose up inside of him. By the time he reached the door and coded himself back into the carriage house, he'd broken out in a cold sweat and his hands were shaking. But they weren't shaking as bad as they had been the day before. Or the day before that.

A cold blast of air hit him when he entered the kitchen and Axel was sitting at the table, his iPad in his hands and a cup of coffee within arm's reach. He quickly blanked the screen when he saw Deacon, but Deacon pretended like he didn't see it and went to the fridge for a bottle of water, guzzling it down in one long gulp.

The kitchen was large and built family-style, though it was rare for all of them to be in it at the same time. They were all solitary by nature, and had their own habits and ways of doing things. But he'd lived in worse places, and no one could say that Eve Winter didn't provide for the men who owed her servitude.

The kitchen was bright and airy and extremely modern, which Deacon didn't particularly care for, but it was more than functional. The floor was big slabs of stained concrete and the walls were a horizontal wood paneling. The appliances were stainless steel and oversized, and every dish in the cabinet was white. Once a week several boxes were delivered that contained groceries for the week. They all foraged for themselves since no one was much good in the kitchen, and Tess was even worse, so there was no use trying to bum a meal off her.

The kitchen was in the back corner of the house and looked out onto a courtyard garden protected by an eight-foot stone privacy fence. There was a fountain and a couple of benches hidden between shrubs and flowering bushes, and more often than not it was the most likely place to find Axel at the end of the day, just as the sun was going down.

Of all his brothers, Axel was the one he was closest to. But he didn't know how his friend did it. How he managed to wake up every morning and get out of bed—put one foot in front of the other—knowing his wife was a thousand miles away, going on with her life under the assumption that her husband was dead. Axel had watched her grieve. He *still* watched her grieve. And there wasn't a damned thing he could do about it. He was hanging on by a thread, and one day it would snap.

The stakes were too high for Gravediggers. They were dead men. Their lives belonged to Neptune and the talking heads who were playing a game of chess with real lives—at least they belonged to them for the ten years they'd signed on for servitude. Or until they died for real. But you didn't sign your name to that contract without understanding the ramifications of what happened if it was discovered that you weren't as dead as the rest of the world seemed to think you were. That was why it was so important to stay away from anyone in their former lives. The second their true identity became known, not only their lives became forfeit, but the lives of their family as well.

So Axel watched the woman he loved from a distance, using satellite imagery and the surveillance cameras that he'd had installed. He'd watched her grieve with such intensity that the child she'd carried hadn't been able to withstand the stress on her body. And he watched her still, as she tried to put the broken pieces of her life back together. Axel wasn't a man of many words. He did the job, and did it well. But there was a loathing rage inside him that bubbled just beneath the calm surface. And Deacon couldn't blame him one bit if he decided to erupt one day.

"How's the new guy?" Deacon asked.

"About how you'd imagine. It never gets easier. Bringing them in and watching them, knowing what they're going through."

"On a scale of one to ten, how pissed is he?"

"About a fifteen, but he's hiding it well. He's a dangerous son of a bitch. You read his file?"

"Yeah, I read it. And he'll be a hell of an asset. If he doesn't try to kill me. Eve's not very good about the transition once she has their signature on the contract. All of a sudden you're surrounded by men who hold you down and inject you with whatever the hell that stuff is."

"Hurts like a bitch," Axel said. "Like molten lead going through your veins. You can actually feel yourself dying. Feel your heart slowing, even though your brain is working just fine."

"Yeah, she doesn't explain that part to you," Deacon agreed. "Now I have to go convince this guy we're not actually here to harm him, and hope like hell I don't have to fight him. I'm getting too old for this shit."

"And you might lose, mate," Axel said, grinning. "He's fucking *Kidon* Mossad."

"Thank you," Deacon said dryly. "That's very helpful."

"Hey, mate, that's why you're the team leader," Axel said, saluting him with two fingers.

"I'll give him another thirty to cool off while I take a shower."

"Good luck."

Deacon tossed his water in the trash, took the stairs to the second floor, and walked to his suite of rooms. Once the new guy was acclimated, he'd take the rooms across the hall from him. Axel and Colin lived up on the third floor. All four suites were identical to each other, but Deacon's was larger since he'd been the first.

His heart rate had finally slowed and the paralyzing fear had ebbed. He hated the weakness—a weakness brought on by what Eve had put him through when he'd been reborn as a Gravedigger. The serum had still been in development when it had been tested on him, and he hadn't had the luxury of coming back to life in a room aboveground where oxygen had been readily available. He'd woken up trapped in a seven- by two-foot box, buried six feet underground.

He'd have preferred a real death.

When they finally dug him out of the ground, he'd been more animal than man. Fear like nothing he'd ever experienced before had seized him as he'd clawed and pushed at the sides of his cage, his every breath growing more shallow.

He shook himself from the memory and stripped out of his clothes, and then turned on the shower. While it heated, he took a moment to shave. He'd barely nuzzled Tess's neck that morning, but when he'd stepped back he could see the marks from his beard. And he couldn't say it displeased him to see them there, especially with the sheriff knocking at the door.

Cal Dougherty would've had to be an idiot not to notice, and Dougherty wasn't an idiot. Deacon had run a thorough check on the sheriff when they'd first set up headquarters, and Cal was so overqualified for his job it was laughable. But the sheriff had secrets he wanted to keep, and Deacon was more than happy to let him keep them. Until it was no longer convenient.

What Deacon didn't appreciate was Cal's interest in Tess. He'd sniffed around for the last couple of years, but fortunately Tess was pretty oblivious when it came to men noticing her. That was one of the things he liked about her. She had no idea of her appeal to the opposite sex, and she seemed to cloak herself with an invisible sign that read "Keep Away."

That fiancé of hers had done her a favor by calling off the wedding, and Tess hadn't seemed to notice men even existed since then. Until that day he'd almost kissed her in the kitchen. She'd most definitely noticed him then, and he'd almost laughed at the surprise that had come into her eyes at the realization that he was very male and very interested. Fortunately for both of them, they'd been interrupted before things could go any further.

He'd wanted her to wake up. To see him as a man. But he hadn't thought things through on what he'd do when she finally did. They had rules as Gravediggers, and it wasn't a job conducive to relationships. Sex, yes. But relationships, no. For all intents and purposes, they "worked" together. She was their cover, and seducing her for the sake of a few moments of pleasure that could never lead to anything else wasn't fair to her.

Now, if only he could get his body to listen to his mind. The second he'd started thinking about that kiss he'd gone hard as a rock, and he shook his head as he looked down at his undisciplined body. He stepped into the hot spray and let out a sigh as the heat pounded against his muscles.

It would've been easy to bring back the taste of her—the way her breath caught when their lips met. It had taken every ounce of control he had not to put his hands on her. And when she'd touched him . . .

He groaned and turned off the hot water so only the cold blasted across his heated skin. It wouldn't have taken much more than a touch for him to relieve the god-awful need that had been building inside him since he'd kissed her. But if he couldn't control those basic needs, he couldn't control anything.

He showered quickly and dried off, cursing the erection that had a mind of its own. He pulled his hair back into a stubby tail while still wet, dressed in khaki BDUs and a black T-shirt, and laced up his boots. When he looked at his watch, he was satisfied to see that he still had two minutes left of the thirty-minute reprieve he'd given the newest recruit.

The two minutes was up by the time he made it back to the kitchen and the locked door that led into their headquarters. Tess had been right when when she'd spoken of the hidden passageway inside the casket warehouse. There was also a passageway from the kitchen inside the carriage house to the underground bunker that housed the kind of equipment and resources that would blow most people's minds.

He typed in the code and pressed his index finger to the fingerprint scanner, and he heard the quiet snick of the lock open. He turned the handle, walked down the darkened stairwell to the next locked door, and typed in a different code. When the door opened, his options were to go left or right. The left would take him to the secret escape tunnel that had become his personal hell every morning. The right took him to another locked door, embossed with a gold trident in the center.

A cool blast of air hit him as he entered the inner sanctum of Gravediggers HQ. There was no one in sight. Considering the night they'd had, it was more than likely the others were catching a couple of hours of sleep.

He left the control room and headed toward the isolation rooms. It was necessary for new Gravediggers to be contained until their bodies had completely detoxed from the serum and any ill effects it might have. Once they passed the psychological and medical evaluation, they could be briefed and slowly implemented onto the team.

He stared at Levi Wolffe through the window in the isolation room. Levi never looked up. He sat on the edge of the bed, his head resting on his hands. Deacon knew he had a hell of a headache, along with a powerful thirst. Dying wasn't easy.

As if he'd heard the thought, Levi lifted his head and stared at him out of cold, black eyes. Deacon was familiar with the look of a man who could and had killed. They'd been monitoring him from the surveillance system inside the house, and when the stages of paralysis looked like they were starting to pass, they'd gone in to retrieve him, he and Axel supporting the other man between them as they guided him to the isolation room. It was easier to move a man the size of Levi if he was able to stand on his own two feet and help a little.

Levi was just over six feet, and his Israeli heritage was strong—his skin swarthy and his dark hair cut close to the scalp. He had several days' worth of beard on his face that he'd get the opportunity to shave off once they let him have a shower and knew he wouldn't try to slice his own wrists with the blade. He still wore the flight suit he'd been buried in, and there were two empty bottles of water at his feet.

Deacon went to the mini fridge outside the room and grabbed a couple more bottles, and then he unlocked the storage cabinet bolted to the wall and took out a painkiller that would take care of the sledgehammers in

Levi's head. Once he had the supplies, he punched in the code on the keypad and let himself into the lion's den.

"I know you're thirsty," Deacon said, coming boldly into the room.

He didn't fear for his life; he'd never feared another man. They were both trained to fight—trained to kill—and there could be no fear when you always expected each fight might be your last. He also knew Axel was watching on the camera feed.

"And you'll probably want this," he said, holding out his hand with the small white pill. "I imagine your head is about ready to explode at this point. It's always bad right after you come back."

Levi just stared at him, but he eventually took the water and gulped it down. He didn't touch the pill.

"It's a standard prescription painkiller," Deacon said. "Nothing more. But I don't blame you for not trusting it. None of the others did either, and I was so fucked up coming out of the ground I don't think they even offered one to me. I'll leave it on the nightstand in case you change your mind. The headache usually lasts six to eight hours without the drugs."

The isolation rooms weren't prison, but they were built with the idea in mind that whoever was occupying the room might not care about his personal safety. They were kind of like hotel rooms, only there was a lock on the *outside* of the door instead of inside. There was a queen-size bed, a small table and two chairs, and a toilet. There was no shower or kitchenette. The isolation room across the hall was equipped with more amenities, and once Levi passed all the evaluations he'd be moved over there.

Deacon grabbed one of the straight-backed wooden chairs and straddled it so he faced Levi.

"She didn't explain what would happen to you, did she?" Deacon asked.

Levi continued his silence, but Deacon wasn't deterred. He'd done this with each of his brothers. They were all different, but in many ways they were all the same.

"It's a shock, isn't it?" he continued on. "All of a sudden this woman shows up out of nowhere, usually when things are about to go straight to shit and you're wondering not *if* you're going to be taken out of the game, but *when* you're going to be taken out. Then Eve Winter shows up like the Angel of Death and tells you since you're already marked for death you might as well come to work for the devil and live a little longer. We're all going to die eventually, right?"

"I believe the life we live on this earth prepares us for the life that comes after. I'm grounded in my faith, and I did not sell my soul to the devil. I've seen the devil and her name is not Eve Winter."

"But she got you to join us?" Deacon asked, surprised at Levi's first words.

Levi picked up the other bottle of water and drank it slower this time, contemplating his answer.

"I agreed to fulfill the contract in hopes of continuing my quest for justice. There is still work to be done on this earth, and my destiny hasn't been fulfilled."

"You seek vengeance?" Deacon asked, unsurprised.

"Don't we all?"

"To a point. There's a lot of good in humanity, but in our line of work we rarely see it. We're protectors."

"That we can agree on, though I'm wondering now who exactly I've agreed to protect."

Deacon knew the feeling. When Eve Winter showed up and told him the only options he had were death or a new life created by her, his first response had been to tell her he would gladly choose death. But Eve knew things. Things that no one else could know. And she knew exactly the buttons to push to make a man agree to her proposition instead of choosing death. He didn't know what had made Levi Wolffe make the decision, but he did know it was deeply personal. It was deeply personal for all of them.

"You're working for the good guys, but it's no different than any other covert ops mission. Sometimes you wonder. And sometimes you don't know which devil you're working for."

"She told me I had to die and be reborn. That my family and friends could never know my fate or they would suffer and meet me in death. Most of my family was killed during a Palestinian rocket attack. They were at the market and there was no warning. Only mayhem and death. My younger sister was the only one to survive, though her injuries were grave. I was willing to leave that life behind. But that doesn't mean that life won't revisit me. We can never truly separate ourselves from our pasts."

"I know. But we can live now and ask for forgiveness later."

A hint of a smile quirked Levi's lips, but it was gone almost before it began. A shudder wracked his body and his hand went back to his head. Then he very deliberately looked at Deacon and then over at the white pill sitting on the nightstand.

"It's a bitch of a headache," Deacon said.

"Yeah," Levi answered. He reached over and grabbed the pill and popped it in his mouth, swallowing it down with a gulp of water. "I don't know what happened to me, but I figure you've had plenty of time to kill me if that's what you wanted to do."

Deacon smiled, but there was no happiness in it. Only bitter memories of his own transition from life to death to life.

"Once you sign that contract, there's no going back. There are no other meetings or negotiations. All you know is they'll do all the work and bring you over. They don't tell you they'll ambush you when you least expect it, to the point you think whatever is happening is real. They don't tell you about the serum they shoot through your body, or that you can feel yourself dying. That your fully functional brain panics as you lose control and begin to feel your heartbeat slow. That you'll be paralyzed just before you slip into unconsciousness."

Deacon watched as Levi's knuckles turned white, but he didn't stop there. "You were lucky. I was the first. And all I can remember is my eyes opening to complete darkness, and trying to suck air into lungs that couldn't remember how to breathe. I remember not being able to move my legs, because it takes a while for the paralysis to completely disappear, but I could move my arms. I didn't know I'd been buried underground. I only knew I was trapped in some kind of box. I clawed and pushed at the sides and top until my fingers bled, and every minute that passed it was harder to breathe.

"Then there comes a point when you're hovering just on the brink of death, where pain and fear disappear and it's nothing more than waiting to take the last breath. All the prayers you know have been said at this point, and there's peace."

"Yes," Levi said, in complete understanding.

"It was then I heard the thump of something hitting the top of my cage, and I was jostled around as they pulled me from the ground. They were as surprised as I was when they opened the casket and I crawled out into the fresh dirt."

Levi raised his brows and said, "I bet so. You're lucky some trigger-happy cowboy didn't fill you with lead because he thought you were a zombie."

Deacon did smile at this. "That's the thing about this organization. There aren't any cowboys. It's a fluid unit, from the most insignificant job to the most important. And everyone is the best at what they do. Eve Winter sought you out for that reason and brought you here."

"And yet, I still don't know what I'm supposed to do."

"How's your headache?"

"Gone," Levi answered. "Thank you."

"We've got your background and service file. You

were Kidon Mossad. Everyone here comes from similar agencies."

"Mossad has no equals."

Deacon smiled. "We can put it to the test once you're back to full strength. We train together and spar together, sometimes just for the hell of it. You'll get your chance to show us what you're made of."

"Where do you come from?"

"Originally? From a little town in Louisiana. But I was recruited by the CIA about a dozen years ago. I worked covert ops eight years of that. My last four I was taken off the books completely and spent so much time in deep cover I forgot my real name. I took over the identity of Syan Ackbar and infiltrated his ISIS terrorist cell. I spent four years there, slowly cutting the heads off the snakes until the cell had been completely destroyed."

"We have agents as well who have infiltrated these cells," Levi said, nodding. "It is a dangerous game we play with each other. Many lives are lost. But more are saved."

"That's why we do it," Deacon agreed. "You'll meet the others over the next few days. All are allies to your country and to you. Dante is former MI-6, Elias was a Navy SEAL, Colin is French Intelligence, and Axel is Australian Intelligence. We no longer fight for our individual countries, but for one world. That allegiance to each other is important.

"You've got to go through psychological and physical testing over the next couple of weeks. You're feeling a little better now after the pain pill, but when it wears off that headache will come back with a vengeance. You might also have some hallucinations and some out-of-character behavior—meaning you're going to get mad as hell and want to pound on whatever's closest to you. You'll also have some nightmares. It's all part of the process.

"Once those symptoms pass, we'll move you to the room across the hall. It's bigger and you can rehabilitate in more comfort. There you'll start the debriefing process and learn about the organization, as well as be updated on current mission status. You should only be there a couple of days. Then you'll move up to your permanent quarters on the second floor. Unless you want to find a place of your own. Dante and Elias both live off-site."

"Ten years seems like a long time," Levi said.

"It's the blink of an eye when it seems like the world might not last that long."

"How do you stand it?"

Deacon shrugged. "We're not prisoners. We train, we fight, we work hard. But we're free to come and go as we please. Elias likes to go to his cabin in Colorado. Dante will disappear for a few days at a time when things are slow, and no one knows where the hell he goes. It's up to you. Ten years isn't forever. It's important to remember that."

Deacon decided not to tell him there were times being a Gravedigger felt as if it'd last an eternity. And who knew what was in store for any of them? It was something that occupied his mind from time to time. When the ten years were up, would Eve really let them leave?

CHAPTER SIX

Tess considered herself a patient person. Sometimes. But after searching for Deacon for a good hour, she definitely wasn't feeling patient. She still had no answers as to why the sheriff thought they'd been involved in some kind of commando raid robbery, she still didn't have a van, and she assumed there was still a body on her table, though to be fair she hadn't looked, and she figured Mrs. Schriever was good on ice awhile longer.

She knew Deacon had to be around somewhere because his motorcycle was parked in the carport next to the carriage house. She'd braved the rain and pounded on his front door, but no one had answered. She'd even tried to figure out how to access the hidden room in the casket warehouse, but by the time she'd knocked on all the walls and tried every combination of things she could think of, she was starting to wonder if she'd imagined the room to begin with. Maybe Axel hadn't disappeared through the wall that day. Maybe she was just crazy.

Fortunately, no one had witnessed her attempt, as

she'd more than likely looked like a madwoman. The rain and humidity made her hair about twice the size it normally was, and she'd alternated between muttering niceties and curses as she looked for the switch to open the wall. She'd even tried ramming her shoulder against it, but that had led to nothing but a sore shoulder and more curses.

Tess returned to the house a little defeated and a lot wetter. She ran upstairs and changed clothes, opting this time for black leggings and a pale blue summer sweater. She also dug out of the bottom of her bathroom drawer the wrist brace from when she'd had carpal tunnel— the pain was getting worse, and as Cal had so adroitly pointed out, there was definitely some swelling around her wrist and fingers. The pressure of the brace immediately felt better, but she was going to have a heck of a time getting Mrs. Schriever prepared.

She glanced in the mirror and decided her hair was a lost cause. It was still damp, and fuzzy tendrils were sticking out in every direction. She looked at her watch and decided there was no more time to waste. Either the man who wasn't dead was gone from her table so she could work on Mrs. Schriever, or she was going to move him herself. Even if she had to roll him out the door and leave him in the hallway.

By the time she was unlocking the embalming room door, she'd talked herself into quite a temper and was ready to go head-to-head with anyone who got in her way. The bodies that came through her funeral home deserved respect and her time and attention. She didn't care that Eve Winter's name was on the deed to the house. It was *her* funeral home.

But when she pushed open the door to the embalming room, the table was empty.

"Well, then," she said into the silence. "That's more like it."

Her heart thudded in her chest as she scanned the room quickly to see if he was hiding behind anything, and then she turned around to see if he was behind her. She didn't like the idea of a strange man on the loose.

Tess left the door open and went to the large walk-in cooler at the back of the room. Her pulse pounded and her hand trembled as she reached for the latch on the door. No one in their right mind would hide inside the cooler. Unless he wasn't in his right mind.

There was no reason to delay the inevitable. She looked around for a weapon and picked up the trocar, which was what went into the belly button and drained fluids from the body during an embalming, and then she wondered how she was going to hold it and open the cooler door at the same time with her damaged wrist. She finally decided to hold it under her arm so she could open the door with her good hand, since the door was heavy.

Once she got everything situated to her liking, she pulled at the handle and slid the door back with a *whoosh*. Fog from the cold crept from the cooler, and she grabbed the trocar and held it up, ready to impale anyone who jumped out at her. Fortunately, the only person in the cooler was Mrs. Schriever, and Tess let out a nervous exhale and leaned her head against the cooler door.

"What in the world are you doing, Tess?"

Tess shrieked and wielded the trocar like a sword as she turned.

Coming face-to-face with none other than her mother.

Theodora didn't look the least bit concerned that Tess was brandishing a weapon. Of course, Theodora never looked concerned over much of anything. She said worry didn't do anything but give a woman wrinkles.

"Mama," Tess said, putting her hand to her heart. "You scared me to death. What are you doing here so early?"

"I asked Sissy to do my roots and give me a trim, but she said she could only do them early because her husband had to leave for work by eight, so she had to be home for the kids. I tell you, people are too soft on kids these days. Nothing wrong with leaving them home alone for a couple of hours. Gives them a sense of independence. Look how great you turned out."

"Sissy's kids are two and four," Tess said, putting the trocar back where she'd gotten it. "It's generally frowned upon to leave toddlers alone."

Theodora waved that bit of information away like she did anything she deemed unpleasant. "It's neither here nor there. The point is I dragged myself out of bed at an ungodly hour, and I'm not even sure I like the cut she gave me. It's so hard to let another stylist work on me. With my level of expertise, I guess I'm just too critical."

Tess wasn't sure what level of expertise her mother was talking about. She'd dropped out of high school at sixteen when she'd become pregnant with Tess, and her grandmother had made her enroll in beauty school so she'd have some means to support herself and a new baby. In many ways, Theodora still had the naïveté of that sixteen-year-old girl, plus she had narcissistic tendencies, was a pathological liar, and an unapologetic gambling addict. It had made holidays growing up extra special, especially the Christmas Tess had gotten the penny gumball machine and then one day realized Theodora had taken all the pennies out of it to play the slots. But like her grandmother said, Theodora had a sickness. She always had, and all they could do was love her the best they could. Some days were easier than others.

Theodora had technically never graduated from beauty school, but she'd opened the Clip n' Curl with the money her daddy had left her when he died, and she'd paid fifty dollars for a beauty license she'd ordered off of the back of a magazine. No one had ever bothered to question if it was legitimate. Theodora could sell snowsuits to Satan.

Tess had to admit, her mother was a beautiful woman. At forty-seven, she could've passed for at least a decade younger. Glamorous was one of the words that came to mind whenever Tess thought of her mother—the other words weren't as nice, but Theodora was still her mother at the end of the day, so Tess tried not to think them.

Her mother had good qualities too, not to mention that not everyone had the personality to grow up in a house with a woman who'd been raised by the Russian Mafiya. Theodora's free spirit didn't do well under strict conditions. And there were moments during Tess's childhood, when she'd needed the hugs and affection that her grandmother didn't easily give, that she'd been able to turn to Theodora and cry or tell her whatever was on her heart. And then most times they'd sneak out for ice cream. More often than not though, after those bonding mother-daughter moments, life would get too heavy for Theodora and she'd take off for a week or two. But she always came back as if she'd never been away.

Tess had never known her father. He'd come to Last Stop for a meeting at the mayor's office. He'd been some kind of big-city attorney according to Theodora, but he could've just as easily been a trucker passing through. No one would ever know the truth, as Theodora preferred to believe her own truths.

He'd stayed a full week once he'd set his sights on Theodora. Of course, he hadn't known she was only sixteen at the time, as Theodora had developed into a bombshell rather early in life, and she made it a habit to lie about her age. She even had a fake ID she used when she and a couple of her girlfriends would drive across the border to the casinos. Between her curves and the fact that Theodora was nothing if not experienced, even at sixteen, he'd fallen hook, line, and sinker for her seduction.

Theodora always said it was the best week of her life. He'd given her a good-bye tickle and headed back to his real life and family, and that was the end of that. The last tickle had resulted in Tess, and she'd always figured her mother never married because she was waiting for Tess's father to waltz back into town one day and pick up things where they'd left off.

And when Tess heard the happiness in Theodora's voice when she retold the story, it was hard not to wish the best for her. She'd been miserable living at home, as Tess had always heard horror stories about her grandfather. He'd been abusive and enjoyed Stoli vodka more than most Russians, and that was saying a lot. Her grandmother had not only been raised in the Russian Mafiya, she'd also married into it.

He'd been dead long before she was born, which Tess was eternally grateful for. Her grandmother loved her and Theodora in her own way, and she'd been able to show it more after her husband's death.

"Your hair looks lovely," Tess said, knowing that's the only thing Theodora wanted to hear. "Sissy did a great job." And Tess wasn't lying. Her mother's hair was a little shorter than it had been and cut in an asymmetrical bob. It was cute and sassy and fit her mother perfectly.

Theodora put her oversized Chanel bag on the counter and pulled out a couple of cases of hair supplies.

"You're white as a sheet, Tess," she said in response. She looked concerned and came over to put the back of her hand to Tess's forehead. "Cool as a cucumber. You need a man in your life. A live one. Men always put the color back into a woman's cheeks."

Tess thought of the kiss Deacon had given her earlier that morning. It had definitely put color in her cheeks and heated her from the inside out. She was almost afraid to imagine what would have happened if he'd actually put his hands on her.

"I've never defined my worth by having a man around to put color in my cheeks." Tess almost rolled her eyes because she sounded like a prude, even to herself. She wasn't a prude. She just didn't want to be like her mother, looking for the next man she could depend on.

"Your grandmother has been a bad influence," Theodora said, pulling a thermos from her bag and taking a long sip. "After Daddy died she decided she never wanted to look at another man. But it would've been a lot easier on her if she'd kept her sheets a little warm instead of ice cold. All that feminism stuff. God didn't create women so they could take the trash out."

Tess figured it was a great time to disappear inside the cooler and retrieve Delores Schriever. Talking feminism with her mother was like explaining to the pope why prostitution should be legal. It was a task best saved for never.

She rolled Mrs. Schriever from the cooler and moved her next to the large metal table they used for embalming, which had the proper drain pans and other accessories to make Tess's life easier during the process. As she'd told Cal, Mrs. Schriever had been embalmed the afternoon before, when she'd been brought in. It was always best to do it as close to death as they could because the body started decomposing immediately, and Tess was pleased to see Mrs. Schriever was holding up nicely.

People were always under the impression that embalming preserved their loved ones forever, but it only slowed down decomposition. Everyone eventually ended up as bone and dust, no matter what chemicals flowed through the veins.

It was easier to do hair and makeup on the larger table with the drains because they'd wash her down one more time before applying the makeup, and they'd wash her hair good before drying and styling it. The water would just flow into the drain below the table.

"What's in that thermos?" Tess asked, arching a brow at her mother.

"Orange juice. I'm trying to be healthy."

"Really? Because all I smell is vodka."

"Just a splash," she said, pursing her lips. "Vodka is a vegetable and oranges are fruit. It's like a vitamin juice. Which means I can have chocolate cake for dessert."

It was hard to argue with that kind of logic. "Put my watch back on the table with my keys, please," Tess said. She'd seen her mother pocket the watch and not think twice about it. She had to watch her constantly and always made her empty her purse and pockets before she left to go home.

"It's a lovely watch," Theodora said, smiling dreamily as she took the watch out of her pocket and put it back next to Tess's keys. "I could get a solid seventy-five for it at the Prance and Pawn. There's a Powerball drawing next Wednesday. If you'll front me some cash, I can pick some numbers for you too. We can split it seventy/thirty."

In Theodora's mind, a seventy/thirty split was perfectly reasonable for her taking the trip to the gas station and letting a machine randomly pick five numbers for her.

"I'm good. But I'll see if I can find you a watch for Christmas."

"That'll be nice. And maybe a new set of martini glasses. One of them broke, so I only have three. It's bad luck to have an uneven number."

Tess sighed and focused on the job at hand. Work was the greatest escape there was. Delores's body was covered with a white sheet and she was lying on a blue tarp that had two handles on each side. It was always best to jostle the bodies as little as possible, especially with the elderly because the skin was so thin and fragile. Tess snapped the four carabiners onto each of the tarp handles, and then she hit the switch. She kept her hand on the body to guide it as the pulley system lifted Mrs. Schriever off the gurney and onto the table.

"Lord, I want you to just cremate me," Theodora said. "I'd never want people to see my body looking like that. I'd want them to remember me in all my glory."

"So you've mentioned," Tess said, unhooking Mrs. Schriever and pushing the gurney and pulley system out of the way. Theodora never missed an opportunity to tell this to Tess, over every corpse they worked on together.

"You'd think with all the advanced technology nowadays they could figure out how to stop the aging process. Thank God for plastic surgery."

"You've never had plastic surgery," Tess pointed out.

"No, but I know a doctor who said he'd fix me right up the second I started to notice any sagging. I've got his number listed in my emergency contacts." Theodora snuck another drink of her vitamin juice and then said, "How much are you paying me? You know I don't like working on the dead. It gives me the willies. And I had to turn away a couple of clients for this. You know how things start to ramp up before school starts."

"Fifty dollars, like always," Tess said.

"You think I could get away with charging fifty dollars at the shop? I mean, it's a spa *and* salon, so they're getting a full experience, not just a cut and style."

"No, I don't think you could get away with it," Tess told her. "A seventy percent increase in prices probably won't be good for business."

Tess tacked the enlarged picture of Mrs. Schriever to the board so they could look at it for comparison. It was always best to have a recent picture of the deceased so they could make them look as much as possible like the way people remembered them. The only problem was that Mrs. Schriever's family had given her a picture from 1962, complete with a jet-black beehive and blue eye shadow.

"Now, what was Esther Schriever thinking giving you that photo?" Theodora said. "What are we supposed to do with that? I'm a beautician, not God."

For once, Tess agreed with her mother. "We'll have to go as close to memory as we can. Esther dropped off all her mother's makeup when she brought her clothes last night, so at least we know we'll have a pretty close match. Go ahead and start washing her hair and I'll do the body."

They each donned a plastic gown and gloves, and Tess soon realized she was going to have a problem with the wrist brace. She removed it, put on a glove, and then put the brace back on top of it. Her mother didn't seem to notice the brace, and if she did, it didn't cross her mind to ask about it, which didn't surprise Tess since, after all, it didn't directly affect her. They also put on polycarbonate face shields that looked a lot like welder's masks, but they were made of clear plastic. Hair and makeup could be a messy business.

Theodora got started washing Mrs. Schriever's hair, and Tess took a bucket and filled it with tap water to sponge Mrs. Schriever down one last time and massage the hands into a position where the makeup would be easiest to apply.

"Last time I saw Delores was at the Fourth of July parade downtown," Theodora said. "Never would've known by looking at her she'd be dead a couple weeks later. She had a prime spot right on the corner. Parked her wheelchair out there all afternoon to make sure nobody took her spot. That's dedication. She was wearing a baseball cap, so I didn't see what her hair looked like, but if I recall she was always fond of pin curls. I'll get her set and then tease them up real nice around her face to give her some volume."

Tess kept her fingers crossed she wouldn't have to minimize the damage too much. She didn't remember ever seeing Mrs. Schriever with teased anything. She went to look through the makeup bag and found a bottle of foundation inside. There was enough to cover Mrs. Schriever's neck and hands as well.

"Ooh, that's the good stuff," Theodora said, looking at the makeup. "It's real expensive."

There were tricks to applying makeup to the dead. Once a body was embalmed, the skin was no longer as soft or pliable, and it no longer absorbed anything, so using a sponge to apply regular makeup could be challenging, to say the least. But Tess had learned a cool trick at her last conference. She poured Delores's foundation into an airbrush gun, along with a small amount of epoxy and water so the color would stick to the skin. It was also important for older people to thin the foundation down with water because you still wanted the age in their skin to show to some degree. The last thing the family wanted was to see their loved one as someone unrecognizable.

Tess gently put a headband around Delores's head, to keep any makeup out of her hair, and then pulled down her face mask to get to work.

The quiet was the part of her job she enjoyed the most. Being with the dead never bothered her, and there was something comforting in the fact that she was entrusted with the job of making sure the family had a great last memory of their loved one. It wasn't something she took lightly.

Tess turned on the airbrush and started at the neck to make sure the color came out right, and then she got down to business.

"You don't suppose that Dante is around somewhere, do you?" Theodora asked. "Talk about putting color in a woman's cheeks. He gives me hot flashes and I finished menopause two years ago."

"Don't hit on the help," Tess said. "And stop biting him. That's just weird."

Theodora growled like a feral cat and then laughed. "I just can't help it. He's very bite-able. I just want to pounce on him every time he walks by."

"That's called assault. Don't do it. Besides, he's young enough to be your son."

"Who cares?" she asked. "Good grief, when did you get that stick lodged so far up your behind? It must be mighty uncomfortable. I could tell you stories about what younger men can do."

"Please don't," Tess said. "What happened to the therapist?"

"He certainly makes our sessions more entertaining. I don't have to worry about all that *'Why do you make such destructive choices, Theodora?'* crap. But Herald just isn't marriage material. I'm sure I'll be back on the market once he signs my release papers for the judge."

"Hmm," Tess said, but Theodora didn't hear her since she'd turned on the hair dryer. Tess was tempted to give her mother the fifty dollars and finish the job herself. It had already been a long morning, and a headache was brewing behind her eyes.

Family was often a burden. It was what it was. But she wondered what life would be like without worrying if the sheriff were visiting because her mother was behind bars, or what it would be like to skip a Friday morning visit to the Clip n' Curl. She loved her family . . . really, she did. But love and sanity didn't always go hand in hand. Cutting the strings to Last Stop was seeming more and more like the right idea.

CHAPTER SEVEN

Deacon hadn't managed to catch any sleep before the briefing. He was exhausted. He'd been awake all night, and he'd pushed himself through his morning run. And then meeting with Levi had taken more of a toll than he'd thought it would, speaking aloud what had happened to him when he'd been buried alive.

By the time he'd lain down on his bed to catch a quick half hour of sleep, his mind had been spinning with an odd combination of memories he'd rather forget and those of a temperamental redhead whose lips tasted like sugar and sex. He'd finally given up on sleep completely and headed down to the briefing room.

For two years he'd avoided tangling himself with Tess. For good reason. She fascinated him on a level he knew was dangerous for both of them. Dead men didn't have personal connections. They didn't have family or lovers or friends. They did the job until their time was up. If they lived to see their last day. The risk of loving someone was too great. If he was captured or killed, then so would she be. He had enough deaths on his conscience without adding any more.

But he was drawn to Tess like a moth to a flame. He found himself lingering in the house when she was around, just to talk with her, and he'd made it a point to help out as much as possible, just on the chance that he could look at her.

She was unlike any woman he'd ever known. She was smart and funny and kind—too kind if you asked him—but there was a sadness at the core of her he wanted to understand. She'd gotten the raw end of the deal when they'd come to Last Stop, and everybody knew it. But she'd kept that stubborn chin pointed high, and she'd done the work without the reward of having the funeral home to call her own.

She may not have been beautiful in a conventional way—her hair was unruly, and freckles covered the bridge of her nose and cheeks—but she smelled of lemons, and she had the clearest green eyes he'd ever seen. He was halfway in love with her, and the only thing holding him back was fear for her safety. Otherwise he would've said to hell with rules and contracts. She bewitched him.

And late at night, when his mind and body were relaxed, those eyes would haunt him in his dreams. He'd wake up with the sheets twisted around him and his heart hammering in his chest, the scent of her wrapped around him and his body throbbing with need.

He'd made a mistake in going to rescue her from Levi earlier that morning. He should've sent one of the others, but there'd been no time for him to hunt someone down. Levi could've killed her before any of the others would have gotten to her. As it was, it had been nothing but luck that Levi had only grabbed her wrist and not her neck. Seeing her in danger had pushed Deacon over the invisible line he'd drawn for himself. It had been too close of a call, and he hadn't been able to stop himself from kissing her. He'd wanted to do a lot more than that.

When Tess had looked up at him, both fear and irritation in her gaze, he'd been struck dumb. She was no shrinking violet, that was for sure. And the daggers that shot from her eyes when he'd made the first smart-ass comment had him going hard as a rock. He'd always gotten a perverse sense of satisfaction from seeing a woman in full temper. And Tess's full temper was a sight to behold.

Technically, personal relationships were only frowned upon, not forbidden for Gravediggers. But the penalty was so severe it wasn't worth testing the waters. Physical releases were easy enough to come by. There was always an available woman, though since he'd set his sights on Tess no other woman had come close to holding his interest.

The worst thing he could do was let anyone know he had a weakness, especially Eve. It was her job to look for those weaknesses. Whether hungry, thirsty, or wounded, it was best to keep it to oneself. And emotional attachments were especially important to keep silent about. In his line of work, weakness was synonymous with unnecessary. Meaning those who were weak didn't deserve to live.

And Tess was fast becoming a weakness.

Deacon sat at the head of the large conference table, turning slightly so he could watch the surveillance cameras at his back while pretending to read a report. He was preoccupied, and he was vaguely distracted by the good-humored banter from the others at the table. They were all low on sleep and running on exhaustion, but they found their entertainment wherever they could.

They were well secured and protected behind the reinforced steel doors and within the underground rooms. Each of them had their own personal code, plus a fingerprint analysis. They'd installed cameras, not only all over the property, but in strategic locations around town, so they could always see if trouble was coming. And if they got in real trouble, there was the escape tunnel Deacon made it a point of running through every morning. It led all the way to the lake and the private property they owned. It was easy enough to fly in some of their larger supplies and equipment and then haul it underground to the compound. The tunnel was big enough for a full-size vehicle to drive through, though they used four-wheelers that could carry high-capacity loads.

On each door around the compound was a trident, the only indication that Neptune existed. Each of the three points of the trident represented the three directors—the secretary of defense, the assistant attorney general for national defense out of the Justice Department, and the CEO of the largest private weapons manufacturer in the country. They were The Directors, and they had more power than God. And worse, they thought they were gods, making deals, moving chess pieces, and putting lives at risk on a daily basis. But even with the corruption of politics and private enterprise, they were the best hope there was.

Headquarters space was large and utilitarian. The "deck," as they called it, was built more like the interior of NASA than like a regular conference room. It was dimly lit, and one entire wall was covered with three large screens. The screens were used for conference calls and team briefings. To either side of the screens were the flags of the allied countries to remind them they were fighting wars that affected all of the nations on a global scale.

On the wall to their right were computer stations, the technology so advanced that not even the Pentagon had the same level of access. Though The Gravediggers were first and foremost a strike force, a lot of their job required the proper intel and investigative work. The back wall was another set of computer monitors, but they were hooked up to the surveillance system. They had cameras everywhere on the grounds, interior and exterior. They used satellite and radar for potential air strikes.

As far as anyone besides the people in the room was concerned, The Gravediggers didn't exist. They'd all been considered a threat to their governments—rogue agents—and the sanction had gone out for their deaths. That's when Eve Winter would pay them a visit and tip them off. And then she'd let them make the decision to come with her or die with disgrace.

She was brilliant at what she did. Just as he'd told Levi, Eve would show up like the Angel of Death and make it look like all hell had broken loose while making it appear that each of them had lost the battle. As far as their governments knew, they were dead men— disavowed and dishonorable—though in reality they were anything but. They might have lost the battle, but there was still a war to be won.

Deacon's eyes skimmed over the report and then cut to the monitor. He couldn't stop watching her. One of the screens showed Tess and her mother working together in the embalming room. He'd already watched Theodora pocket some of the makeup that had been with the deceased's belongings and some kind of lapel pin that had been on the burial suit. Theodora was an interesting woman, but he could tell by the line between Tess's brows that she had a killer of a headache, and she'd about reached her limit with her mother.

Since sleep hadn't been on the agenda, he'd spent the time reviewing the video from earlier that morning. From when she'd first found Levi. He and his brothers had been left with a choice, and they hadn't been wise in that choice. Actions had consequences. Always. And anyone who thought otherwise was a fool.

The priority had been getting the van out of sight so The Shadow could repair the area where the bullet had damaged the door. If they hadn't gotten it out when they had people would have been up and starting their days, and there was no doubt in his mind *someone* would've noticed the bullet hole. People in Last Stop noticed every damned thing.

So they'd had no choice but to make a quick stop and unload Levi's body. The embalming room had been the closest location that could be kept secure, so they'd moved him quickly, and then Dante and Axel had hauled ass out of town to get the van repaired, while Colin and Elias took the opportunity to catch a couple of hours of sleep.

If she'd stayed asleep as was her normal habit, none of this ever would've happened. She wouldn't have been in danger. And he wouldn't have kissed her.

He'd watched the video over and over again as she'd struggled with Levi—her fear tempered with determination. She was a sight to behold, and he wanted her. Bad.

He'd only let himself watch a replay of their kiss once before deleting the footage. Lack of privacy had been another factor in him keeping his hands off of Tess over the last couple of years. Thank God she'd never had male company over. He doubted he would have let the man live if he'd had to watch it unfold on the screen. She was imprinted on his soul, and though he hadn't claimed her, she was his.

He'd thought more than a time or two that he should thank Henry Pottinger for changing his mind about marrying Tess. She'd been mad as hell, but she hadn't been brokenhearted, which told him right there it was a marriage for a specific purpose instead of a marriage of love. Tess was a woman who craved family. Her own family situation was unique, to say the least, and she wanted to be part of a stable family unit. She was the kind of woman marriage and children meant something to.

Henry's rejection, in front of a crowd no less, had closed Tess off to the possibility of other men. At least for a while. And that had been just fine with him.

Except now her eyes were wide open, and they were directed at him. It would've been so simple to gather her in his arms and devour her. And he wouldn't have wanted to let her go. Especially once he'd reviewed the video. Because the look on her face had held every bit of desire, and longing, and need that he knew had been reflected on his.

What he had to figure out was how he could have her and deceive The Directors at the same time. They'd never allow him happiness. His life belonged to them. But he wanted Tess and he was determined to have her. No matter how he had to go about it. When he'd worked for the CIA, his life had revolved around the art of deception. Of believing the life and lies he told people about. It was a web of deceit that had been easy to become tangled in. He lied to everyone, even his superiors if the need called for it.

He'd have to lie to them again. And he'd have to lie to her. What he did was classified, and even if he could share it, most people wouldn't have been able to comprehend the horrors that he dealt with. The taking of life to save others. The deception. When his parents had still been alive, they'd thought he was a schoolteacher.

He scowled as he thought of the other surveillance video he'd watched. The sheriff could be a problem. He'd anticipated Cal's visit—anticipating the worst was part of his job—but the sheriff's inquiries were easy enough to deflect. The van was being detailed and the back doors replaced where the bullet had hit. The tires would be replaced with ones with a slightly different tread, and there were no mud samples to collect. All the police had to go on was the rambling story of the criminal who'd been shot, and he was going to want to make himself the victim to lessen the charges. But there was no proof left verifying what he'd said.

What had caught Deacon off guard was when Cal had asked Tess to dinner. It made the muscles in his stomach tighten with dread each time he watched it. If Deacon was a different kind of man, he would've backed off and let things take their course between Tess and the sheriff. She deserved someone who could give her the possibility of a long-term relationship. Deacon couldn't promise her anything except the moment. And he was a real bastard, because it didn't seem to matter. The moment would have to be enough. Because now that he'd tasted her, he wasn't turning back.

The trident in the center of the large middle screen flickered and Eve Winter's face appeared. The others stopped talking and the atmosphere in the room changed.

Eve's age was indeterminate. She could've been twenty or fifty, but Deacon figured she probably fell somewhere in between. None of them knew exactly what her background was. Her name wasn't one that was well known in any of the agencies—if Eve Winter was even her name at all.

Eve was small of bone and mighty of personality. She was Asian-American, and her features were a delicate mix of the two heritages. Her cheekbones were sharp, and her upper lip was slightly fuller than the lower and slicked in the red lipstick he'd never seen her without. Her hair was dark and rich and hung halfway down her back. But it was her eyes that made people stare. They were an unusual shade of gray, fringed with thick, black lashes. They were beautiful until you looked past the surface to what lay within.

Deacon had always felt a little bit sorry for Eve. And despite the way things were, he knew her burden was the heaviest to carry and the hardest to uphold. The Directors had created Neptune for one specific purpose. And they'd chosen Eve to run the entire organization. The Shadow and The Gravediggers all reported to her, and she was the mastermind behind coordinating the efforts between the two sectors. Her mind was like a computer, and she did nothing without purpose.

She was the person who made the hard decisions most people couldn't bring themselves to make. Those kinds of decisions—where humanity was forsaken for the greater good—chipped away at a person's soul until there wasn't anything left. He often wondered how much of Eve Winter's soul remained.

"On June twenty-third of this year, five thousand and sixteen people were killed in the bombing at the College World Series in Omaha, Nebraska." There were no greetings of hello. Just business. Just the mission. "It's the largest death toll since the 9/11 terror attacks, and it could have been much worse than it was. Not all of the explosives detonated on the side of the stadium where there was a larger concentration of people."

Her voice was smooth and didn't hint of any geographical dialect or accent. She could've been from Texas or Wisconsin and no one would've been the wiser. She'd erased all traces of her past, whatever it might have been. *Everyone* had a past.

Images popped up on the screens on each side of Eve, and she clicked through several pictures of the destruction and aftermath of the bombing. Deacon had seen most of the images already, but the devastation was still a kick in the gut.

"Men, women, and children," she said. "Young and old. Families out for the day, many of whom were watching their kids play ball." All of the players survived, though there were some critical injuries, but the stadium collapsed around the field. Those in the stands and beneath didn't fare as well.

"An attack of this size has many components and players. It was well orchestrated and organized. But it was practice. We've found other practice sessions that had similarities in different parts of the world. As you all know, terrorists generally like to start small and work their way up to their final goal. In an attack of this size, there's considerable planning and logistical requirements that have to go into each stage of their mission. Not to mention the equipment and weapons."

Two more pictures came on the screens and she continued. "The picture on your left occurred at an open market in Dubai. The one on the right at a mall in São Paulo. There are several others. Casualties ranged from fifty-five people to just over seven hundred. But it's the materials used that link these attacks together."

"I take it the similarities have something to do with the Russian tanker we've been keeping an eye on?" Deacon asked, knowing that Eve didn't give them orders without a purpose in mind, even if she didn't have all the pieces to the puzzle yet.

"You are correct," she answered. "The Jihadist terrorists call it The Perfect Day. The Russians call it *Den' Sud'by*."

"Day of Destiny," Dante interjected.

"But it all means the same thing," Eve went on. "It's a terrorist's wet dream. One day where everything falls into place. Where chaos and confusion and death ensue to the point that there aren't enough first responders, nurses, doctors, or hospital beds for survivors. It's 9/11 times a thousand.

"Russia has been waiting patiently and biding its time. They're at a place politically where they have the money, the weapons, and the power. They've spent decades living here, setting up communities and infiltrating all areas of the government. They've perfected what it means to be American."

"While many Americans have forgotten what it means to be American," Dante said, straightening the cuff on his silk dress shirt. "The irony isn't lost on me."

"The fact is they're here," Elias said. "And once they've achieved their Perfect Day, it's easy enough to shut down electrical grids and put everyone into darkness. To shut down radar and air traffic control. They'd create a society of chaos and anarchy, and we all remember what happens to people when they're put in those conditions. We all remember Hurricane Katrina. You take away people's resources and throw them into the worst of the worst conditions and there's no hope for peace. They turn on each other and it's every man for himself. The human instinct for survival is strong, and a person will resort to whatever is necessary to make sure they're the last one standing."

"Which is one of the reasons this team was assembled," Eve said. "The College World Series bombing used a new gas called XTNC-50 in its explosives. It was created in a Russian lab, and as of now, there aren't many documented instances of its use. It's been thrown around as a threat, but we have yet to see its full potential. It's more than a hundred times the fatality rate of sarin gas. It takes seconds to kill. And there is no antidote."

"Is that the common denominator between this practice session and the others?" Deacon asked. "This is the first we've heard of the attacks in Dubai and South America. There's nothing in the intel we were given."

"An oversight the Department of Defense will hear about," she said, and Deacon felt sorry for whoever was on the other end of that conversation.

"But yes," she continued. "XTNC-50 is one of the commonalities. These are terrorists on a suicide mission, and their goal is to send a message and incite worldwide panic. The best way to send the rest of the world into a panic is by putting the United States in a panic. It's not only domestic destruction with the bombings, it means global economic destruction. And Russia is sitting pretty at the top of the food chain. They love it when the world is in chaos, because they thrive under those conditions. Their money and banking systems aren't dependent on Wall Street or the World Bank. They're financed mostly through the Mafiya.

"The explosions went off in timed intervals, and the XTNC-50 gas takes very little time to work. Those who managed to escape the gas and explosions headed toward the exits, but the terrorists used marked first responder vehicles to block exits from the stadium. They were also dressed as first responders, adding to the confusion.

"By blocking the exits they were herding the survivors to exactly where they wanted them to go. They left only one path of escape, and those who took that path were met with another surprise. Snipers waited for them, so as they ran toward the exit it was like a firing squad. Eventually the storm calmed enough for people to realize they were better off staying put, though many succumbed to the gas."

"Jesus," Elias said, rubbing a hand over the scruff of his face. "None of that information was released by the Justice Department, and there wasn't even a whisper in any CIA correspondence. We have their servers under surveillances, and we get flagged with any internal information on the terror attack."

"They're on a budget crunch," Axel said. "Maybe they're trying to be efficient."

"And effective," Eve said. "But like I said, this was practice. Their Perfect Day has been years in the making."

"What is their idea of the Perfect Day?" Deacon asked.

"That's what we don't know and what you're going to find out," she said. "These are your targets. Jorgen Yevorovich, Mikhail Petrov, Sergey Egorov, and Ivan Levkin. Egorov is a distant relative of Vladimir Putin. They're all second- and third-generation Americans. They have businesses and families here. And they're coordinating the largest single terrorist attack the world has ever seen. Study them. Find them. Leave one of them alive for capture. Kill the others."

"And the tanker?" he asked.

"That's part of your mission. At this moment, the tanker you've been surveilling is headed toward U.S. waters under the guise of carrying machine parts. It's also loaded with several crates of XTNC-50 gas. That tanker can't get anywhere near land. You've got to destroy it before it gets in range. You'll coordinate a HALO jump onto the tanker and take care of any guards. We think Yevorovich and Levkin are on the tanker. Set the explosives and then the Zodiac will be waiting for you to take you to the submarine. You should be well out of range when the explosives sink the tanker."

"How much time do we have before the tanker hits U.S. waters?" Axel asked.

"A week. You'll find schematics and other pertinent

information in your inboxes." The screens on either side of her face cleared and she looked at each of them. "How is the new recruit?"

"He's awake and in holding," Deacon said. "He's stable enough. He remembers you and signing the agreement, but there's still some memory loss and disorientation. He was under longer than I'd have liked, so it might take him a couple of extra days to adjust."

"Good," she said. "We need him now. Go ahead and administer the psych evaluation."

Deacon raised his brows. "That thing is brutal. An hour ago he could barely stand by himself."

"Then give him until noon." Her smile wasn't a friendly one. "Moving on: I've been alerted that there could be some pressure from local law enforcement. Something about an armed robber identifying the transport van."

"We've got it under control," he said. There was no point in asking how she knew about the situation. She knew everything. "There's nothing to substantiate their claims, and the van is being serviced. I'd say the biggest issue is Tess at this point. She's got it in her head that she wants to resign and move out of Last Stop."

"Tell her no," Eve said, her eyes narrowing.

Deacon almost grinned. He'd done just that, but he didn't think Eve would appreciate the humor.

"What's the big deal if she decides to go?" Elias asked. "She got shafted on this deal and we all know it."

"Tess is useful," Eve said. "It's by no coincidence that we chose Last Stop for Gravediggers HQ. We scouted locations for several years and put chess pieces into motion long before anyone was brought on board. This is a prime location. We're close enough to the city that we've got major resources available, and we're in a central location so we can be anywhere in a matter of a few hours. This town is perfect because of the soil. Every town around us for a hundred miles is mostly built on limestone. Do you know how hard it is to dig tunnels and passageways through limestone?"

"Pretty hard?" Elias asked sarcastically, drawing a chuckle from Dante and Axel.

"How is Tess useful?" Deacon asked, going back to her original statement. He'd gotten a cold chill down his spine the moment Eve uttered her name.

Eve's gaze lasered in on his, and he wondered just exactly what she saw there. "She's what we needed for a solid cover. I watched her for a couple of years, found out what her goals and plans were. Checked her background and her family life. I knew if we came in and bought the funeral home out from under her that she'd stay if we asked her. She doesn't have the courage to pick up and start somewhere new. And she's a direct connection to keeping us plugged in without being in the middle of things.

"She also has indirect ties to the Russian Mafiya. The Mafiya is a closed community. They still speak 'Old Russian' that dates back to the time of the tsars. It's like a foreign language within their own country. She speaks the language, and there are possibilities her grandmother could still be connected in some ways. No doubt she knows things. We've had her monitored for years. Tess too, just in case Tatiana ever feels the need to absolve her conscience to her granddaughter. We've not had reason to pull her in for questioning on the past at this point, but we'll see where this particular mission takes us. They treat her like an outsider, but Tess belongs here. She's too entrenched. She'll never leave this place."

"And yet I've heard her tell two people she's leaving," Deacon said.

"Then give her a reason to stay," she told him flatly. Her tone was nonnegotiable. "I don't care how you have to do it. Threaten her. Seduce her. Give her a purpose. She's a mousy bookworm who spends more time with dead people than with the living. Make her feel needed and important. She speaks that particular dialect of Russian better than any of us could hope to. She may not realize it, but she was raised with the same traditions, information, and survival skills that the Mafiya passes on to their families. Hell, bring her in on the mission and give her a job on a need-to-know basis. Do whatever it takes."

"Mousy" was the last word he'd have used to describe Tess. "Fiery," "passionate," "hardheaded," and "opinionated" would have come long before he ever thought the word "mousy." It looked like Eve didn't know everything after all.

"And what happens if she has more courage than you give her credit for and down the road she decides to leave anyway?" Deacon asked.

"Then we'll take care of her."

"That's cold," Colin said.

Eve's glare cut to him and her gaze was glacial. "It's reality. If we bring her in and tell her classified information, her contract would be much like yours. The only thing that can separate you from The Gravediggers is death. Or if you term out."

She added the second part as an afterthought, and Deacon felt like he had a pretty good answer to his wondering whether or not she'd actually release them from their bonds to go back out into the world as civilians.

"We're not an assassination squad," Dante said.

"You're what you're told to be," she countered. "Don't act as if your armor isn't tarnished, Dante. You've somehow managed to seamlessly meld your life before death and this one. It's because I allow it and nothing more."

Deacon stared at Dante, but the other man's face was unreadable. They all knew Dante took his trips from time to time, but they never knew where he went or what he did. But the information was curious, and though he would've said he could trust Dante with his life, now he wasn't so sure. There was no place for secrets like that in the brotherhood.

"There are bigger things at stake than a Russian mortician," Eve said. "We either use her or dispose of her. End of story. Don't forget why you're here. And don't forget I don't need your permission to do what I think is best. It's my mercy that allows Tess Sherman to continue as she is. Just as it's my mercy that allows you to be here."

"Our countries betrayed us," Axel said, the anger in his voice palpable. Of all of them, he'd lost the most.

"Some of you, yes. And some of you betrayed yourselves. It doesn't matter. You didn't follow orders and you had to die. End of story," she said with a shrug.

"We're not puppets," Deacon said. "And none of us will condone cold-blooded murder of the innocent. We've all walked in the gray areas. But we have a moral compass. Just because the pencil pusher at the top doesn't have one doesn't mean that we have to lose our sense of right and wrong."

"It's a moot point," she said. "Your countries considered you traitors. Maybe you should've followed orders for the greater good. Now you'll never know. In the end, the legacy you've left behind is that of a traitor."

"And yet it's us you wanted for this team," Colin said. "Knowing we'll disobey orders if we feel it's necessary."

"Do you think you're irreplaceable?" she asked coolly, arching a brow. "Do you really think that The Gravediggers' inception began when I brought Deacon back as the first of you? Ten years is how long this project has taken to get where we want it to be. And we're not there yet. Do you think there weren't others before you? That we haven't put millions of dollars into finding the perfect candidates. To test and discard them?"

"What's that supposed to mean?" Axel asked.

"It means you are an experiment, plain and simple. And the alpha team of this particular experiment didn't work out the way it should have. They were terminated. Once we changed the selection criteria and focus, we got better candidates. *You.* But everyone is replaceable. You, me, The Directors," she said. "Everyone."

Deacon froze, as did the others. He'd had no knowledge of others who'd come before him and failed. It was a sobering thought. The crux of it was that if he wasn't here, living on the mercy of Eve Winters, he'd be dead anyway.

"The Gravediggers were created for one purpose—they are a strike force that puts an end to domestic terrorism. Period. Terrorism is a moneymaking business and our lawmakers know this. Terrorism feeds billion-dollar weapons contracts, and global fear allows these contractors to push the lobbyists' agendas through.

"It's taken years of research and resources, and billions of dollars to fund this brainchild. You've been selected from a global database of the most skilled agents in the world. This is not a United States problem. It's a worldwide problem. The United States is the center. Nothing can shut down global economics and trade faster than a terror attack on U.S. soil.

"I don't have to tell you what a well-strategized terror attack can do. The Perfect Day is about hitting us where we'd hurt the most and doing the most damage. Schools, commerce buildings, media outlets, the United Nations building, Wall Street, Silicon Valley, and banks. Their goal is to shut everything down. Once it's shut down, it'll be that much easier to do the same in other countries, one after the other.

"To be successful at this we have to focus our energy on what's around us. You have access to all agency databases. It's something none of the other agencies have. And our technology is able to match and discard possibilities with impressive accuracy. We are able to move without restriction, and we eliminate problems without having to gain permission or cut through red tape. We have autonomy where all other agencies have their hands tied. But there are sacrifices that must be made and consequences if the rules aren't followed."

"We're at your mercy," Colin said, the bitterness in his voice thick.

"Yes," she said, and then she looked back at Deacon, her face unreadable. "Bring Tess in. At this point in the game she's a possible asset, and we still don't know if her family has potential Mafiya information that could be of use. I don't care what you have to do to convince her to stay. Just do it. And if we discover we don't need her, then we'll cross that bridge when we come to it."

The good news was that he no longer had to think of a way to deceive The Directors into letting him pursue Tess. The bad news was she was now on their radar. The fault was partly his. Eve had seen something in the way he'd talked about Tess, and she'd pissed him off by saying Tess's life would be forfeit if things went south. He'd given Eve a weapon to hold against him.

They'd be lucky if they all came out of it alive by the end.

CHAPTER EIGHT

Tess tried her best to avoid Deacon the rest of the day, but she found herself sneaking glances, looking for him as she went about her day-to-day business.

She didn't need complications in her life, and she had a feeling Deacon would be a big complication. Once she'd finished working on Mrs. Schriever and the lady was presentable, Axel and Elias helped Tess lift her into the casket and roll her into slumber room one.

Something weird was going on. Elias and Axel had both given her an odd look, and they were both quiet. That wasn't unusual for Axel, but Elias pretty much talked all the time, so she knew something was up when he barely uttered a few words and got to work.

She'd had no clue where Deacon had spent the rest of his afternoon. He was almost always there to help her set up a viewing. Setting up the guestbook, chairs, and preparing the cookies and coffee. And if there was rain, like there had been all day, then he made sure there was space for umbrellas and wet things, so people weren't dripping all over Mrs. Schriever.

Elias and Axel knew the drill as well as Deacon, but their silence was so unnerving she gave them a shopping list of supplies she needed from the mortuary supply center and had them make a trip into the city just to get them out from underfoot. They were being too weird. Or maybe she was just being weird because one kiss from Deacon had made her an insane person.

Deciding that if she didn't get a fresh cup of coffee now she probably wouldn't get one before the end of the night, she headed out of slumber room one and put her hand on the newel post on the stairs to swing around the corner. Deacon stood about a foot in front of her, and she let out an unladylike squeak before slapping her hand over her heart in surprise.

"Good grief. You're quiet as the dead. You just missed Axel and Elias. They headed over to Keaton's to pick up a few things."

She decided to give him a taste of his own medicine and move around him like he'd done with her earlier that morning.

He moved to the side and blocked her.

"Your pipes are rattling in your bathroom. I can hear them outside."

She raised a brow in confusion. "Oh, did you want me to go put on my overalls and grab a wrench? I'm sure I can have it fixed in a jiffy."

He rolled his eyes and she tried to move past him again, with no success. "If you weren't so quick to interrupt, you would've heard me offer to fix them for you."

"Oh," she said.

"Do you mean, 'Oh, Deacon, thank you so much for offering'?"

She narrowed her eyes. "Don't push it." He grinned and she tried to move around him once again. He was making her crazy. She wasn't sure she'd ever seen this playful side of him before.

"Don't worry," he said. "I'll make sure I'm done by the time guests start arriving."

"I . . ."

But he didn't hear what she was going to say. He moved around her and headed off to presumably go get his tools. Her mouth hung open, and she found she was a little perturbed that he'd once again been the one to walk away.

"I was going to say thank you," she yelled after him. "You rude . . . man." She heard his chuckle just before she heard the door close to the garage. She shook her head and stomped off toward the kitchen for her coffee.

———

SHE WAS MAKING him crazy.

He'd spent the better part of his afternoon observing Levi while he went through each stage of the psych evaluations. It wasn't pleasant. He'd strapped him into the chair and attached the virtual reality goggles to his head. And then he'd punched play on the program that had been designed specifically for Gravediggers, and hoped like hell Levi was strong enough to withstand it. Each phase of the testing got more difficult. It wasn't easy for someone with the most rested mind and body.

He couldn't imagine what it was like after just having woken up from a death induced by medication that caused hallucinations, when it was a struggle to keep the contents of your stomach down and the headaches were debilitating. It was normally a five-day minimum before psych evals could be administered.

Tess had never left his mind. And that was dangerous. Distractions in his line of work could be catastrophic. After watching Levi tortured for two hours, recalling Eve's words about using Tess however he could, and thinking of kissing Tess again, he was in a damned foul mood by the time he unhooked Levi and all but carried his sweat-soaked body back to the bed.

What he needed was physical labor, which immediately made him think about laying Tess out on the first available surface and doing wicked things to her. Since that wasn't the best idea, considering all the cameras, he figured hammering something might be the next best option. And Tess's pipes were at the top of the list.

He'd caught sight of her on the cameras, and he could tell she was agitated about something because her hair had grown a couple of sizes by the time she finally told Elias and Axel to hit the road. He waited until they were out of the picture to tell her about her noisy pipes, and then it didn't take much poking and prodding to get her all riled up.

He must have some kind of sickness, because watching her cheeks color and her hair practically crackle with energy had made him feel a whole lot better than he had when he'd walked into the house. And now he had the plus of putting tools in his hand and getting rid of the rest of his frustration.

"Ohmigod," she said, standing in the doorway of what had been her bathroom.

He'd been waiting for it.

"Ohmigod," she said again.

"You already said that," he said. "It'll look worse before it looks better. Trust me."

Tess threw up her hands in frustration. "I thought you were just going to fix the pipes. How am I supposed to shower? Where are the walls? Where's all my stuff?"

"That's a lot of questions," he said. "And I am fixing your pipes. But the pipes are the least of your problems in here. The floor is rotted and none of the plumbing or electrical is up to code. It's amazing you haven't electrocuted yourself. No wonder your hair always looks like you've just been shocked."

She scowled at him and he couldn't help but grin. Her freckles had turned white with rage. Boy, was she mad. Her jaw was clenched tight, and he was willing to bet her fingernails were making little indents on the palms of her hands.

"How long is this going to take?" she asked hotly. "About a hundred people are going to be walking in the door in the next half hour to pay their respects to Mrs. Schriever, and it sounds like a demolition derby up here."

"It'll take a couple of weeks." He remembered the time frame for the mission and then added, "Maybe longer." Like several months, he added silently. Because though he could do the work, he wasn't a contractor.

"How much longer?" she asked, eyes narrowed.

"Maybe four weeks."

"My bathroom is going to be a disaster area for a month?" Her voice was hoarse with the restraint she was showing. "So for the next month I'm supposed to haul all my stuff to the first floor to shower? That's super-convenient."

The sarcasm wasn't lost on him, but he played along anyway. "I think so. You'll be right there by the coffee-maker, and after you do an embalming you can walk straight into the shower so you're not trailing that smell all over the house."

"The smell is part of the job," she said primly. "And it dissipates."

"Right," he said and then changed the subject. "I'll get the guys to give me a hand up here when they're not doing anything else. All you need to do is pick the tiles and fixtures. It's going to look great."

Her mouth opened and closed a couple of times, but no more words came out. "Are you saying the smell doesn't dissipate?" she asked, going back to the other topic.

"I'm teasing. Of course it dissipates. The smell of you drives me crazy. Lemons and sunshine. Tess, I've got to tell you something," he said, taking a step toward her.

"Is it that you can have everything in here put back together by midnight tonight?" she asked.

"No."

"Then I don't want to hear it."

He grinned and she narrowed her eyes in warning as he took another step closer. "You should probably watch your blood pressure. It can't be good for your health to repress all that anger."

She took a deep breath. And then another. He was surprised fire didn't shoot from her nostrils. He took another step closer, but she was concentrating so hard on breathing he wasn't sure she noticed.

"I don't think I started having blood pressure problems until you decided to kiss me," she said. "Then it ramped up pretty good. Why did you do that again?"

"Because I couldn't stay away from you any longer," he rasped. "I can't stop thinking about kissing you."

Her eyes widened and she looked up as he took another step closer. "You can't?"

"Maybe if I kiss you again I'll be able to stop."

She nodded. "I'm a scientist," she said.

He paused and looked at her with confusion. "Okay." And then he started to lean down to take her lips.

"I just mean I like experiments. And it's like an experiment to see if you'll want to kiss me again after you kiss me one more time. I talk a lot when I'm nervous, by the way."

"I've noticed that. Let me help." He leaned down and took her mouth before she could say anything else.

He was almost positive she'd stopped breathing. Hell, he wasn't sure *he* was still breathing. He nipped at her bottom lip and her mouth opened with a gasp. And he devoured. His tongue swept into her mouth and tangled with hers, the taste of her dark and rich and intoxicating. And this time he put his hands on her.

Blood rushed through his veins and his heart hammered in his chest. He knew what it was to want a woman. But he'd never known what it felt like to *need* a woman. Not just any woman. Only Tess. She'd bewitched him, and one kiss would never be enough.

When he finally pulled back, Tess's eyelids blinked open and she looked a bit dazed. Her breaths came in rapid pants and her pulse fluttered at the base of her throat.

She hadn't let go of him. He hoped she never would.

"Did it work?" she whispered.

"Did what work?"

"The experiment. Do you still want to kiss me?"

"No," he told her.

Her head jerked up in surprise, but he tightened his arms around her before she could pull away.

"I want to do more than kiss you." He kissed the corner of her mouth and then kissed his way down her jawline and to her neck. "I want to strip you out of that ugly jacket and see where these freckles go."

"You think my jacket is ugly?" she asked.

"Hideous. It covers up that beautiful body."

She snorted out a laugh. "I'm built like a boy."

"I've been a boy. I can tell you with certainty I never looked like you do."

His hands traced the subtle curve of her hips up to the slight indentation of her waist. She sucked in a breath as his fingers trailed higher, over her ribs and to the soft swell at the bottom of her breasts. She was small-boned and the curves she did have were slight and delicate. But there was no mistaking her for a boy.

He pushed the jacket from her shoulders and it fell to the bathroom floor. She wore a simple camisole beneath it, and he could see the tight beads of her nipples through the thin fabric.

"That's better," he said.

"That's my funeral jacket."

"We can bury it later." He bent to kiss her again, but her head snapped up. If he hadn't moved out of the way, she would've snapped his jaw closed.

"Funeral!" she said. "There's a viewing downstairs. I've got to go." She looked around and then noticed her jacket on the bathroom floor. The grimy, Sheetrock- and tile-covered bathroom floor.

"Oh, no. No, no, no." She picked up the ugly jacket between two fingers, shaking off the dust. "What have you done? You're complicating my life."

She turned and walked out of the bathroom and into her bedroom suite, muttering under her breath. He followed behind her and hoped she didn't look in the mirror. He'd mussed her hair and the side of her neck was red from where he'd kissed her.

"How am I complicating your life?" he asked, leaning against the door frame.

She was constant motion and energy, and he could've watched her all day. She disappeared farther into the closet and his brows rose as the silky shell she'd been wearing came flying out of the closet. She came out a few seconds later buttoning a black blouse with thin white pinstripes.

"What kind of funeral home director goes to a viewing without a jacket?" she said, her irritation obvious.

"I'll get you a new one," he told her. Her scowl could've melted a lesser man.

"Size four," she said. "Nothing fancy."

It was everything he could do to hold in a laugh. He couldn't remember the last time he'd just had . . . fun. Since his first day at the CIA fifteen years ago he'd had nothing but the weight of the world, literally, on his shoulders. There'd been no family he could share it with. No wife he could confide in. Only his own thoughts and the knowledge that if he didn't get the job done, then no one would.

"Try not to destroy anything else," she threw over her shoulder, heading toward the door.

"You never told me how I'm complicating your life. You like kissing me."

Tess turned back around. "Let's not get cocky," she said. "Of course I like kissing you. But the timing is bad. I'm leaving Last Stop. I've got other things on the horizon."

"Your grandmother will miss you."

"She can come visit. When did you learn to speak Russian?" she asked, changing the subject. She did that often. Talking with her was like following a tornado. "You answered me this morning when I swore at you."

"That's top secret information, and you've got other things on the horizon. Where are you going to go?"

"Maybe Austin or San Antonio. Somewhere with a population large enough for a steady business."

"That's morbid."

"Morbidity is my business," she said with a shrug. And then she looked at him oddly. "Yours too."

"You have no idea," he said. "Have dinner with me."

"I told you. I'm leaving."

"Okay, let's skip dinner and go straight to bed."

She laughed.

"No," she said, grinning, and she was gone back down the stairs almost before he could blink.

"Stop telling me no," he called after her, repeating her from earlier that day.

Her laughter followed her down the stairs.

Deacon felt a pang of remorse for what he was doing. There was no question he wanted her. He *liked* her. But he was pulling her into a game she'd never be able to escape. And she might very well hate him for it someday.

Suddenly, he wasn't sure he could stand to be hated by Tess Sherman.

CHAPTER NINE

Friday mornings gave Tess heartburn. Theodora had that effect on people.

The viewing the night before had gone off without a hitch, and no one had mentioned the fact that she wasn't wearing a jacket, though there'd be another opportunity to notice the following morning when they put Mrs. Schriever in the ground.

The rain had finally stopped sometime during the night, and since it was summer and they were in Texas, it meant stepping outside felt like being in one of those microwaveable steam-fresh bags.

She dressed in a pair of white capris and wore a loose linen shirt in light beige. She put on white sandals and slathered moisturizing sunscreen on her face. Her hair was its usual mass of curls, but it was a little more subdued today so she left it down.

Tess winced when she looked at the clock, and then ran down both flights of stairs, cursing Lucifer as he hissed at her and wove between her feet. When he got to the bottom he lay down right in front of the first step and stared at her, daring her to step on him.

"It'd serve you right," she said, hopping over him and heading toward the garage.

Her grandmother liked to be driven around in the black Suburban that was used for funeral processions. She said it made her look like the Secret Service. Tess grabbed her purse off the hook by the door and went into the garage to get into the Suburban. She dropped her keys, and they managed to go under the Suburban just far enough that she had to get down to look for them, so she put down her purse and bear crawled, wishing she hadn't chosen white pants for the day.

Time was her enemy. The sooner she got out of there the better chance she had at not running into Deacon. She'd delayed going back upstairs the night before, wondering what she'd do if he was still in her bathroom wearing ripped jeans and a tool belt. It was a hell of a time for her sex drive to make an appearance—right when she was making plans to change her future. The smart thing to do would be to stay far away from Deacon Tucker.

She'd never been any good at resisting things she wanted. Like when she was eight and found three kittens in a drainage ditch. She'd put them down her shirt and told her grandmother they'd followed her home. Of course, her chest and stomach had been scratched to pieces, so that story hadn't gone over so well. Or when she'd had tickets to see the Backstreet Boys in concert, but she'd been grounded. She'd decided the consequences of standing in that sea of hormones would be well worth the punishment she'd receive when she got home. She'd been right.

She had a feeling whatever happened between her and Deacon would be pretty similar—a sea of hormones followed by a great deal of time in the confessional. She was non-practicing Russian Orthodox.

She hit the button on the visor and the garage door opened. She backed out quickly and got a quick glimpse of Deacon's motorcycle and a flash of movement as he came around the side of the carriage house in badass boots, jeans that fit like a glove, a tight white T-shirt, and his helmet in his hand.

Their gazes locked and her eyes widened with what might have been panic. It was funny that she could be totally calm at the sight of a twitching dead body, but the sight of a healthy and virile man sent her into a panic. It was probably something she should ask her therapist about. Though it had been several years since she'd been to see him. You couldn't grow up with a mother like Theodora and not need a little therapy. It had taken her a lot of years to understand that Theodora did love her as much as she was capable of loving anyone.

Tess pressed down on the gas and shot backward out of the driveway, her left tire rolling over the curb, and then she threw the car in drive and burned rubber down Main Street. Her heart was pounding and there were little beads of sweat above her upper lip.

Her phone rang and Deacon's name appeared on the

caller I.D. She took a deep breath and reminded herself she was an adult before answering.

"Tess Sherman," she said. She was proud of her professionalism.

"Hello, Tess Sherman," Deacon said. "You sure left in a hurry this morning."

"Busy day," she said, overly cheerful. "It'll probably be a while before I'm back. Maybe even late tonight. You probably won't see me again today."

"Uh, huh," he said. "Listen—"

"It's just I'm really busy with all this planning for my future, and what to do once I leave Last Stop. I've been sending out my résumé." Which was a lie, but she was going to make sure to do it as soon as she got back home. She was babbling. She always babbled when she was nervous.

"Listen, Tess—"

"Okay, look. I'll be honest. I'm attracted to you. And I really like kissing you. I just think the timing is all wrong. I don't even know much about you. Do you have hobbies, interests, or felony convictions? These are things people should know before they keep kissing like we've been kissing."

"I agree," he said. "But I—"

"I'm very conflicted. You're making me crazy. But I really want my bathroom finished, so maybe you could spend some time in there today. And don't forget your tool belt. Wait, forget I said that last part."

"Tess!" he finally said, the exasperation clear in his voice.

"What?"

"I just called to tell you you left your purse on top of the car. You probably want to stop and get it."

Tess's mouth dropped open, and she felt the hot flush of embarrassment spread across her skin.

"Oh," she said. "Thank you."

"You're welcome. Say hi to your grandmother." He paused for a couple of seconds and then said, "I really like kissing you too." And then he hung up.

Tess stopped the Suburban right in the middle of the street, got out, and grabbed her purse from the top of the car. Then she got back in and kept driving toward Dallas and the Back Acres Retirement Village.

She pulled into the gated community and waved at the security guard in the little hut. People who lived in the village took turns working at the security gate, and one time when she'd come to visit there was a man there who had to have been at least a hundred years old, wearing his old SWAT clothes and an AK47 slung across his chest.

It hadn't filled her with loads of confidence, and some of the others must've complained as well, because now there was a sign attached to the guardhouse that said all security guards were unarmed.

She passed the hedge sculptures and the big fountain, and pulled in front of the main house, where there was a little grocery store inside, as well as a couple of clothing boutiques, a spa, and a bar. Tess had decided the first time she'd seen the place that retirement looked pretty awesome, and she was going to find a place like Back Acres the minute she was old enough to qualify.

It was 9:47, which meant she was two minutes late. Her grandmother was sitting on one of the little white benches out front, with her hands folded neatly in her lap. She gave Tess a glacial stare and then sighed as she gathered her handbag and stood to her feet.

Tess had gotten her height and willowy frame from her grandmother. Even in her seventies, Tatiana Sherman—Tati to her friends—was striking. She wore long linen pants and a white linen blouse, and she'd used a wide sash for a belt and tied it in a sassy bow at her hip. She wore the same pearls Tess had seen her in every day of her life—pearls given to her by her father when she'd turned sixteen.

She had the bones of royalty—high cheekbones and cat eyes that tilted up slightly at the corners. Her hair was a shock of creamy white that she wore short, curled, and teased. She had as much Texan in her as she had Russian. There were a few fine lines around her mouth and the corners of her eyes, but she'd aged well. She liked to give credit to the vodka, which she drank each night before bed. Tess had been embalming people long enough to know that's basically what her grandmother had done to herself while living.

Tess got out of the car and went around to open the passenger door and help her in.

"Sorry I'm late," she said, kissing her on each cheek. "I put my purse on top of the car and drove halfway here with it like that."

"Three minutes, dear. You know if we don't get there right at ten Debra Lassiter tries to take my chair. That girl has spent her whole life trying to take people's hard-earned stuff."

Tess wasn't sure Debra Lassiter qualified as a girl since she had to be pushing sixty, and she really wasn't sure how her grandmother had come to the conclusion that the center salon chair at the Clip n' Curl had been hard-earned. Mostly she'd bullied everyone out of that chair until every woman in town was afraid to sit in it.

"Your mama came and got me a couple of weeks ago for Julie Schleiger's baby shower. Lord that girl looks like she's carrying triplets. I've never seen cankles like that. Anyway, I saw Debra out in someone's yard pulling up a sign. She's got no respect for personal property."

"She's a Realtor," Tess said. "She was probably pulling up one of her 'For Sale' signs."

Her grandmother let out a stream of Russian curses that would've made a sailor blush, and Tess just stared straight ahead, pushing down on the accelerator to get back to Last Stop as fast as possible.

"You know it's a terrible idea to get into the habit of putting your purse on top of the car. I saw a special on *60 Minutes* once, and they did a whole segment about these lowlifes that just sit around looking for people driving by with their stuff on top of their car. Before you know it they've walked off with your identity and your favorite lipstick."

Tess saw the Last Stop city limits sign and let out a breath. Her hands were gripped tight on the steering wheel, so she relaxed them and had perfect clarity as to why Theodora religiously swore by her vitamin juice every morning.

The Clip n' Curl was on Main Street, right smack-dab in the middle of everything, which was just how Theodora liked it. The street was packed with cars, which wasn't unusual since there were so many businesses on the strip. It was a simple storefront with two large square windows and a glass front door. Someone had painted a summer beach scene on one of the windows, and there was a little display in front with sand and a beach bag filled with hair products. The salon opened right at ten o'clock.

"Look there," her grandmother said, pointing down the street. "That's Debra and she's already got a parking spot. You're driving like the bus driver at the retirement home. Get a move on, girl."

Tess felt her blood pressure spike, and the fear of competition took over. It was just like every sporting event she'd ever tried to participate in while at school. She was never as fast or aggressive as all the other competitors, and she could still hear the criticism in perfect Russian as it boomed over the cheering crowds.

She screeched to a halt right in front of the Clip n' Curl's doors to avoid the pressure, and she let her grandmother out with only seconds to spare. She saw Debra pick up the pace, but she'd had a hip replacement last year and couldn't move as fast as Tatiana. Tess unbuckled and reached over to pull the door closed since her grandmother had left it open in her hurry, and she immediately felt the relief of being alone.

Tess shifted the air vents so they blew on her armpits, and then crept along the street, hoping someone would pull out. She got lucky at the end of the block nearest the courthouse, and somehow managed to squeeze the Suburban into a space that was clearly meant for a much smaller car.

She grabbed her purse from the backseat and had her handle on the door when the door opened for her. Cal Dougherty stared at her through the window, and she let out a quiet sigh, thinking she would've been better off all around if she'd pretended to be sick for the day.

"Hello, Cal," she said, sliding out of the Suburban.

"I figured I'd let you get parked before I tried to get your attention. I could hear you muttering in Russian from the open car door."

"It's been that kind of morning."

"I just wanted to make sure I didn't freak you out about asking you to dinner yesterday morning."

"Oh, no," she said. "I always get accused of crimes and hit on at the same time. Story of my life."

He rolled his eyes and fell into step beside her as she made her way to the Clip n' Curl. "No one's accusing you," he said. "But you've got five men working for you that you don't know a thing about."

"Six," she said, thinking of the not-so-dead body who she was assuming would become her employee.

He raised his brows at that. "I've run background checks on them."

"For what?" she asked, horrified. "That's a violation of their privacy."

"You're a single woman with five . . . *six* . . . very dangerous-looking men living right under your nose. I wouldn't be looking out for you if I didn't do some checking."

"It's still rude," she said, even though his thoughtfulness went a little ways in helping repair the damage of his accusations the day before. "But I appreciate you thinking of me." She paused again and pursed her lips before asking, "So . . . did you find out anything?"

He grinned and shook his head. "Nope, clean as a whistle, every one of them. Too clean if you ask me. But I don't want to start digging and get in over my head. I can tell you with certainty they're skilled. I can recognize men who are trained to fight."

"And why would you be able to recognize men like that?" she asked.

He just smiled again and said, "I wasn't always sheriff. Do you mind if I head over to your place and check the transport van? I'm assuming it's back?"

The change in subject threw her off guard and she stopped in her tracks. "Cal Dougherty, I thought you said you weren't accusing me? I take back all those nice things I was thinking about you just now."

"Nice enough to go to dinner with me?"

She narrowed her eyes at him and his smile widened.

"I don't know why the men I know think it's so goshdarned funny when I get mad. But no, I won't go to dinner with you. Ever. Unless it's potluck at the church, and then I guess I won't be able to help it, but it doesn't count because there will be lots of people around."

She was babbling again. It was the first time in her life she was actually anxious to get inside the Clip n' Curl.

"That's harsh. But probably best. I've got dinner plans tonight anyway. I don't think she'd be into a trio."

Tess's mouth dropped open and she shook her head. "Help yourself to the van. I'm sure one of the guys can let you in if the door is closed. And stop running background checks on my employees. They're all very nice men who don't accuse men of crimes and try to double book me for dinner. Don't be a cad, Cal."

He winked and shrugged. "I'm pretty sure that's why Victoria divorced me. Catch you later."

He strolled in the opposite direction, toward the funeral home, and she realized she was standing right in front of the Clip n' Curl. Several pairs of eyes inside were staring straight at her.

"Well, this will be fun," she said in Russian and opened the door.

"He'd be an excellent choice for you, Tess," her mother said by way of greeting. "He seems very stable. Though I've heard he's not the most endowed, if you get my drift." Theodora waggled her eyebrows and pointed to her privates.

"Very subtle, Mama. I think everyone gets the drift."

Theodora was dressed in head-to-toe black, like she normally wore when she was cutting hair. She had a chain belt around her hips, and she was wearing a pair of leopard-print ballet slippers. Seeing mother and daughter standing next to each other was one of those *WTF* moments. They couldn't have looked or acted more different.

"You're looking a bit peaked today, Tess. I've got some of my vitamin juice in the fridge if you want some."

Tess thought it over for a second or two, tempted, but she declined. "I'll stick with coffee."

She poured a cup from the pot and doctored it up, and then took her place on the stool behind the counter. Taking the money and booking appointments kept her busy for the next hour and a half.

Besides her mother and grandmother, there was Debra Lassiter, in the chair next to her grandmother, looking sour, probably over the fact that Tatiana had beat her inside. Though if it bothered her so much, Tess wasn't sure why she kept booking her appointments on Fridays, when everyone in town knew Tatiana *always* had her hair done on Fridays at ten o'clock. Debra was round, and there was no differentiation between her head and her neck. But she wore bright red lipstick with confidence, and she was sucking down one of Theodora's vitamin juices, so Tess had a feeling she'd be pretty relaxed before long.

Twenty-year-old Crystal Rose sat behind the nail counter on the other side of the salon, waiting for her first customer. Theodora hated doing nails, but she hated Hard As Nails, which was two shops down, to get business she could steal a piece of the pie from. So she'd hired Crystal fresh out of beauty school.

Crystal's parents were Bobby and Lynette Rose, and Bobby owned the mechanic shop a couple of blocks over. They were good, blue-collar people who worked hard and went to church the occasional Sunday. So it was a little disconcerting to see the three of them together, since Crystal was more suited to the Addams Family.

Her jet-black hair was shaved to the scalp on one side of her head, and she'd dyed the other side a bright blue. She had piercings in both eyebrows, her nose, and her lip, and she had circles in both her earlobes big enough to throw darts through. From a conversation that had taken place at the Clip n' Curl after Crystal had started working there, Tess also knew she had her nipples pierced and she'd tried having her clit pierced, but it had hurt so bad she ended up throwing up on the piercer, and she'd had to pull the needle out herself because he was so pissed.

Her eye makeup was dark, and her lipstick was black. In a place like Last Stop, when Crystal Rose walked down the street, people stopped to stare. She might look like a freak, but she did a mean set of nails.

"I'm just saying," Theodora continued. "You could do a lot worse than Cal Dougherty. And you're not getting any younger. I know women are waiting longer to get married these days, but you've got to think about your eggs. There's a shelf life on those babies."

"Nonsense," her grandmother said. "I was almost forty when I had you, and I breezed through pregnancy and delivery. I was out of bed and working the next day. Age makes you tougher. Your memories are clouded because you got pregnant with Tess so young. You didn't have any fortitude. Never did I hear such wailing and complaining while you were giving birth."

"She was breech, Mama. It fucking hurt."

"*Kiska*," Tatiana said with a snort of derision.

Tess's eyebrows shot up to her hairline. It wasn't often one heard one's grandmother call someone a pussy. Much less if that someone was her own daughter.

Fortunately, the little bells above the door chimed as Jo Beth Schriever and Carol Dewberry walked in.

"Sorry I'm late," Carol said. "I was picking up my prescriptions at the Drug Mart, and I wasn't sure I was going to make it out of there alive. Mavis Beaman was in there."

There were several sympathetic groans that accompanied the news. Tess waited while Carol put her purse in one of the cubbies, grabbed one of Theodora's special vitamin juices, and sat down across from Crystal at the nail table.

"What can I do for you today, Jo Beth?" Theodora said. "I don't have you in the appointment book. Did I forget to put you down?"

"Oh, no," Jo Beth said a little breathlessly. But that's how Jo Beth did everything. Like she full-out sprinted everywhere she went and could never quite catch her breath. She'd worked at the post office since she'd graduated high school about twenty years before. She was a mousy woman with forgettable brown hair, brown eyes, and thin lips.

But Tess knew a side of Jo Beth most people didn't

get to see. They'd once attended a bachelorette party together, and after three or four Slippery Nipple shots, Jo Beth had given one of the strippers a lap dance instead of the other way around. She'd also ridden a mechanical bull and made out with a waitress name Lucille, so it was hard for Tess to see Jo Beth back in her normal habitat.

Jo Beth's eyes got wide when she saw Tess sitting behind the counter. "Umm . . . Hi, Tess." And then she looked back at Theodora. "I was going to see if you could squeeze me in. Aunt Delores's funeral is tomorrow."

"If you don't mind waiting a little while, I can squeeze you in," Theodora said.

"I appreciate it. I was real close to Aunt Delores. She and I had a lot in common."

Tess wanted to ask if Delores had also been fond of giving lap dances, but instead asked Carol, "What's wrong with Mavis Beaman? I haven't seen her in years. I thought she'd moved."

"She's been going through the longest menopause in history," Carol said, rolling her eyes. "She was in the pharmacy line waiting for her hormones and started having hot flashes. She stripped her shirt off right there in front of everyone, and then she burst into tears because Wally McAlpin screamed out loud at the sight of her. You know how excitable he can get."

"Bless her heart," Debra said, shaking her head. "I remember those days. I threw a brick right through Harold's windshield. The hormones made me do it."

"Yeah, that was a good one," Tatiana said, her smile

nostalgic. "That's the first time I ever had any respect for you."

Debra gave her a puzzled look, not sure if she should be insulted or not.

"What happened to Mavis?" Tess asked, drawing the conversation back on point.

Carol stuck her hands in two bowls of hot sudsy water, and there was an unholy glee in her eyes at the idea of being the first to impart such a great story.

"She dropped like a stone onto the floor. Just *splat*, like an overgrown toddler at the grocery store. She looked like a fool flopping around down there and carrying on. I'm telling you, she's faking it. Nobody has menopause for eight years. I think she just likes being crazy and getting away with bad behavior. On her way down to the floor I saw her grab a bag of M&M's right off the shelf and shove them in her purse."

"My goodness," Theodora said, scandalized. "You just can't trust anyone nowadays."

The irony of Theodora making that statement wasn't lost on Tess.

"Well I'd like to get back to the subject of Tess and the sheriff," Tatiana said. "You should try him on for size. Sometimes men have to grow on you."

"You and the sheriff?" Jo Beth asked, blinking rapidly.

"There's no me and the sheriff," Tess assured her. "I'm not interested."

"It's because that Henry Pottinger broke your heart," Carol said, sagely. "You can't put a timetable on grief and moving on. You take your time. When you're ready to take the sheriff for a ride, I'm sure he'll still be available. I think he's allergic to marriage since Victoria up and left him."

"Henry didn't break my heart," Tess said. "Mostly he made me want to slash all his tires. But that was just because I'd basically wasted a year of my life trying to plan a wedding he never intended on going through with."

"What the hell did you do with all those flocked Christmas trees?" Tatiana asked. "I've never seen such a thing. It would've been a beautiful wedding. Very Russian."

"I put them in the front lawn of the funeral home and sold them all at a discount," Tess said. "My first inclination was to set them all on fire, but Miller talked me into getting a little money back."

"I can't blame you for wanting to slash his tires," Jo Beth said timidly. Her breaths were coming in and out so fast Tess wondered how she wasn't hyperventilating. "The way he called off the wedding in public like that was just awful. He just ruined that whole Fourth of July parade. He really thought the crowd would be on his side when he got up on the bandstand like he did and told everyone he couldn't marry you because he had to follow his heart."

Crystal hadn't said a word, but she snorted and muttered, "Asshole," under her breath.

"And then he called up Tammy right there in front of God and everybody and told her he was in love with her and wanted to spend the rest of his life with her."

"You forgot the part where he asked Tess for the ring back so he could give it to Tammy," Carol said. "I thought Tess's hair might catch on fire. It got pretty entertaining after that with you tossing the ring in the Dumpster like that."

"She's a Sherman," Tatiana said. "We always think on our feet. And if her grandfather had been alive, Henry probably wouldn't have kneecaps."

"It was a real spectacle," Debra said. "I don't know how you showed your face in public after that." She pursed her lips judgmentally and said, "If he didn't break your heart that means you never really loved him. And I just don't see how that's possible. He's an excellent dentist."

"That's ridiculous," Theodora piped in. "Women marry men they don't love all the time. She had her reasons. And if Henry was such a hotshot dentist, his front cap wouldn't have popped off when he climbed into that Dumpster."

"It only popped off because he landed on his head," Carol said. "He was never very coordinated. You dodged a bullet there, Tess."

"A bullet would've been too merciful for that bastard," Theodora said. "If it was up to me, I'd have taken my shears and cut out his cold, black heart."

And that right there was why Tess had suffered through the ups and downs of her mother's sickness. There was love there. It only got redirected from time to time.

"Thank you, Mama. But I'd prefer you stay off death row. Henry has never been worth it."

"Don't worry, baby," Theodora said. "You'll find a man who is. Maybe one of those nice young men who works for you. Except for Dante. I've already called dibs."

"And she's back," Tess said, but Theodora had the water on full blast and was scrubbing away at Debra's scalp.

"THIS DOESN'T SEEM right," Elias said.

Water sprayed from one of the pipes in Tess's bathroom, and Deacon was getting blasted in the face as he tried to tighten the valve where the leak was.

"No shit," Deacon said.

"Next time just get her flowers, mate," Axel said. He placed a bucket to catch the drips that weren't spraying in Deacon's face. "Women are only impressed by home improvement projects if you can actually do them."

"I can do it," Deacon said. "I wasn't expecting pipes to start disintegrating the minute I touched them. This could've happened at any time. Only now I know where the major problems are."

"Right," Elias said. "Nice save. I don't see why Eve picked you to seduce the delectable Miss Sherman. I think I'm much more qualified for the job." Elias smirked and leaned on the shovel he'd been using to fill the wheelbarrow with broken tiles and Sheetrock. "How about we we shoot for her at the range? Whoever is most accurate with the fastest time gets to take her to bed."

"Hold on a sec," Axel said, moving out of the bathroom. "I want to get out of the way before Deacon kills you."

"What?" Elias asked, his grin widening. "Seems fair to me. What if she likes me better?"

Deacon growled and said, "She doesn't."

A gleam of the devil was in Elias's eyes and he kept pushing. "Want to put it to the test?"

"I will kill you, and I'll make it hurt. No one touches Tess."

"Staked a claim, have you, brother?" Elias asked. "Why didn't you just say so? There are plenty of fish in the sea."

"You have so much to learn," Axel said from the doorway.

"What are you guys, a hundred? We're in the prime of our life. Women are meant to be savored and enjoyed. Like an eight-course meal, except there's a different woman at every course."

"You're an idiot," Deacon said, blotting his knuckles on a rag. "A woman is going to come along someday and make you forget about your eight-course meal. And then she's going to make you beg and knock you off that pedestal you've put yourself on as God's gift to women."

Elias snorted out a laugh. "No woman will make me beg. That's when you know it's time to move on to the next course."

"This conversation is making me oddly hungry," Axel said. "It's still stupid, but I guess it could be worse. He could be using an all-you-can-eat buffet as an example."

"Yeah," Deacon said. "He's all class with his eight-course meal analogy."

"Shut up, the both of you," Elias said. "If you want to limit yourself to one woman, then it's your loss. More for me."

Deacon felt the panic of those words prickle beneath his skin. "Just stay away from Tess," he growled. "Can we please get some work done here, ladies?"

Deacon had decided that if Tess's bathroom ever had a hope of being finished he was going to have to recruit some help. So after they finished training for the day, Elias and Axel had grabbed their tools and followed him up to the mess.

They were supposed to be on a rigorous training schedule—after all, that was their actual job, not working for the funeral home. So they had spent the afternoon first at the range, each of them put through the rigorous target drills and then eventually progressing to the moving targets. Their speed and accuracy were required to be twice as fast as any other agency's. They were all exceptional shots—better than exceptional—but Elias was fucking phenomenal with a weapon in his hand, and it was a beautiful thing to watch.

After they'd finished at the range, they drove out to what had once been a small three-story hospital. It had been built in anticipation of the population boom in Last Stop, but the bypass had taken care of that and they'd left it unfinished and never inhabited. It was a great location to run scenario training. All they had to do was pick a random scenario and upload it to the

VR goggles. They could work anything from a terrorist scene to an active shooter to biological weapons and run it through start to finish, using Simunition weapons to make it as real as possible.

Today's scenario had been particularly rough—it always was when it involved children—and Colin had ended up with a deep gash across his cheek when he'd rappelled into a window that had a broken shard of glass still attached. He was lucky he hadn't lost an eye, and Dante had taken him to get stitched up once the scenario had been completed.

Manual labor or sex were the two best ways to work off the adrenaline after a particularly high-rush training session or an actual op. Since sex wasn't on the menu, manual labor was the best option. And Axel and Elias had jumped at the opportunity to help Deacon since they were in the same situation.

"So when you say major problems," Elias said, "you pretty much mean everything, right? Because this is not even a shell of a bathroom. If we weren't on the third floor, I'd tell you to knock the whole thing down and start over."

"Eve should've taken care of this during the renovations," Deacon said. "There was no reason not to other than she just wanted to make her usual power play. She knows Tess's psychology well enough to know that she won't complain about the conditions, and she was already living here anyway. But she always likes to see how far she can push people, how bad she can make their circumstances, before they'll break. It's the same reason she had Levi go ahead and do the psych evaluation, even though he was still orienting himself after waking up, and his body was still weak."

"Yeah, she's a bitch. We all know that," Elias said.

"How's Levi doing?" Axel asked.

"He's holding on, which I'm sure she knew he'd be able to. He was Kidon Mossad, so she'd know he can withstand torture at an elevated level."

"Just because she knows he'll succeed doesn't make her any less of a bitch," Elias said. "It's a harsh thing to do to put someone through that when your head is pounding and you have flashes of complete memory loss. Or flashes of too many memories."

Deacon finally got the water shut off and flung his head to the side, tossing wet hair out of his eyes. He looked down at his scraped knuckles that were oozing blood.

"You got the Dumpster?" Axel asked.

"Yeah, they delivered it this morning," Deacon said. "It's right outside."

Axel walked into Tess's suite and toward the window and looked down at the lawn. "Looks like a perfect shot to me," he said, grinning. "Elias, help me lift that toilet. Might as well start with a bang."

"It's a good thing Tess isn't here to see this," Deacon said, bothered by the sight of dusty boot prints messing up her bedroom.

"Don't worry, it won't be long before she hears about it," Elias said with a chuckle.

Up until now, Deacon had been the only one to invade her personal space, and he didn't like the idea of other men seeing where she slept and dressed. How they casually looked at her belongings and photographs, or moved her things around to make a path to the window. The territorial instinct was strong, and his adrenaline was still high. He had to talk himself down from those basic, gut reactions.

They laid plastic across the floor to keep the wheelbarrow from leaving marks, and then Deacon picked up the sledgehammer and decided the best way to take out his frustration was on the shower and what was left of the walls.

"You think we can get this done in less than six months?" he asked.

Axel started laughing, and then he kept laughing as he shoveled debris into the wheelbarrow.

"I think what he's trying to say is, 'Hell, no,'" Elias said, joining in the laughter.

Deacon sighed and hoped this wasn't the thing that would push Tess past her breaking point. Maybe Eve knew what she was doing after all.

CHAPTER TEN

The next day, Mrs. Schriever was buried. *With* her broach.

There had been no sleeping in on Saturday morning, and Tess had desperately needed it after spending a majority of her Friday at the Clip n' Curl, and the rest of it keeping herself preoccupied while Deacon worked shirtless in her bathroom. When he'd finally come downstairs sometime after ten, covered in sweat and dust and looking just a little bit frustrated, she was sitting on the bench seat in the kitchen trying her hardest to concentrate on her crossword puzzle book and wondering if she'd be able to button her pants the following morning if she went ahead and ate all the cookies that had been left over from the viewing the night before.

The look in Deacon's eyes when he'd seen her sitting there had made her feel hot all over. And a little afraid. There was a lot of passion in his gaze. She wasn't used to that kind of intensity when it came to physical matters, and for a split second she wondered if he was going to pounce.

He'd taken a deep breath, tossed his shirt over his shoulder, and then walked straight up to her and given her the sweetest kiss right on the forehead. It had taken her completely off guard. He'd whispered good night and then left her sitting there without a thought in her head.

Saturday morning, Tess had sighed at the memory and forced herself out of bed and down to the kitchen for coffee. Esther Schriever had chosen a nine o'clock funeral, which meant Tess had to be up at five thirty and dressed by seven.

She had a slight moment of panic when she got to the bottom floor and remembered she didn't have a jacket to wear. But the worry was short-lived when she walked into the kitchen and found a new suit jacket in a hanging bag lying across the table.

She unzipped it and there was a note pinned to the lapel that said: *"It's not too fancy. I hope this one ends up on the floor too. ~S"*

She found herself smiling before she took her first sip of caffeine, and she stroked the collar. And then she realized there wasn't just a jacket inside, but an entirely new pantsuit.

There was another note attached to the pants. *"Scowling will give you wrinkles. It came as a set. The size should be right since I had the chance to measure you at length. By the way, when can I get my hands on you again? ~S"*

"Incorrigible," she muttered. "And charming. Good move, Deacon."

She had taken her coffee and the suit halfway upstairs before she remembered that her bathroom was a construction zone, so she headed back down to the large bathroom next to the embalming room. In all honesty, this one was much nicer than the one she was used to upstairs. The downstairs bathroom had been completely remodeled, with travertine tiles and heated towel bars. And the walk-in shower had so many shower heads she felt like she was in a car wash.

Her mood was pretty darn good by the time she got out of the shower and toweled off. She slathered herself in cream with the light lemon scent Deacon had commented on and then pulled on plain black underpants and a matching bra. And then she stood there staring at the suit hanging on the hook on the back side of the door.

Deacon had said it wasn't too fancy, but from where she was standing it looked like the fanciest thing she'd ever laid eyes on. There was no label, and that was a bit worrisome, because she'd read in *Cosmo* one time that clothes without labels were really expensive. She stroked her fingers down the lapel and bit her lip. It *felt* really expensive.

"Here goes nothing," she said, and pulled it from the hanger before she could talk herself out of it.

She put the whole thing on before she looked at herself in the mirror, but just the feel of the material against her skin was a new sensation. And when she turned around, she almost didn't recognize the body in the mirror. She had . . . curves. And what looked like cleavage.

"Holy smokes," she said, turning so she could see her

butt in the mirror. She'd never thought much about her butt before, but after seeing it like this she decided it wasn't half-bad. The jacket was form-fitting and emphasized her breasts and the smallness of her waist.

"It's like a magical suit," she said in awe. And if she could manage to make it through the day without getting it dirty or tearing a hole in it, she'd consider it a success.

Friends and family came to lay Delores Schriever to rest. The rain had started up again sometime during the night, so everyone huddled under the tent as the preacher gave the CliffsNotes version of her life. Jo Beth had a freshly colored and styled mane of hair, and she looked an awful lot like Peppermint Patty from the Peanuts gang, only the wet had made the whole thing fall flat so she looked mousier than ever. But Tess had a new respect for Jo Beth after hearing her opinions on Henry the day before. And no one would ever hear it from her about the mechanical bull or the lap dance.

Delores had had a good and fulfilling life, and Tess guessed that, in the end, that's all you could ask for. She waited until the crowd dispersed and then gave Axel and Elias the go-ahead to lower the casket into the grave and fill it with dirt. She left them to the job and then drove the Suburban from the cemetery back two blocks to the funeral home. By the time she finished up the final paperwork and put on an old pair of sweats and her University of Texas T-shirt that was so worn and thin it was indecent, it was well after three o'clock.

That's when her best friend, Miller Darling, showed

up with two bottles of wine and her emergency bag of supplies. The emergency bag included a cookie mix, binoculars, chocolate-covered almonds, nail polish, *The Breakfast Club*, and a forty-eight pack of condoms.

"Emergency" was kind of a loose term where the emergency bag was concerned. It might be brought out for anything from a bad breakup, to PMS, to having weird hairs show up on your body that had never been there before. It was an all-around emergency bag. And Tess hated to even think about how long that forty-eight pack of condoms had been in there unopened. The rest of the supplies had been refilled as the years passed and the movie changed from time to time.

"My God, would you look at that?" Miller marveled as she peeked out the window of the kitchen. With binoculars. "You think they do that on purpose?"

Miller was wearing a pair of tight jeans and a sleeveless black shirt that draped open in the back, showing the tattoo of an open book on her left shoulder. Her hair was dark brown with several lighter shades woven in—at least for now, since she tended to change it like underpants—and she had it pulled up into a loose ponytail that looked beachy and arty at the same time.

Miller had been Tess's best friend since the first grade, when her family had moved to Last Stop. The Darlings were still considered outsiders, which was probably why she and Miller had hit it off so well. They'd both been outcasts. And Miller had given Libby Barlow a fat lip when the bully had thrown Tess's sandwich on the ground during lunch.

"Do what on purpose?" Tess asked, opening the oven door to check on the cookies. "Are they supposed to be black like that around the edges?"

"No, black isn't good for cookies. Take them out."

Tess opened the oven door and black smoke billowed out. The smoke alarm shrilled, but she didn't see any flames, so she figured that was a step above the last time. Miller glanced over and sighed before opening the kitchen door and letting some of the smoke out. Then she went back to watching through the binoculars. Apparently the view was much more appealing than burnt cookies.

"Damn, they're leaving," she said. "Do you think they exercise like that on purpose? With their shirts off and bodies gleaming all seductively?"

"Yes, I'm sure it's all very intentional," Tess said sarcastically, grabbing the hot mat and pulling the cookies out of the oven. "I'm sure that's all part of their devious plan as they work out inside their *private* gym. They take their shirts off and wear those shorts that hang down low on their hips. And then they slick their bodies up with fake sweat and pose seductively, hoping above all hopes that the creeper staring at them through binoculars might come fulfill their every sexual fantasy."

Miller put down the binoculars and gave her a droll stare. "I see what you did there. And I don't think I care. If they really wanted privacy, they'd close the blinds."

"Ahh, the Peeping Tom credo."

"Shut up and give me a cookie. I can tear off the

black parts. And it's not like I didn't notice you sneaking little peeks too."

Tess pinched her lips together and didn't bother denying it. She'd done nothing but think about kissing Deacon again. It had been almost forty-eight hours since his lips had touched hers, and she was going through withdrawal. She hadn't told Miller about their kisses, and she wasn't sure why. They told each other everything. But kissing Deacon had been different, and she wanted it to be something that was just hers.

She and Miller made an odd pair, but maybe that's why they'd always meshed so well. Tess was the more introverted of the two, preferring to spend her time with dead people, and also the fictional people in the books she inhaled like oxygen.

Miller was the exact opposite. She loved people—their quirks, habits, facial features, and conversations. She studied them like a scientist would a bug under a microscope. She asked them questions and wanted to know everything about them, and she was genuinely interested in their answers. She said it was all research, and Tess guessed she could get away with that excuse because Miller was a romance novelist. Which was ironic, because Miller was pretty much the most unromantic person Tess had ever met. She was logical and straightforward, but Miller liked to say that it was cutting through people's bullshit that made her write such great characters.

When she'd hit thirty, Miller had had one of those freak-out moments where she was afraid her body would immediately start going south and that her chances of marriage were all but in the toilet. And like with most things, she took it to the extreme. So now Miller was one of those CrossFit junkies who showed up at six-in-the-morning workout like it was church and posted the WOD—or the Workout of the Day to non-CrossFit folk—on Facebook every day. The only reason Tess knew about WODs was because one time Miller had dragged her to one of those god-awful classes at the crack of dawn. Tess hadn't been able to sit for three days afterward because her body hadn't bent in the places it was supposed to. CrossFit hurt. Which was why she did yoga.

Miller was what the guys liked to call "packed." The transformation in her body since she'd started working out only made Tess a little jealous. She'd kill for those arms and shoulders. And probably her ass too. And she was really envious that Miller could go out in the sunlight without burning to a crisp and come away nice and bronzed. Tess had freckles for a reason.

Tess consoled herself by remembering that women's bodies were all built differently—*blah, blah, blah*—and that one day she was going to be grateful for her willowy figure and the fact that she had no boobs to worry about sagging. She never had to count calories or forgo cheesecake. Or burnt cookies. And Deacon had seemed more than pleased with her body. Either that, or it really had been his hammer pressing into her stomach the night before. Either way, it was an impressive hammer.

Miller put the binoculars on the table and then went to get the wine from the little fridge under the island and two wineglasses from the cabinet.

"What do you think?" she asked. "Are the cookies salvageable?"

Tess paused mid-chew. "Yeah, the middle tastes fine. I think there's something wrong with the oven. There's no reason for the oven to smoke like that."

"I hate to be the bearer of truth, but I'm pretty sure it's you and not the oven. Something always goes wrong when you cook. Like when those kabobs caught on fire."

"I didn't know you were supposed to wet the sticks first," Tess protested, using a spatula to put the rest of the cookies on a plate. She set the plate in the middle of the table and waited for Miller to uncork the wine. "Why don't they ever tell you stuff like that in the recipe books? It's amazing anyone ever learns how to cook."

"People have different gifts. Cooking just isn't yours."

"Oh, yeah? Then what's my gift?"

"You're really great at embalming people."

"That's my job," she said, rolling her eyes. "I'm *supposed* to be great at it. I mean what am I great at other than my job? I feel like I'm in this perpetual rut. I don't know what to do with myself."

"Is this one of those midlife crisis moments?" Miller asked. "You should go shopping. It always makes me feel better."

"That requires putting on clothes and going out in public."

"No way. I do all my shopping online now. I think the UPS man thinks I'm trying to seduce him, because he literally delivers packages to my door every day. He keeps looking at me expectantly, and I don't have the heart to tell him I'm just excited because he's delivering my new waxing kit."

"Waxing kit?"

"I'm part Arabic. I wax everything," she said. "Now, stop trying to change the subject. You're amazing. You're good at lots of stuff that has nothing to do with your job. Except cooking. You're terrible at that. And you could use some wardrobe help, but that's only because you hate your body."

"I don't hate my body," she said, surprised. She replayed the scene from the night before when Deacon had told her she was hiding behind the ugly jacket. "It's just a body. Clothes are used for covering it. Because it's illegal to be naked."

"Yeah, yeah. I'm just saying no one in Last Stop is going to stone you because you're not wearing an oversized man's shirt. You're not your mother."

"For that, we give thanks," she said.

Miller had poured them glasses of wine that were full almost to the brim, and they toasted each other with that statement.

"You're excellent at yoga," she said. "You can do all those bendy moves that I can't because my boobs are too big."

"Yes," Tess said wryly. "That's making me feel much better."

"No, seriously. You're like a pretzel. Men love that in bed. They'd much rather have creativity and athleticism than boobs. At least after things get going."

"This is a weird conversation. Maybe move onto the next topic."

"You're funny, you're really good at *Jeopardy*, you speak Russian for Pete's sake, and you can play pool like a boss."

"It's all geometry."

"Which does me no good since I'm a writer."

"Thanks for the pep talk," Tess said, taking a cookie and snapping off the burnt edges. "I feel better about myself now."

"You'd have done the same for me."

Tess took a deep breath, needing to share what had been on her mind more and more the past few days. "I'm pretty sure I'm going to move," she said at length. "Away from Last Stop."

"O-kaaaaay," Miller said after a long pause. "Where are you moving? You've got a pretty sweet setup here. Think of all the gas you save not having to drive to work. And there's no mortgage payment."

"I need a change. I've started sending my résumé out to a few places, just to put some feelers out."

"Whoa!" Miller's dark brown eyes were wide with surprise. "You're serious?"

"As a heart attack. It's time to make my escape. This place will never be mine. And I just need some distance. I want a chance at anonymity. Or at someone getting to know me first without knowing the infamy of my mother. I want to get married and have children, and the pool is very, very small in Last Stop."

"Thank you," Miller said. "That's making me feel much better about my own circumstances."

"I'm all about harsh realities today."

They sipped their wine in silence for a few minutes, and Tess opened up the chocolate-covered almonds.

"Well, I think it's a great idea," Miller said at last, topping off their wine.

"You do?" Tess asked. "Really?"

"Sure." She shrugged. "I've always thought you needed to escape. You're not like me. You're a romantic at heart. And though you don't particularly like people, you crave family. Probably because yours was so abnormal growing up."

"Thank you for the armchair analysis, Doctor Darling."

She grinned, unfazed. "You're welcome. A change of scenery might be good for you. A little adventure, a little romance. I can work from anywhere, so I can visit anytime. Unless you're thinking of moving really far away; then we'll have to reevaluate. Because if you have an emergency, it'll take me too long to get there to water your plants or take care of your kids." She picked up the binoculars again and looked back toward the gym.

"I wonder where they went," she said. "That Elias guy is an interesting character. He'd make a fabulous hero for one of my books. He's sexy and funny and always has a clever word. But you can tell he's got some baggage. There's a broodiness to him when he doesn't feel like he has to be 'on' in front of people. He's got some pent-up aggression for sure. I bet he'd be fabulous in bed. Or on the couch or in the shower. There are some men you can just tell by looking at them that they don't need a map to find a clitoris."

"Henry couldn't have found one with a GPS and a personal guide," Tess said. "But I don't know about Elias. He's a good guy, but you seem to gravitate towards guys with baggage."

"They're just so much more interesting."

"But one day maybe you should try sizing up a guy for potential relationship material instead of potential fictional character material."

"Again, my characters are so much more interesting than real men. Real men leave the toilet seat up and can belch the alphabet. At least with Elias I'd know what I was getting into. He's got a hot body and exudes sex appeal. And sex is all I need. I can fulfill my emotional needs by watching *Dr. Phil* and *Fixer Upper*."

"That show makes me have all the feels," Tess said. "If I get my own place, maybe they'll come do a show on me."

"And maybe one of the carpenters will be a hot ticket with a tool belt and a million-dollar smile."

An image of Deacon dressed very much the same flashed through Tess's mind, and she shoved another cookie in her mouth.

"Where'd you find Elias, anyway? I know he's from Texas, but I always find it fascinating that anyone would end up here when there's so many better places to be."

"You ended up here," she said. "And I'm here."

"We're here because of our parents. And I stay here because moving is a pain in the ass, my house is dirt cheap but still awesome, and I can travel all over the world and not have to worry about someone breaking into my place while I'm gone for weeks at a time. But why would anyone seek out Last Stop on purpose?"

"Beats me," she said, shrugging. "Eve sent him to me."

Miller swirled her wine around her glass. "I wonder if she's got a catalog of sexy men she orders from. What do they do around here?"

"They stay busy enough," she said. And then she thought of the new guy who had appeared on her embalming table. Deacon had said he'd be sticking around too. Maybe Eve did order them from some kind of catalog.

"I think I've ruined myself," Miller said. "No man could possibly live up to what I've created in my head. Besides, the last few guys I've dated have seriously left me questioning where the future of our society is heading. It's not normal that three out of the four of them still lived with their parents. Their mothers still folded their laundry and set it neatly outside their doors, and made their lunches for them before they went to work every day."

"Sounds like a pretty sweet deal," Tess said. "I'd probably stay too. But you want to avoid those kinds of men. They're going to be looking for a wife who will fill the role of their mother."

"Yes, I know." Miller nodded sagely. "Considering I'm not particularly interested in shooting out a small person from my loins in a painful manner, I certainly don't want to adopt a man-child through the guise of wedding vows."

"Maybe you should get a cat," Tess said.

"I'd rather watch you settle down and have babies so I can spoil them. That way my loins stay intact and I can leave when I get tired of your kids. But you're doing your best to avoid any potential relationships."

"Henry pretty much cured me of that," she said.

"Henry was a horse's behind. I told you that from the beginning. He kept looking at my ass."

"You do have a great ass," Tess admitted. "I sometimes stare at it too."

"Thank you. And I probably won't have to do extra squats to burn off these cookies since they're so bad. I don't even think they qualify as dessert."

"Yet you're eating them anyway."

"It's a weakness." Miller took a bite out of the center of her cookie and then chased it with the wine. "You've got to get out of this house. The only men visiting you in here are the ones you're filling with weird chemicals and gluing their eyes shut. They're not interested in you. Come out with me tonight. Your funeral is all done for the day, and you've got nothing better to do than sit here, finish off these cookies, and watch a *Murder, She Wrote* marathon. Though if I were you, I'd spring for some night-vision goggles and see what else you can see in the carriage house after the lights go down," Miller said, waggling her eyebrows.

"They have a right to their privacy," Tess said primly, though her cheeks heated.

"Oh, she blushes," Miller said, chortling. "*Tess likes a bo-y*," she said in a singsong voice. "Who is it? You didn't put money in the pot at the Clip n' Curl, did you?"

"Of course not!" she said. "It'd be a waste. I don't stand a chance with a man like that."

"Because I'm such a keen observer of human nature, I just noticed two things. The first is that you said you don't have chance with a *man* like that. Meaning, you have a very specific man in mind. The second is that you are truly clueless when it comes to your looks. For heaven's sake, Tess. You've got a mirror. You also have a hairbrush and concealer for those dark smudges under your eyes, so maybe work on that part. God wouldn't have invented that stuff if he hadn't wanted you to use it."

"I'll make sure to tell Father Murphy that the next time he preaches on vanity."

"This is Texas. People here don't go to the Dollar Store without their full hair and makeup done. Half the congregation left during the middle of that sermon, and the only reason the other half stayed is because they were men."

Tess laughed until tears rolled down her cheeks. "Stop it."

Miller grinned, flashing the lone dimple in her cheek. "Seriously, Tess. Henry did a number on you, and I hate him for it. He stripped away all your self-confidence when it came to your looks and your God-given talents. All he wanted was for you to fill the role of 'his' wife. Like it's some big deal to be the wife of the only dentist in Last Stop. *Whoop-de-friggin-do*."

"Tell us how you really feel," Tess said, arching her brow.

"He's an idiot, and you should thank the good Lord every day that Tammy got stuck with him instead of you. He had a twelve-step program for everything, from doing the laundry to wiping his ass. You would've ended up strangling him in his sleep, and then you'd have gone to jail and we wouldn't be sitting here drinking wine and eating bad cookies."

"You're a good friend," Tess said, wiping her cheeks.

"Damn straight I am. You're gorgeous. And I say that with no bias whatsoever. Your looks are just a little more subtle than some women's. You've got that wholesome, girl-next-door thing going. Like those Ralph Lauren models. Men like that."

"Which men?"

"Well, the sheriff for one. I heard at the grocery store *and* while I was filling up the tank that Cal has been all over you like white on rice."

"Yeah, that was a little weird," Tess said. "Surprised the hell out of me. He didn't seem too brokenhearted about the rejection though."

"I wouldn't think so. He's been banging Mandy Simmons for the last few weeks, but she's been yapping about marriage to anyone who will listen, so my guess is he's ready to move on. Probably a good call on turning him down."

"Thank you," Tess said. "Not to mention that I'm not the least bit attracted to him."

"But you *are* attracted to someone. You always get

that dopey look in your eyes when you've got the hots for someone, and I could tell you were thinking about him earlier when I mentioned the guy in a tool belt."

"That's ridiculous. I do not get a dopey look on my face."

Miller rolled her eyes. "Whatever you say. But take my advice, don't ever play poker. Now, tell me which one you've got your eye on. If it's Elias, I'd pretend to play the martyr and let you sleep with him, but I'd probably hate you forever. And then I'd immortalize you in a book and probably kill you off somewhere along the way."

"I appreciate your non-sacrifice," Tess said dryly. "But you don't have to worry. I'm not going to sleep with any of them. I'm moving. Remember?"

"That's why it's so perfect," Miller said excitedly. "It's like one last *hurrah* before you go."

"I don't just sleep with men for *hurrahs*, no matter how great they might be at *hurrah-ing*."

"Okay, okay," Miller said, holding up her hands in surrender. "It's part of that girl-next-door thing I guess. You've always been that way. I'm not even sure you've ever had a real orgasm before. I worry about your sex life."

"Very comforting to know. And I have too had a real orgasm before," she said, straightening her shoulders. "Just never with an actual man."

Miller's mouth dropped open and a piece of cookie fell out. "Remind me to send Henry's Tammy a card with my condolences. I'll send it with flowers to his office since she's a hygienist there. Poor thing probably spends all day sitting on one of those electric toothbrushes."

Tess snorted out a laugh. "She certainly has my sympathies. But sex with Henry was one of the most productive six minutes I had every Tuesday and Friday."

"Your sex schedule was the same as trash pickup?" Miller asked drolly.

"Yeah, but it wasn't too bad. It was just enough time to figure out what was for dinner the next night and to mentally pick out my clothes for the next morning. And having it on such an exact schedule was pretty nice. Foreplay always lasted from eight twenty-five to eight thirty, and then we wrapped up the grand finale by eight thirty-six. Henry spent the next twenty-four minutes checking his work emails before lights out at nine o'clock, while I adjourned for a twenty-four-minute shower that involved that Christmas gift you got me in 2004."

"Geez, I don't actually think you're supposed to keep them that long. Seems like it might short-circuit or be a fire hazard at this point. I'll get you a new one for this Christmas."

Miller pulled out her phone and made a note, seemingly satisfied with herself. Tess stifled a laugh. This was classic Miller. She was one of those people who ordered gifts all through the year and put them in a closet somewhere so she'd be prepared, because she almost always had a deadline right before Christmas and didn't have time to think about the holidays.

"Don't think I'm going to let you ignore my question," she said, putting her phone down. "Which one is he?"

CHAPTER ELEVEN

Deacon was never quite sure what day of the week it was. When you tended to work all seven, the days didn't seem to matter all that much. There were no such things as weekends. Downtime came when it came, whether it was a Tuesday or a Saturday.

The sheriff had come by to check out the van, but he hadn't found anything. The Shadow could always be trusted to cover tracks completely, and this time was no exception. Deacon could tell the sheriff was annoyed not to have found any trace of mud or the bullet hole the perps had spoken of, but there was nothing there for him to find. Which was fine by him. The farther away the sheriff stayed, the better. He didn't like the way Cal looked at Tess, as if he were thinking about trying her on for size.

The only reason he did know that it was Saturday was because Tess had had the funeral to see to, and it was Axel and Elias who'd been up for the burial rotation. He'd watched them leave the house in the Suburban and the newly repaired transport van that morning.

After the funeral, Deacon, Elias, and Dante finished a solid workout in the gym. When they'd finished, they took quick showers in the locker room and coded themselves into HQ. They heard Colin laughing the moment the door popped open with a tiny click, and when they entered the room they found him working at one of the computer stations, but he had the volume turned high for the cameras inside the house.

"What are you doing?" Deacon asked, instantly recognizing Tess's voice.

"Tess is baking cookies," Colin said. "The smoke alarm just went off. I think she caught the oven on fire."

"How does she keep doing that?" Deacon asked, grabbing a bottle of water and taking a seat at one of the workstations.

"Hey, that's Miller," Elias said, very interested all of a sudden. "You shouldn't be listening to their personal conversation."

"That Elias guy is an interesting character. He'd make a fabulous hero for one of my books. He's sexy and funny . . ."

"You were saying?" Colin asked as Elias turned up the volume a little.

"Quiet," Elias hissed. "I'm trying to listen."

"That's wrong," Deacon said. "She would kick your ass all over the place if she found out you were doing this."

"I don't see you putting in earplugs," he shot back. "Maybe because you want to see if Tess thinks you're as spectacular in bed as Miller thinks I am. Lord, that woman is a temptation no man could resist."

"She's managed to resist you for months," Dante said.

"That's because I haven't tried. It's hard to resist all this charm when it's coming at you full force."

"Just like every other cocky SEAL I've ever met," Colin said. "Care to put a wager on it?"

Deacon rolled his eyes, and then caught Tess's words—*Just never with an actual man.*"

"Holy shit," Deacon said, leaning forward.

"Poor girl," Dante said sympathetically. "Maybe we should find this Henry and make sure he has a bit of an accident."

"This place could use a little excitement," Colin said. "I'm in."

Deacon wasn't sure what he was doing, but the direction of the conversation had him racing out of the room and up the other set of stairs that led to the casket warehouse. He didn't want the others hearing whatever Tess was about to say. He pressed his thumb to the keypad and the door that led into the casket warehouse swung open.

He'd spent most of the day away from her, determined to give her some space and put some distance between them, hoping she'd be thinking of him like he'd been thinking of her. But knowing that a man had never pleased her as she should've been pleased made him angry and unreasonably possessive all at once.

He knocked once on the kitchen door and then stepped inside without an invitation. Both women stared at him in surprise. They were sitting in the same position they had been in when he'd been watching on the screen, but up close he noticed the flush in Tess's cheeks.

"I need to talk to you," he said to Tess. "It's really important. Come riding with me."

"You're not extending the length of my bathroom renovation, are you?" she asked, narrowing her eyes. "You said four weeks."

"I don't know why you're so obsessed with timelines. You're getting a new bathroom out of it."

"Timelines are essential to life. And so are showers. I want my space back."

"Speaking of, we should probably fix the floor of your bedroom before your bed falls through. Might as well do all the renovations at once."

"Except I won't have a place to sleep."

"There's always slumber room number one," he said, lips twitching.

"I don't mean to interrupt," Miller said. "But what the hell is going on here? I feel like a third wheel. Should I leave y'all alone?"

"Yes," he said.

"No," she said at the same time.

Miller turned to look at Tess with a twinkle in her eye. "Never mind my earlier question. I think I have it figured out."

"We're having girls' night," Tess said to Deacon. "Thank you for the suit, by the way. It was very nice."

"Did it fit?" he asked.

"Perfectly."

He grinned and crossed his arms over his chest. "I'm an excellent measurement taker."

Tess turned crimson.

"Hello." Miller turned to Tess inquiringly. "You left a lot of information out just now."

"I was getting to it," Tess growled.

He turned his attention to Miller. "I need to talk to Tess. It's important."

"If it's so important, why didn't you come earlier instead of going to the gym for a workout? You've been wasting all this time."

"Because we didn't want to deny you the opportunity to use your binoculars."

Tess snorted out a laugh and Miller pinched her lips together. "You left the blinds open."

"That's a Peeping Tom's favorite excuse," he said.

Tess laughed even harder at that and tears rolled down her cheeks. "That's what I said too."

"Remember what's in the emergency supply pack," Miller said, looking pointedly at Tess. "Maybe take it with you. Just in case. Though I think that box has been in the bag four years now. I'm not sure what the shelf life is."

"Hush," Tess hissed.

Deacon was pretty sure he was getting the gist of the conversation. "What's in the emergency supply pack?" he asked. "I thought we'd take the bike out for a ride. Bring it with you."

Miller broke into hysterical giggles, and Tess groaned.

"Y'all should go," Miller said. "I just remembered I have some errands to do."

"You just remembered?" Tess said. "How very convenient. You never do errands on the weekend because of the crowds." Then she turned to Deacon. "I've never been on a motorcycle."

"You'll love it. Nothing makes you feel freer than riding the open road."

She pushed her wineglass back, though it was half-full. "If I go with you, I'd like some explanations please."

"You'll get them," he promised. "As much as I can."

"This is super-awkward," Miller said. "I'm going to go now." Miller stood and started gathering dishes. She tossed the cookies into the trash and rinsed the wineglasses in the sink.

"Can you cook?" she asked Deacon.

"Yes. But mostly out of necessity."

She nodded. "That'll be good enough. I approve."

Tess sputtered. "You approve what? My life is not your next romance novel."

"This is what I like to call backstory," Miller said. "This is the part of your life where you do something wild and crazy and have the best sex of your life. This is the part of the story that has to happen so you can learn from your experiences and find your true happily ever after."

"She gets philosophical after a couple of glasses of wine," Tess said apologetically.

His lips twitched. "I'm okay with it. I like this story. Best sex of your life?" he asked, brows raised.

"Hmm . . ." Tess said for lack of anything better. "Maybe we should talk about my bathroom. It seems like safer ground."

"You'd think that," he said, "but I wouldn't bet money on it."

"Y'all stop talking about bathrooms and go have fun. Don't forget the emergency supply pack," Miller said, dropping it in Tess's lap. "My work here is done. Call me tomorrow if you're free. Just don't call before noon, because it's my morning to sleep late."

"It's always your morning to sleep late," Tess said. "Do you even know what before noon looks like?"

"Sure," Miller said. "I see it around six a.m. when I'm heading to bed." She grabbed her purse and blew Tess a kiss.

"Hold on, cowboy," Deacon said, stopping her in her tracks. "You've had about one glass of wine too many to drive home."

"I live three blocks from here," she said.

"Most accidents happen less than a mile from a person's home."

"You made that up," she said, hands on hips.

"I never make things up," he retorted.

"Well, I make up stuff for a living, so I can recognize a good bullshitter a mile away. But I'm happy to leave my car here and walk home since the rain has stopped. When Tess and I move to the city, we'll never have to worry about having too much wine because we can just take the train wherever we want to go."

"Are you moving with me?" Tess asked.

"I just decided. Is that okay?" Miller asked. "I don't want to live with you though. I'll get my own place. Maybe next door. You know I don't like living with other people."

Deacon was starting to think maybe Miller had

had more than two glasses of wine. She hadn't stopped talking since he walked in the door.

"No need to walk," he said. "Just a second."

He pulled out his cell and dialed Elias. Since he knew he'd been watching the cameras, Deacon didn't have to explain what he needed, but he did it anyway.

"I need a favor," he said.

"I can see that," Elias said. "I'm happy to take her off your hands. What the hell is in that emergency bag? I can't decide if she terrifies me or if I'm turned on."

"I'll let you be the judge of that," Deacon said. "Can you give Miller a ride? I think she lives near your place."

"This day is getting better by the minute," Elias said. "I'll be right there."

Elias knocked on the kitchen door a minute later and opened it without being invited in. "Looks like I missed the party," he said, winking at Miller. "What do I have to do to get an invitation next time?"

"Have a vagina," Miller said deadpan.

Tess burst into laughter and said, "She's an acquired taste."

"My favorite," Elias said. "What do you say? Want to hit the open road and see where it takes us?"

Miller arched an eyebrow and said, "As long as it takes us to my front door."

"And I thought you were the one who liked to take chances."

"I'm letting you take me home," she said. "That seems like a pretty big chance to me."

Elias arched a brow and moved in closer. "How's that?" he asked.

"If I have to explain it to you then maybe you're not as smart as I thought you were." Miller gave Tess a hug and tossed her keys to Elias. "Looks like I'll be eating ice cream and watching movies tonight. Don't forget to call me tomorrow. And for Pete's sake don't forget the emergency pack."

"I really want to know what's in that emergency bag," Deacon said as Miller and Elias left.

Tess just smiled, two streaks of color painting her cheeks. "Hmm. I'm at a loss for words so it seems like a good time to change the subject. Did I tell you I'm thinking of getting a motorcycle when I move to the city? I hear they get great gas mileage."

Deacon stared at her blankly for a moment. The thought of her decked out in leather, straddling a bike, made him go temporarily mute.

"Do you have leather pants?" he asked.

"No, should I get some?"

"It's essential," he said stoically.

CHAPTER TWELVE

Tess was afraid she could get used to living on the wild side.

She'd always made it a point to be extra-responsible and make good decisions. But within three days of being in Deacon's company, she wanted to do what she wanted and say to hell with everyone else. Deacon was a bad influence on her. And she liked it.

Common sense had her running upstairs to put on a pair of jeans, an army-green tank top, and a pair of cowboy boots she never got to wear because it was usually too hot. She braided her hair down the side and put on the extra helmet he'd given her. *Everyone* in town was going to be watching them. And those who weren't watching would hear about it and start talking.

Tess didn't know squat about motorcycles, but she pictured herself on something small and bright red. Something fun and zippy and cute. Deacon's motorcycle wasn't cute. It was black and chrome and looked like it belonged in the middle of a pack of Hell's Angels.

There was something very primal about watching a

man straddle a motorcycle. The way his jeans conformed to his muscular thighs and the way his biceps strained beneath the tight sleeves of his T-shirt as he revved the engine. And when he started the engine and it rumbled to life, she shuddered at the pure unadulterated sexiness of it all.

She listened to his instructions as he told her where to step and put her feet. If she'd been thinking clearly, she'd have realized ahead of time how intimate it was going to be to sit behind him.

"Relax," he said over the roar of the engine. "Put your hands at my waist, and lean into the turns with me."

"Right, easy for you to say," she muttered under her breath.

She took a deep breath and relaxed, her breasts pressing into his back. And then she placed her hands at his waist like he'd told her and said, "Holy cow."

"What was that?" he called back.

"Nothing."

The seat vibrated beneath her, and the heat from the engine rebounded off the driveway and surrounded them. It was louder than she'd thought it would be, and she restrained herself from reaching farther around to cop a proper feel of the hardest abs she'd ever touched in her life. Sitting behind him on his motorcycle was the biggest sensual rush she'd ever experienced with a man.

"And isn't that a damn shame," she whispered. "Lame ass."

Henry would have a cow if he could see her now. She held on a little tighter just because she could.

She didn't know how long they rode. Once they got on the road and picked up speed, the temperature dropped drastically and she was more grateful than ever that she'd changed clothes. He drove up and down the streets of Last Stop and around the outskirts of town. He finally turned the bike onto a narrow, graveled road and then walked it up to a metal gate that said "No Trespassing" and had a keypad. He typed in a code and they waited as the gate swung inward. Then he revved the engine once and they took off down the graveled lane, dust flying behind them.

She recognized the area they were in, though she hardly ever came out this direction. It was nothing but fields with tall amber wheatgrass that blew in the wind and a small lake that had been used as a fishing tank when she was a kid. It was an area that had once been used for carnivals when they passed through town, but that had been a long time ago. She hadn't realized Eve had purchased the land along with the funeral home.

He took them all the way down, between the tall grasses and toward a bank of trees that hovered over the lake. Her ears rang as he cut the engine, and she wasn't quite sure what to do next.

"You might be a little stiff," he said over his shoulder. "Can you get off?"

She held onto his shoulders and swung a leg over, keeping her hand on him to maintain her balance. And then she pulled her helmet off and took a deep breath.

"Holy cow," she said. "That was intense."

"What do you think? You going to get your own in the big city?"

"The jury is still out. We might have to do more riding first." Her hair was damp at the temples from the helmet, and her arms and neck were pink from the sun. She hadn't thought about that part.

"Whose property is this?" she asked.

"Eve purchased it when she bought the funeral home." He took off his helmet, and a couple of strands hung loose, and the look in his eyes was so intense it almost took her breath away. "There's no one here but us."

The late afternoon sun gleamed off the water and filtered through the trees, and the tall wheatgrass blew softly. The smell of mud and ozone was heavy—the lake water had been stirred up by all the rain, and it was murky. There was a small breeze, but the air was humid and the dark clouds in the distance showed there'd be more rain to come.

He dismounted the bike and took her helmet, hooking it to the back of the bike with his. And then he came toward her and heat spread like wildfire low in her body. She'd always had such great self-control. She could compartmentalize her needs and be satisfied without ever feeling . . . enough . . . sexually.

But Deacon made her a liar. She would never be able to compartmentalize again. She knew what need was now. What it was to want something so desperately that the body physically ached for it.

"I've got some things to tell you," he said. "Do you want me to tell you before or after I kiss you?"

"After," she said without hesitation. "Long after."

He pulled her to him, and his mouth was suddenly on hers. Hot and wet, and there was a desperation he hadn't let slip through when he'd kissed her before. She clung to him, her body molding to his, and her fingers tangled in his hair. She kissed him recklessly, as if she were dying and he was the elixir of life.

Light danced across her closed eyelids, and everything around her faded away in a whoosh as the blood drummed in her ears. Every sound was distant—the leaves as they rustled in the wind, the water as it lapped against the land, and the low rumble of thunder growling in warning in the distance.

He tasted of something dark and dangerous. Something she hadn't known she'd wanted until she'd sampled the power of it. She'd never been so aroused in her entire life. Not with just the touch of lips. Her nipples rubbed against his chest, hard and aching for more.

She'd never thought of her breasts as an erogenous zone. She always thought them too small to feel pleasure. But now they felt full and heavy, and each time her sensitive nipples scraped across his chest she could feel the echoing sensation between her thighs.

His erection pressed against her stomach, hot and hard, but it wasn't where she wanted it. She wrapped her leg around his waist and his hands cupped her ass, lifting her so the hard length of him notched exactly where she needed it to.

He spun her and she went dizzy at the sensation, her pulse pounding and her body throbbing. She barely noticed when he sat her on the cushioned seat of the motorcycle. But the second he tried to pull away, her eyes snapped open, wild with lust.

"Lean back on the seat," he ordered. "And grab onto the handlebars."

She did as he asked and then waited. His face was dark, almost angry in its intensity, and his eyes blazed with desire as his gaze traveled down her body. He tugged at her boots, pulling each one off and letting it drop to the ground, and then he did the same with her socks.

"I've got a confession to make," he said.

Another rumble of thunder sounded, low and lazy, and his hands trailed up her legs to the button on her jeans.

"What?" she said, barely able to get the word past her lips. She couldn't think. Didn't *want* to think. There was too much to feel.

He tugged at her jeans and pulled them past her hips, down to her knees, and then past her ankles. She'd never felt so exposed, even though she was still wearing her tank top and white bikini panties. She'd also never felt so desired.

His fingers danced up her legs and teased at the edges of her underwear. His thumb traced just over the swollen bud of her clit. Her back arched off the motorcycle and her legs hooked around his waist, trying to pull him closer.

"Don't you want to know my confession?" he asked, his voice hoarse and low.

"It seems there could be a better time for it," she panted.

He choked out a laugh and then tightened his hold on her underwear, ripping it off with one tug. She squeaked in surprise and her eyes widened as he bent and kissed the inside of her knee.

"I heard you earlier. When you said you'd never had an orgasm with a man." He kissed his way up her thigh and maneuvered her legs so they were wrapped around his neck.

She knew that what he'd said was significant somehow, but her brain wasn't functioning well enough to figure out *why* it was significant. And then his mouth was between her legs, kissing and suckling the taut ball of nerves. His finger slipped inside of her, and then a second finger joined it, and he curved them up inside her, pressing against something she hadn't even known was there, but that felt so good she almost melted off the back of the motorcycle.

"Ohmigod," she called out.

"Mmhmm," he said against her, the vibration adding yet another sensation to the storm brewing inside her body.

Her heels pressed against his back and her thighs were like a vise around his head. Her hips moved rhythmically against his mouth, and tension built and twisted inside of her. Cool droplets of rain splashed against her heated skin, but it didn't bring relief. She was on fire, burning from the inside out, and the pressure built and built until the first surge of pleasure ripped through her with the force of a lightning bolt, going on and on until she saw stars and then her body went liquid and pliant.

"Wow," she said, letting the rain fall against her closed eyelids.

After a few moments, she finally found the strength to open her eyes, and she looked up at the wet shirt molded to his chest. He stood rigidly, his face pointed toward the sky, his breath heaving in and out of his chest. His muscles trembled with restraint, and his erection seemed almost painfully constrained behind the zipper of his jeans.

"Deacon?" she asked, wanting to give him the same pleasure he'd given her.

"Just give me a second," he said, sucking in a deep breath.

"I want to . . ."

"Not this time, baby. This one was just for you."

And then she remembered his confession. She rolled awkwardly off the bike and searched for her panties. "You said you heard what I said. About never having had an orgasm with a man. How could you possibly have heard that? It was just me and Miller in the house."

She pulled on her underwear and then grabbed her jeans. She had a feeling she wanted to be dressed for whatever was coming. The rain was a slow and steady drizzle, so she grabbed her boots and moved under the shelter of the trees. Deacon grabbed something from the saddlebags and followed after her.

He unfolded a couple of blankets and laid one on the ground. "I told you I would tell you whatever I could. That's what I'm going to do. Maybe you should sit down."

"I think I need to stand for a little while," she said, pacing back and forth in front of the blanket. Her jeans were wet and there was no way she was getting the denim over her legs until they dried a little, so she pulled them right side out and lay them flat on the blanket. The canopy of the tree cover was dense enough that water wasn't seeping through the branches. If it rained a little harder, that might be a different story.

Deacon nodded and folded his long legs as he sat down on the blanket. "None of us are what we seem," he said slowly, looking up at her. "Four years ago I was a contract agent for the CIA."

She stopped in her tracks and stared at him as if he'd sprouted two horns. "You're kidding me."

"Unfortunately, I'm not. I'd been assigned a mission I didn't morally agree with, and I refused the job. They decided I was too dangerous to keep around after that, so they disavowed me and sanctioned my death. I didn't have any family still alive. My dad died of cancer about a decade ago, and my mom died a few months after with undiagnosed ovarian cancer. They'd always thought I was a teacher. My cover was that complete—from the diploma on the wall to pictures of me with some of my students. They never knew any differently.

"I lived a lie my entire time with the CIA. My house was staged to be what people needed to see. And I was always careful not to collect personal items—photographs or heirlooms. I always lived with the assumption that one day I'd have to walk away from it all. And that's what I did after they sanctioned my death. I packed a duffel bag, torched my house, and went rogue.

"I was on the run for six months before Eve Winter found me." He leaned his back against a tree and tried to get comfortable. Thinking about his past was never easy. "I was bone tired. The agents they'd sent after me were good. I was better. But I was getting desperate."

He looked at her and grinned, the cocky expression on his face almost reassuring. Chills pebbled on her as the sky turned brilliant orange with the setting sun, and the slowing raindrops looked like molten fire as they fell from the sky. She moved closer to him, and he handed her the other blanket to wrap around herself. She took a seat across from him, somehow feeling like what he was sharing should be done in whispers.

"I was laying in bed one night in Austin, in a run-down motel that catered to druggies and prostitutes. I'd only been there for a night, and was only planning to stay one more. I'd picked a unit right in the middle of several other units. There was no back exit or window. Just a single door and a small window to get inside. I'd set little traps when I was sleeping. A chair under the knob. Glasses in front of the door. Blackout paper taped on the window. And I'd sleep with my gun under my pillow, with my hand resting on it, just in case.

"I remember when I woke up, knowing something was wrong. I was sleeping on my back and both my hands were crossed over my chest. I opened my eyes and listened, but there was nothing. There's something about the silence of a room that isn't empty. A feeling. An intuition. All I knew was that I wasn't alone. And when I moved my hand back under my pillow, my weapon was gone.

"I moved fast, grabbing the lamp from the bedside table and throwing it as I rolled to the floor. It was then the lights came on and I came face-to-face with Eve. She just stood there like the Angel of Death. And when she told me she was there to recruit me, I thought she was working for the enemy. No one in my own government would touch me. She told me she was there to help me die, but then she'd bring me back from the grave."

Tess's head was spinning. It was like one of Miller's novels. "Who is she really?"

"She's a troubleshooter for a covert organization, and I'll spare your life by not telling you the name at this point. It's so covert not even the president knows of its existence."

"That seems dangerous," she said.

"It can be," he agreed. "But there are a lot of things the president doesn't know. Knowledge is best used when it's shared by many people.

"After a surge of domestic terror attacks in 2005, it was created as a counterterrorism unit strictly within the U.S. borders. It was actually spearheaded by a woman name Celia Kyle. She's the CEO of the largest weapons manufacturer in the world. She's our supplier, from helicopters to scuba gear to submachine guns. She convinced the secretary of defense to come on board. The third party is the assistant attorney general for national defense out of the Justice Department. The three of them make up Neptune."

He took off his G-Shock watch and turned it over so she could see the trident etched on the back.

"The trident?" she asked.

"It's our symbol. It stands for the three who allowed us all to live by dying, though I've always believed Eve is the real mastermind behind the whole organization. They'd be nowhere without her. But the three of them are called The Directors.

"Only Eve really knows what's going on between all the moving parts. And she reports what she deems necessary to The Directors. There are two factions within Neptune. The first is called The Shadow. They're the organizers. They make sure supplies are where they're needed, when they're needed. They're the cleanup team that hides bodies and makes sure everything looks exactly as it did before all hell broke loose."

"What's the second?" she asked.

"The Gravediggers," he said. "That's what we are. We're strictly an intelligence strike force. When Eve told me she'd help me die and bring me back from the grave, she wasn't kidding. The Shadow helped stage my death. The body the CIA recovered was a match for dental and other key indicators.

"I had to disappear completely for a short time in case they weren't a hundred percent convinced of my death. And the safest place for me to go was underground. I was given a serum, like the one you saw me administer to Levi the other morning. It simulates death, and then we're buried in a special casket that has a limited supply of oxygen capabilities. We're then shipped to an undisclosed location and given a serum to bring us back from the dead, so to speak. We're given new lives and new missions, and as long as we serve Neptune we can live for real.

"Eve and The Directors scouted locations for a long time before they decided Last Stop was the perfect place for headquarters."

"Why?' she asked, hoarsely. "Why is it the perfect place?" Tess shivered, and it had nothing to do with the cool summer rain. She'd known somewhere in the recesses of her mind that she wasn't going to like whatever he told her.

"The setup was perfect. We're close enough to Dallas for there to be a legitimate reason for unusual aircraft to be in the area, and the funeral home provided the perfect cover for the bodies we'd be bringing in. The land in Last Stop was ideal. Almost every town around us is built on limestone, but Last Stop has a soft soil that can be easily excavated for different things. There's also a lot of land. We needed space, a funeral home, and a good location, with easy access to anywhere we needed to be if there was a terror strike. We can be anywhere in the country in a matter of a couple of hours.

"When we checked into Jessup's background and then yours, Eve knew you'd stay on if she bought him out. She didn't think you'd ever leave your grandmother, and she knew even though you weren't owner, that you'd like running the place as if it was your own. And then there's the fact that you're descended from Russian Mafiya."

Her eyes widened at that and a chill went down her spine. "So what? What does that have to do with anything at all?"

"Nothing that Eve's been able to find. And believe me, she's looked. She's always looking for ways she can use people. You serve a double purpose for her. You're a fixture in the community and have an established place in the funeral home. And you speak Russian. Not just Russian, but you speak Old Russian. It's like a lost language."

"Really?" she asked, genuinely surprised.

"You didn't know?"

"Why would I?" she countered. "I'm an American. It just so happens that my grandparents were Russian. I knew about their connection to the Mafiya, but I didn't realize there was a language difference. From what I understand, my grandmother's father was the head of the organization until his death. He married my grandmother off to his next in command when she was only sixteen, things started getting unstable in Russia, my great-grandfather died, and the whole Mafiya fell apart. My grandparents came to the United States and changed their name from Syomin to Sherman. Russian was the language they used at home. As far as I knew that was the only Russian there was. Why such a big interest in the Russians?"

"There are waves of terrorism," he said. "And for several years we've seen an uprising in attacks from Russia. Many times they don't take credit for it, so other terrorist organizations step up and claim responsibility. But Russia has been a sleeping giant for years. They've been patient, and their agents so ingrained in our country that it's almost impossible to distinguish them unless there are definite red flags."

She felt hollow inside. "I guess there's a reason you're telling me all this now. You tell me all of this and say flat out that Eve has had an interest in me and my family, and I'm just supposed to believe there's no coincidence that you finally decided to make your move. You must think me pretty pathetic. Poor Tess Sherman, with her gambling addict mother, colorful grandmother, and her ex-fiancé who decided to dump her in front of the entire town. Plain, boring Tess Sherman who wants to live in peace, so she lets people like George Jessup, Eve Winter, Deacon Tucker, and her own mother screw her over again and again." She dashed a tear from her cheek, hating that she mad enough to cry. "Dammit!" she said, getting to her feet. "I went through therapy so I could learn how to deal with stuff like this. You'd think after having your mother steal your life savings that it would be about the lowest point in a person's life. Yet I keep finding out other people can dig the hole deeper. This is why I prefer my own company most of the time. This is the perfect example of why I need to get the hell out of this town."

"Now, hold on," Deacon interrupted. "That's not true. I've had the hots for you for two years. And what I told you today has nothing to do with the other. You're the one who wasn't ready to see me. I hated with all my soul to watch you put on a brave face while all your dreams were ripped away. I hated watching how you'd walk into a crowded room and people would whisper about you the minute you turned your back. You had your guard up as high as it would go. I was waiting until the right moment.

"Not to mention that there's more at stake for me and you both if we become involved. It's one thing to have a quick fling and be done with it. It's another to have a relationship. You think there's no loopholes or conse-quences of having a relationship? I want you more than I can ever remember wanting anything, Tess. And to want you and act on it means that both our lives are forfeit if my identity is ever discovered or I'm ever captured."

"This doesn't make any sense," she said, throwing her arms up. "Why are you telling me all this now? Why are you allowed to? You just told me you've spent your entire career lying, even to your own parents. You must think I'm an idiot for it to not cross my mind that you're lying, for whatever reason, to me right now. If this is a covert ops group that not even the president is aware of, why are you telling nobody Tess Sherman from No-where, Texas?"

"You mean the funny, smart-ass, brilliant, kind, sexy Tess Sherman? The one whose taste is on my tongue and who I want to be inside of more than I want to breathe?"

Tess swiped a tear from her cheek, her face heating

at the intensity of his words. "Why are you breaking the rules for me?"

"Because you're worth it. Because we are currently facing down the single most horrific terrorist attack the world has ever known, and I'd rather have you by my side than far from me. Because you're brilliant. Because you speak Russian and you could be an asset. Because you crave adventure and something more than Last Stop can offer you, but you feel duty-bound to stay. You don't really want to leave. This place is in your blood. It's your heart. And lastly, because *I* need you. I've chosen to ignore orders and tell you more than I should have. It wasn't a chance I even took with my own parents. But I can't, and won't, lie to you. You've been lied to too much in your life."

"How? How did you know what I'd told Miller? About my past with men?"

He sighed and she wrapped her arms around herself protectively.

"We've got cameras everywhere. Inside the house, around the property, and at points of entry into the town."

"My bedroom?" she said, bringing her hand to her mouth.

"No, the third floor is a dead zone. The camera range only extends to the top of the stairs on the third floor. It's for everyone's protection."

"You were protecting me by listening in on private conversations between me and my best friend?" Now she was really fuming. "You've been listening *all along*?" She practically screamed the last two words, her vision going slightly blurry with rage.

"No, we haven't," he assured her, but her anger was too great. "Colin had the volume up because you were baking and you have a tendency to set things on fire. But that's no excuse. I'm sorry," he said. "I really am. I can promise it won't happen again. I'll make sure of it. We all feel protective of you. When you started talking about Henry . . ." He shrugged, looking uncomfortable.

Tess was going to commit murder. "I don't give two figs about Henry. I never did. The only reason I agreed to marry him was because I had this idea in my head of what a family was supposed to be. And I wanted it. I want a bunch of children who will one day come home for Christmas and bring their families. I want a husband I can share things with and talk to. It might not have been the great passion of the century, but I'd hoped we could at least be friends."

"You deserve the great passion of the century. You deserve all those things. I'm asking you to stay, Tess. There's a place for you here, in our own unusual family. You belong here until you're ready to make your own."

She blew out a breath and relaxed her arms. A cool head was what was needed now, so she took a couple more breaths and released them. The sun had all but disappeared, leaving nothing but violent streaks of pink as it vanished behind the lake.

"I honestly don't know what to tell you right now,"

she said. "I want to go home and get warm. And I want some time alone to think. I can't talk about any of this until I think."

"However much time you need," he said. "Just knock at the carriage house when you're ready to talk. We're prepping for a mission now. We actually leave for Russia next week. Those Russian terrorists I was telling you about are Mafiya. You could help us do a lot of the prep work. We speak Russian, but there are words and phrases we're unfamiliar with."

"Don't pressure me," she said. "I'm through being nice and accommodating. I'm going to do what I want to do for once, and to hell with everyone else. I've gotten mean." She narrowed her eyes and tried to look tough. More than likely she probably looked like a deranged leprechaun.

"I'm going to go home and drink a gallon of hot tea and read until my eyes fall out. I'm going to avoid my mother, the sheriff, and anyone else who knocks on my door tomorrow. Because thanks to you and the way you paraded me through town on the motorcycle, everyone is going to think I've won the bet on getting you into bed."

Deacon's eyes twinkled. "Technically, you could probably claim the prize. Oral sex is still sex. You'd have to ask if a motorcycle was acceptable instead of the bed. But it's basically semantics."

"Watch it, buddy. I will let my mother loose on that carriage house and laugh with evil glee as she practices her wiles on all of you," she said. "Before she's done, I guarantee at least one of you will have given her money or will take her to the nearest casino. Theodora could convince the pope he was Jewish. She's tricky."

"Wow, you have gotten mean." He handed her the helmet and got on the bike.

"Thank you," she responded primly, hopping on behind him. "I think I'm starting to get the hang of it."

CHAPTER THIRTEEN

"**Y**our mama's gone again," Tatiana said in Russian.

Every Monday morning, Tess woke up at the crack of dawn and drove to the Back Acres Retirement Village for yoga with her grandmother. It didn't do a lot for her pride to sit in a room full of seniors who were sixty-five plus and be breathing harder than they were by the end of each session. But she did it anyway so she could spend time with her grandmother and stay relatively healthy at the same time.

It wasn't doing Tess a lot of good to be in Prayer Pose and talking about her mother. Theodora wasn't good for relaxation techniques. Not to mention there was always a small part of her that held out hope that Theodora had changed. That she was happy running the Clip n' Curl and that she was content to stay and live a normal life with her family.

"Where'd she go?" she asked, keeping their conversation in Russian so the others couldn't eavesdrop.

"I'm not sure, but she left with Carl Robinson."

Tess gasped and broke her pose to stare at her grandmother. "Are you kidding me? Carl wouldn't be that stupid."

"Your mother has spent her life making men stupid as long as they feed her addiction. You know that better than anyone."

Tess sighed and took a deep breath. Then another and went back into Prayer Pose. Meditation wasn't going to work for her today. "It's just that she seemed to be doing better. She was fine when we were at the salon on Friday. And it's been months since she's been to the casino."

"That doesn't mean she hasn't been feeding her addiction in the meantime. There's online gaming and scratch-offs at the gas station. She just hasn't had the cash flow to make a big trip. And apparently she found the cash flow with Carl. She called me Saturday night, and I could tell she was upset about something. She'd heard about your joyride with one of those hotties you've got working for you."

Tess was a little taken aback at her grandmother's use of the word "hotties," but mostly she was just confused. She moved into Warrior Pose and said, "What does that have to do with anything?"

"You know how competitive Theodora is. Part of her problem is she wants what everyone else has, and she thinks she's entitled to it. It's part of her sickness. So once she heard the news about your ride through town, she automatically assumed you got him into bed and won the bet. She was counting on that money, you know."

Tess knew that was part of the sickness as well. Because a normal person wouldn't have counted on money that was never theirs to count on. They all moved to Downward Dog and Tess felt the blood rush to her head. Her hair was up in a bun, but sweaty tendrils were sticking to her face. She wasn't a good sweater.

"But what about Carl?" she asked. "He should know better. They should all know better. It's not like Theodora doesn't have a reputation."

"It's a competition to her, and Carl or the sheriff would be the next best thing to the men who work for you. My guess is the sheriff didn't bite, so she called Carl to come fix a leaky pipe or something. I heard it all from Janet Rhodes, who lives next door to Carl and Tamara. Janet said Carl left for a plumbing call early Sunday morning at Theodora's, and she said there was plumbing going on, but nothing to do with leaky pipes if you get my drift."

Tess's lip curled in disgust and they switched positions again, this time down into a push-up and then immediately into Child's Pose. She was already winded and sweaty, but her grandmother looked like she'd just stepped out of an AARP magazine. Even in her yoga clothes, she was still wearing her pearls, and her hair was perfectly in place.

"You know Carl is well-to-do," Tatiana said. "He ought to be charging two hundred dollars for ten minutes of unclogging a toilet. And money and how to get it is all Theodora would have in mind when she invited him over. How she got him to go off with her is a mystery, but she managed to do it. She'll be back when his money runs out, without a lick of remorse. Whether or not Carl has the guts to come back with her will be the question. Word has it that Tamara is fit to be tied. Their whole savings account is gone. I wouldn't be surprised if the sheriff has to get involved when Theodora comes back. Tamara isn't one of those women to stand by and let people get away with stuff like that. It's disgraceful."

"Tell me about it," Tess said, repeating the positions for the second circuit. "Aren't you embarrassed? She's your daughter. How can you stand all the gossip?"

"Easy," Tatiana said. "I moved to the city where no one knows or cares who she is. You think these old people give two hoots about Theodora Sherman? They're too busy keeping their meds straightened out and regulating their bowel movements."

"That doesn't help me a whole lot," Tess said.

"Buck up, girl," she said. "No one has to answer for Theodora except Theodora. She doesn't define you, and you shouldn't let anyone make you feel that way. Hold your head up high. She is what she is, and you are what you are. One has nothing to do with the other."

The instructor called for the Bridge Pose, and Tess muttered, "Good grief," under her breath, and then worked her way awkwardly into a back bend. She glanced over at Tatiana and saw she'd reached the position easily. "Ridiculous."

"Hey, can you keep it down," the old guy next to her said. "I can't concentrate with all that foreign yapping. This is America for God's sake."

She and Tatiana both responded in kind, neither of their replies something they would've said in English. Fortunately for the old guy, the poses were getting harder and Tess needed all her concentration and air. Old people yoga wasn't for the weak.

When they were finished, Tess lay on her yoga mat and wondered why she put herself through the torture. The only thing that got her up off the floor was the fact that everyone else was already up and out the door, going about their active lifestyles. She crawled onto her hands and knees and then pushed herself to her feet.

"Come on, girl, you're embarrassing me," Tatiana said. "I've got a reputation here."

Tess thought it ironic that *she* was the embarrassment instead of her mother, but that was the point of distancing oneself she guessed.

"If we hurry, we can still make breakfast. They stop serving at eight-thirty to get ready for the lunch crowd. I could use some pancakes."

"Right, sounds good," Tess lied, thinking she'd throw up anything she put in her mouth.

They made it to the little restaurant just in time for breakfast, and the hostess didn't look too happy about the fact. The sun was shining, but it was already close to ninety outside, despite the fact it was still early morning, so they opted to sit inside in the air-conditioning instead of on the covered patio.

Tatiana would occasionally dab at her temples with the blue towel that was draped casually across her shoulders, but that was the only sign she'd spent the morning working out. Tess's yoga pants and tank top were soaked through with sweat, and she'd caught her reflection in one of the windows as they'd walked by and it wasn't pretty. Her face was beet-red and her top knot had slipped to the side of her head. She immediately drank the ice water that was put in front of her and waited for it to be refilled.

"Do you ever think about your time in Russia?" she asked her grandmother. Deacon's words had been on her mind, about how their upbringing and language were different because of their Mafiya ties.

"Of course not," she said dismissively. "Why would I?"

"Maybe because it's where you came from. Those are your roots."

Her grandmother's lips tightened into a fine line and she got that steely look in her eye. "There's not much about those days worth remembering. We lived like royalty. My father was a very influential man. But things change. Politics change. People change. And their alliances change. Much the same happened during the Romanov era. In Russia, people who are in power can fall very quickly. One day we were royalty, and one day my father was dead and we were escaping with only our lives and nothing else. I was just a girl. My life has been here."

"You never keep in . . . contact with anyone from that time?"

"Who's to keep in contact with? Everyone is dead. I'm an old lady."

"I keep hearing the Russian Mafiya has moved back into power," Tess said carefully.

Tatiana was very still as her hot tea was served. How anyone could drink hot tea in this heat after a workout, Tess wasn't sure, but her grandmother lived on the stuff. She took her time adding lumps of sugar and stirring it precisely.

She finally stopped stirring and looked at Tess with those clear blue eyes. "I think you're watching too much television. This is my country now. What happens there no longer concerns me, and it's a time I choose to forget. I had to live with memories of those days while your grandfather was alive. And I don't mean to speak ill of the dead, but it was a big relief when your grandfather died. He courted trouble wherever he went. I've had almost thirty years of blessed peace, and I'm not looking back."

Their food was served, and Tess wondered why she'd bothered to work out at all. The calories sitting in front of her probably doubled what she had burned.

"Now tell me about this motorcycle ride you took," Tatiana said, waggling her brows. "I bet it wasn't just the motorcycle you rode. You've got that look about you. I bet he put that Henry to shame. I never did like that boy. I told you when you were engaged, you can't trust a man who carries a Waterpik in his pocket."

CHAPTER FOURTEEN

Deacon left Tess alone for three days. He avoided her on the cameras, and he didn't venture into the house. Fortunately, there was plenty of work to keep them busy, but it was a long three days.

They were working on a deadline, trying to trace the quartet to ground and get a bead on the different batches of XTNC-50 that could be entering into the country from different points of entry. Headquarters was beginning to feel a lot like prison. He'd scarcely left the carriage house or HQ, afraid he'd accidentally run into Tess and she'd make a rash decision.

His temper was on edge, and when he wasn't sitting in front of a computer or tracking satellite images, he was beating the hell out of punching bags and lifting weights until his muscles burned.

They'd been at it since early that morning. Their time was limited, and they still didn't have a clue as to the targets for the *Den' Sud'by*—the Day of Destiny—though they were slowly putting pieces together.

"You've got to snap out of it, mate," Axel said softly.

"She'll come around when she comes around. I still think you're out of your damned mind, but it was your choice to make. Your chance to take. She'll either take the bait or she won't."

Deacon gritted his teeth to correct him. They all still thought he was following Eve's orders, seducing Tess and luring her in so she'd stay. But that's never what he'd planned. It just gave him the excuse he'd never had before to make his move and claim her before it was too late.

"This job is a game of chance," Elias piped in. "We've got her monitored. She's got a listening and tracking device inside her purse, and we're monitoring her cell phone. Dante went early this morning to the retirement center dressed as a utility worker to plant listening devices at the grandmother's apartment while she was at her yoga class, and we planted another device at Miller's house, though that was a lot trickier because she never leaves. If Tess decides to tell anyone the information you told her, we're going to know about it and we can deal with it accordingly."

Deacon went cold inside. He'd promised her they'd no longer violate her privacy, and now they were doing it worse than they had before. If she found out, she might never forgive him. He looked around the room at the men he considered brothers. Even Levi, who'd only been with them a matter of days. There was an immediate bond when men were joined together for heroic tasks, sometimes unattainable tasks.

Eve had been right about Levi. He'd finished the

psych testing and had managed to do it standing, while still holding onto his sanity. Then they'd taken him out in the field on a couple of test ops to see what he was made of. And Deacon could say with certainty that Mossad agents were not like normal men. They were trained unlike anything he'd ever seen before, and Levi's skills, even when he was at half-strength, were exceptional.

Colin's head was buried in his computer screen, and Elias and Axel were tracking map routes and trying to close in on possible routes the Russian terrorists might have taken. It was a slow and time-consuming process.

"The Russians excel at confusion," Levi said. "We're collecting mounds of data and separating the possible from the impossible. But the data shows a pattern, and that pattern is that they're unpredictable. They hit the College World Series in June, and regular intelligence agencies still aren't a hundred percent sure that the Russians were behind it. They don't have the intel that we have access to. And to throw confusion into the fray, ISIS immediately stepped up and claimed the attack.

"We're following the major players who have spearheaded the current Russian Mafiya, and we know that they have plans much bigger than that of one single stadium's destruction. It's just gathering information at this point and narrowing down the possibilities."

"I think I can help with that," Colin said. "Mikhail Petrov is dead. Border Patrol stopped his eighteen-wheeler outside of San Antonio early this morning. The investigation is still ongoing. He was importing pottery and furniture into Texas. The only problem was when

Petrov was stopped, the police found three underage girls in the cargo area.

"Petrov was also transporting several ounces of an unknown substance, which was his main purpose for coming across the border. It had originally been packaged and airdropped into Venezuela. It turns out Petrov is an acquaintance of Joaquin Ramirez."

Joaquin Ramirez made Pablo Escobar look like a choir boy when it came to drug trafficking. He ran one of the most ruthless cartels in the world. He had deep pockets and a global reach. As of yet, he was untouchable.

"Convenient," Deacon said. "It makes sense for him to be friends with Ramirez."

"Pretty much," Elias said. "The SEALs made several trips to Venezuela to try and make a capture. He's a slippery bastard."

"Petrov was able to retrieve the package, and then Ramirez used his considerable resources to get Petrov into Mexico and set up with the correct papers and an eighteen-wheeler. Ramirez is known for his love of underage girls. He has a party every year and makes all the families gather at his villa. The locals call it *Parte de las Lagrimas.* The Party of Tears. Ramirez makes the daughters of the villagers parade through the streets, and then he selects several to stay with him as personal guests for an 'initiation.' I guarantee those three girls in the back of Petrov's truck were gifts from Ramirez."

"How'd he die?" Deacon asked.

"He went ballistic when they started searching the

cargo hold," Colin piped in. "I guess he remembered he was supposed to be transporting the chemical weapon, and that if he didn't succeed his comrades would slice off his balls and shove them down his throat. Petrov opened fire on the officers and they fired back. A hazmat team contained the unknown substance, and Homeland Security took over. Eve and The Shadow showed up on-site and removed the substance from Homeland Security for testing. It has been confirmed as XTNC-50, and now Homeland Security is throwing a fit, wanting to know who the hell just took over for them. They'll be tied up in red tape for a while and still not get an answer."

"What about the girls?" Deacon asked.

"They were sent back home to their families," Colin said.

Deacon pushed back from his chair and started pacing the length of HQ. "They're not going to stop until they have that stuff exactly where they want it to be. They're hedging their bets. The tanker coming in from the Bering Sea. An eighteen-wheeler from Mexico. You can bet they've got other avenues of backup transport lined up."

"There's still no word on Egorov, but Levkin has been spotted less than fifty miles from here," Colin said, bringing up a photograph on the big screen. "An ATM caught him on camera. The card he used is issued to a Peter Paulson. A quick run on Paulson didn't bring up anything. He's been using cash. And there's no record of hotel or rental cars. But when you put all the data in the computer, the statistics are high that they're using Dallas as their gathering place. It's a great central location. A major city, but not L.A. or New York, which are usually under tighter scrutiny."

"We've got confirmation that Yevorovich is on the tanker. He's our next target. The tanker is slowly making its way towards U.S. waters, its course set for Alaska." Deacon stopped moving and switched the screen to a satellite image. "After doing a little digging, I found that a plane has been chartered and is scheduled to take off from Bethel airstrip in Alaska on Saturday. Reservation was made by John Jameson."

"They're so clever on the aliases," Dante said. "Where was the destination in the flight plan?"

"Dallas," Deacon said.

"Home sweet home." Elias shook his head. "So what's the plan?"

"We'll HALO in and land on the tanker like Eve said." Deacon put an image of the tanker on one screen and its blueprints on the other. "We'll plant the explosives and make sure Yevorovich is dead before we're extracted. We leave in two days. I want our focus to be on pinning down Levkin. He's the weakest link. Egorov has too many political connections to bail him out if he's caught. He won't talk."

"He'll be the most dangerous," Axel said. "He's the one we need to find. Nothing will stop him from his end goal. Egorov has ambition. He's willing to die for his cause, but he wants his name to go down with the greats. Putin will canonize him. His family will be held in high esteem. His children will never want for anything. His life is a sacrifice worth everything."

"Then let's find him," Deacon said. "They have to be communicating somehow. They can't be planning an attack of this scale without some kind of communication. We just have to find the link."

"We've got company," Colin interjected, nodding toward the outdoor monitor.

All the guys turned to see Tess standing with her back ramrod straight as she knocked on the door to the carriage house. The look on her face was pure determination.

"Ooh, I think you're in trouble," Elias said.

"In my country, when a woman looks at you like that, it means you should sleep with the dogs." Levi had been quiet up until that moment, and Deacon scowled at him.

"Not helping," Deacon growled.

"How long are you going to make her stand there?" Elias asked.

Tess looked around and then spotted the camera. She pulled off her sunglasses and gave the camera a meaningful look of expectancy.

"All right, all right," Deacon said. "I don't see any of you rushing to let her in."

"We all know better, mate," Axel said with a grin. "You're the one Eve gave the orders to. Lure her in, using whatever skills you have. And thank God for it. I wouldn't want to face that redhead's temper."

"Right," he said. The weight of Eve's orders was heavy on his shoulders. The outcome of this particular situation wasn't shaping up how he'd planned. But he had no choice. He went to let Tess inside.

———

TESS HAD COME to a decision.

She didn't know if it was the right decision, and her stomach had been in knots over it for the past three days. It wasn't the safe decision. It wasn't the normal, boring, responsible decision. She'd gotten a taste of reckless behavior on the back of that motorcycle, and reckless was starting to look more and more appealing.

Her foot tapped impatiently as she knocked on the door to the carriage house. Once Deacon had told her about the cameras, she felt like an idiot that she hadn't noticed them before. She'd gone through every room in the house, noticing where the tiny devices had been installed. They had coverage of the entire first floor, including the embalming room.

The second floor was full of empty bedrooms and an upstairs living area with a huge fireplace, but when she looked for them, the cameras were there. Now that she knew the truth of who and what they were, she understood the need for the cameras. It also made her realize she'd been glad for her ignorance the last couple of years. It was an entirely different feeling living under a looking glass. Her home would be a target if they were ever discovered. It wouldn't mean much for Eve and her men because they could hide anywhere. But for Tess it would be catastrophic. Her home, her family, and her community could come under fire.

She looked up at the camera and tipped her sunglasses down her nose, raising her brows in question. Maybe Deacon had changed his mind and didn't want to mess with her after all. Or maybe he wasn't home. Maybe he was off on some super-secret mission to save the world and she hadn't even noticed his disappearance.

But almost as soon as she'd had the thought she heard the deadbolt unlock, and the door opened. Three days had seemed like an eternity, and her breath caught as he stood before her. Good grief, he was beautiful. He had a couple of days' worth of beard, and his hair was tied back out of his face. His eyes were shadowed.

Her gaze traveled down in pure appreciation. He was wearing an old gray T-shirt that was tight across the chest and shoulders, and a pair of jeans that had seen better days. When she looked back up at his face, he arched a brow and smirked.

Busted.

"You told me to knock when I'm ready to talk," she said. "I'm ready to talk."

"You want to come in?"

"Not really. Maybe if we can talk somewhere in private? Without a million cameras staring down at us, or people close enough to hear what we're saying. This place has turned into one of those weird reality shows overnight. I can't even get my coffee in the mornings without wondering how many eyes are staring at me. It's not a good feeling."

"It's because you talk to yourself all the time," he said. "You do it out of habit."

"I thought you weren't watching me," she said, her anger building once again.

"I'm not," he said smoothly. "I haven't set eyes on you in three days. It's been a really long three days, by the way."

Placated, she took a deep breath and released it. "Right. Well, it helps when I talk things out. I'm one of those people who can remember something forever if I hear it. If that makes sense."

"Why don't we go to the third floor?" Deacon suggested. "It's the only place we'll have complete privacy. Unless you'd like to make another trip to the lake."

The look he gave her was so sensual and full of desire she thought she might combust on the spot. She didn't think she'd ever thought about sex so much in her whole life as in the last three days. She'd never been so aware of her own body. Her own needs. She was afraid he'd opened up some kind of Pandora's box where her sexuality was concerned.

Sex had always been rather perfunctory up until now. Between Miller and the novels Tess liked to read, she'd always heard people talk about a great sweeping passion and sex as some kind of religious experience, but she always figured that kind of pleasure wasn't meant for some people. Everyone else in the world was perfectly fine, having perfectly average sex, and perfectly mediocre orgasms.

Boy, had she been wrong.

"Yeah," she said, hoping like crazy he couldn't tell what she was thinking about. "Third floor. Good."

Great, Tess. Now you sound like a caveman. She rolled her eyes and turned on her heel, before he could suggest something else or tell her to forget the whole thing altogether.

She led him through the kitchen and up the three flights of stairs. And when she got to the top landing outside her door, she unlocked her door and held it open for him.

"I don't suppose you're going to finish my bathroom anytime soon?" she asked, nodding to the construction zone. "I notice there hasn't been any progress."

Her suite of rooms took up the entire third floor, but the big oak bed dominated this room. It was impossible not to stare at it as they came inside and he closed the door behind them. Six hundred square feet could feel awfully small when Deacon Tucker was taking up space in the room. She'd bought the bed at a garage sale, knowing it was more than she needed and that it would be hell to get up three flights of stairs, but she'd done it anyway because she'd liked the intricate carving on the headboard and the sturdy posts at each corner.

"I didn't want to risk the chance of running into you. You scared me when you threatened me with your mother."

She *hmmphed* and said, "It was an empty threat. She left town day before yesterday. She canceled her appointments and took off. She left Crystal the key and told her to have at it."

"Crystal's the girl with the half-shaved head and piercings?" he asked.

"That's the one."

"I can't imagine she gets a lot of business," he said, smiling.

"She does great nails. And she actually does a decent job on hair. But getting anyone to take the chance is the hard part. People pretty much judge a person on sight in Last Stop."

"I've noticed," he said.

She directed him down the two steps into the living area. She didn't have much furniture, only a chair and ottoman and a chaise lounge she liked to read in. His gaze lingered on the bed and then he moved into the sitting room. It didn't matter. The bed was still visible since there was nothing but a half wall separating the two spaces.

"Whew, it's a little warm in here," she said. "I should probably open a window and turn on the fan."

"Good idea. If you want, I can run the central air vents up here so you've got something stronger than that wall unit." He sat down on the edge of the chaise and said, "Where'd your mother go?"

"I don't know. But my grandmother said she seemed upset by the fact that you paraded me through town on your motorcycle like a common trollop. Those were my mother's words, apparently. She was a little jealous that she didn't get to be the one paraded through town. And it probably didn't help that she was holding out hope all this time for winning the bet. It wouldn't sit right with her for her only daughter to beat her out of the pot. No one beats Theodora Sherman. At anything."

"At least she didn't take your life savings this time," he pointed out drolly.

"No, but she left town with Tamara Robinson's husband. So she was stealing either way." She shrugged and tried to play it off, though she wondered when she'd grow past the age of being mortified by her own mother's behavior. "It's just how she is."

"That doesn't make it right," he said. "And it doesn't make it hurt any less. Narcissistic people don't think about the destruction they leave in their path."

"Before she left, I thought maybe she was going to stick around this time and stay straight. But now that she's gone again, I keep thinking maybe she'll stay gone for good this time."

Tess walked over to the big square window that looked out over the town. "I feel like I should feel terrible for even thinking it, but I don't." She took a deep breath and then said, "I'll help you if you truly need my help with the language. At least for now. Now that I know some of the truth, I won't ever be able to un-know. So even if I moved, I'd be wondering if the world was going to end."

His lips twitched. "So you're joining with us because you're nosey?"

"I'm curious," she corrected. "And I'm looking for a change. I figure this is about as much change as a person can get without dying or switching sexes."

She sat on the edge of the club chair, and then stood back up again. What had she been thinking to agree to meet with him in her room? She hadn't thought about anything but stripping him naked since the moment they'd walked through the door. Maybe that was what her subconscious had been planning all along. She'd never actually seduced anyone before. Maybe it was high time she did.

"You're worried about something," he said. "What is it?"

"You said I could be of use because I speak and read the dialect of Russian you need. I want to make sure there's no chance of anyone tracing anything I do for you back to my grandmother. She told me today she was glad to leave that life behind her. She made a fresh start when she came to America. Reading between the lines during our conversation today, I think my grandfather brought more of the old country with him than she'd have liked, but he's been dead since I was a baby and she said she finally had peace and a life she enjoys living. I don't want to change any of that for her. And I don't want Eve thinking she's some kind of connection or a useful tool. She's an old lady, and she can be a mean one when she wants to be. I'd put my money on her over Eve Winter any day."

"There's always an element of risk," he said. "Nothing is fail proof. Our real identities were scrapped once we joined the program, and if anyone bothered to look closer at the Last Stop Funeral Home and all of its employees, they'd see exactly what we want them to see. Eve and The Directors spent years building a very careful operation. But all it takes is a breach in our systems. We're protected from radar seeing our equipment or the underground bunker. But glitches happen. It's why we have plans B, C, and D.

"And even if someone does take notice of us here, there's no reason for them to think you're involved. You were here long before we set up shop. So there's no reason to think your family or friends might be in danger. But if it makes you feel better, we can put some added surveillance around your grandmother's apartment."

"It would make me feel better," she said. "Do I get government health benefits? Because that stuff is ridiculously good, and I'd like to actually be able to afford to go to the doctor when I'm sick."

His eyes were sparkling with laughter. "Yeah, good luck with that. You're basically an off-the-books contract worker until it's determined your services are no longer needed. You know what we are and what we do, but you're not exactly privy to classified information."

She pouted a little at that bit of news. "Well, that sucks."

"It could be worse," he said.

"How's that?"

"Eve could've ordered us to kill you and hide your body."

"I don't think I like Eve very much."

He laughed full out at that, and she felt her insides heat at the sound. It was rare he laughed, and she guessed considering what he did for a living he hadn't had very much reason to laugh. But damn, was it a sexy sight.

She muscled up some courage and moved to stand directly in front of him, and then she took a deep breath and prayed the words she'd been wanting to say all morning came out clearly. She opened her mouth and nothing came out. And then she tried again, and she could feel the heat rushing to her cheeks.

"What is it?" he finally asked, curious.

"I want to seduce you."

CHAPTER FIFTEEN

All the blood in Deacon's head pooled directly into his lap. His eyes blurred for a second and he shook his head to reorient himself.

"Can you say that again?" he asked, wanting to make sure he heard right.

"No," she said. "I don't think I can."

"You've really got to stop telling me no."

She'd consumed his thoughts for the last three days. He'd been drunk with the taste of her on his lips, and all he could think about was having her again.

"I figure you heard me right the first time," she said, sounding angry about it now.

Lord, he loved her prickly temper. Her hair was practically crackling around her head, and all he could think was that he wanted nothing more than to see it spread out across her pillow and his hands tangled in it.

She was an array of walking contradictions. Sweet and surly. Innocent and experienced. And every facet of her intrigued him.

"I figure I did," he said. "But I thought I might've had a stroke just now, so I wanted to make sure."

"Where are you from? Originally," she added.

He hadn't been expecting that, and he was caught off guard. It had been a long time since he'd thought of home. He hadn't been there since he'd gone back for his father's funeral his last year of college.

"Baton Rouge," he told her. "Why?"

She nodded sagely. "You're too adept at talking like a Southerner. That's something that's inbred. Can't be learned."

He laughed and rubbed his hand over the scruff of his beard. "And here I thought I'd learned to cover it up so well after all these years." He shifted, anxious to get her back on track. "So, how are you going to seduce me?"

"I'm not sure, but it probably won't work if you keep sitting there asking me questions. I guess the first question should be whether or not you want to be seduced."

He arched a brow at her and then stood to his feet, so she could see the erection straining behind the zipper of his jeans.

Her eyes widened and she licked her lips. "I guess you do."

"Oh, yes. I do."

"I babble when I get nervous," she said. "I just thought I should tell you that up front."

"I've known you two years. I'm well aware."

"Oh. Good. I read a lot, so I've got this pretty well planned out in my mind. Knowledge is power."

"Fuckin' A," he said. "Tess, you could stand there in

a paper bag and I'd be seduced. I'm so freaking seduced right now this is probably not going to last very long. You don't have to worry about me. I'm one hundred percent on board."

She smiled and her dimple fluttered at the corner of her mouth. And then her fingers went to the buttons of her shirt and all the spit dried up in his mouth.

"Wait a second," she said, and he bit back a groan. "How does this work between us and . . . everything else?" She waved her hands around as if he was supposed to know what the heck she was talking about.

"I have no idea what you're talking about."

"With Eve and The Gravediggers and all this secretive stuff. You said there were consequences. How much trouble are you going to get in if we go through with this? What will she do to you? Will she let me help you with the translations if she thinks we're . . . you know . . ." She waved her arms around again and he couldn't help but grin.

In Eve's eyes, he was following orders. But he knew it was much more than that. His plan had been formulating long before Eve issued the words to him, and he knew exactly what he wanted from Tess. He wanted *all* of her. The consequences didn't seem to matter so much as long as they were together. But there was always a chance she might not feel the same way.

"Our relationship is ours alone, no matter what she might tell you. We're not breaking the rules, and she'll hate that you're a distraction for me. But there's nothing she can do about it as long as we stick together. With that said, if I'm compromised, both of us will be marked for the kill. You have to understand that going in. It's a lot to ask a person to risk."

"My new middle name is risk," she said softly.

"I thought it was fun," he said, remembering she'd said something similar before the motorcycle ride.

"I changed my mind." She undid the buttons slowly, one by one, and the shirt parted inch by inch, teasing him with glimpses of pale flesh.

"How hell-bent are you on seducing me to completion?" he asked, eyeing the lacy camisole beneath her top. Her nipples were rigid peaks, and he realized the camisole was all she was wearing underneath. For some reason that drove him wild.

"I'm flexible at this stage of the game," she said. "Why? What do you have in mind?"

The way she asked him the question—a little bit taunting, a little bit sassy—had him moving closer. He pulled her into his arms and took her mouth—hard. But she was ready and eager for him. There was no slowing down or pulling back. All she'd had to do was tell him she wanted to seduce him, and it had worked like a charm. He was putty in her hands.

Her hands slid up his shoulders and behind his neck, tugging his hair loose from the leather tie he'd wrapped around it. He tightened his hold on her, his hands molding her, until he gripped her ass and lifted her up against him.

He pinned her against the half wall and her legs twined around him. Her shirt had fallen off of one shoulder, and his hand closed over her breast. He felt her nipple hard against the palm of his hand, and he rubbed it beneath the cotton of the camisole. Every stroke of his hand had her jerking against him, as if he were rubbing her clit instead of her nipple.

He pulled his mouth free and they both gasped in air. Her mouth was swollen and red, and her cheeks were flushed. Her eyes were closed and her head tilted back, red hair hanging gloriously down her back like a bounty spread out for his taking.

He wanted to feast.

"I want you in that bed," he growled against her neck. "From the second I saw that thing all I could think about was you laid out across the covers wearing nothing but me."

His fingers scissored her nipple, tweaking it slightly, and she whimpered with pleasure. And then he couldn't help himself. The sound was so sweet he dipped his head and closed his mouth around her, sucking at her through the thin layer of cotton.

"Ohmigod," she said. "Deacon. Don't stop doing that."

He chuckled against her and pulled the shirt she was wearing down so her arms were tangled in the sleeves. She tugged against them and made a sound of frustration.

"I want to touch you."

"You're about to," he whispered. And then he picked her up and carried her the rest of the way to the bed.

He laid her on the bed and then stripped off his shirt and toed off his shoes.

"Have I told you how much I love looking at you?" she panted.

"I don't think you've mentioned it," he said, grinning. That look in her eyes made him feel like Superman. He'd known what it was to be desired by women. But he'd never been looked at the way Tess was looking at him. As if he was the best thing she'd ever seen. It made him feel invincible. And he would've moved heaven and earth for her to keep looking at him that way.

He removed her shoes and let them drop to the ground, and then his hands went to the button on her jeans. He pulled them down slowly, taking her underwear down with them. Her arms were still caught in her shirt, but she was stock still as his fingers traced her thighs, moving higher to the soft folds of her mound. But he didn't linger. The time for foreplay had long passed.

"I want to see all of you this time," he rasped.

He removed her shirt fully and then pulled the camisole over her head, leaving her completely naked on the white comforter. The sight of her took his breath away.

"More beautiful than I ever imagined," he said. "Almost too delicate to touch. Like a painting."

She was willowy and thin, without many curves. Her arms were resting above her head, and that glorious red hair tumbled around her. She was pale, and a light smattering of freckles dotted her skin. He could see her heart pounding in her chest as his gaze moved down her body. Her nipples were dusky brown and erect, just waiting for his mouth.

He moved farther down to the plump folds between

her thighs. She was wet and ready for him, and he took her long legs and splayed them open, so she was completely bared to him. And then he looked his fill.

"So fucking beautiful," he said reverently.

"Please hurry," she begged. "This is torture."

Deacon unbuttoned his jeans and carefully lowered the zipper. Her eyes followed his every move, and she licked her lips in anticipation. He didn't prolong it. He pushed his jeans and underwear down to his ankles and stepped out of them.

"Oh, wow," she said, her eyes devouring his erection.

He chuckled at the way she said it and then knelt on the bed between her open thighs.

"There are forty-eight condoms in the nightstand."

He froze and stared at her. "That's a lot of condoms."

"We don't have to use them all today."

"Don't worry. We'll make a dent in them."

He reached over and opened the nightstand drawer, shaking his head at the sight of the small Glock sitting next to the box of condoms. Tess was full of surprises. He pulled a condom out of the box, opened the package, and then rolled it on.

He used his finger to part her folds, feeling the sweet syrup of her desire, and making sure she was ready for all of him. Then he leaned over her, nipping at her swollen lip, as his cock nudged at her entrance.

"Look at me, baby," he said, waiting for her eyes to flutter open.

He'd always been captivated by her eyes. He watched as the green deepened to jade and her pupils dilated as he pressed forward, filling her, and it was the most incredible thing he'd ever seen. He hooked his arms beneath her knees and leaned forward so they were pressed to the mattress so she was fully open. And then he slid all the way inside of her, touching her at the deepest point, and holding himself there.

Her breathing hitched and her eyes widened. And then when he didn't move, her body arched against him, seeking more. Her fingers dug into his shoulders and she bit her lip in concentration. And then he felt it. The gentle pulsing around his cock as she squeezed him, milked him, with her vaginal muscles.

"Jesus, Tess," he gasped.

And then he drew back and plunged into her with a force so great the bed creaked beneath them. He couldn't stop himself. He felt like an animal in rutting season. The urge to mate with her was stronger than his self-control.

Her body arched against him, met him thrust for thrust, and he took her mouth in a primal kiss. He felt the texture of her walls change, felt the increase in moisture and heat, and then she moaned, low and long, as she climaxed, pulsing and squeezing around him.

The feel was too much for him to hold back any longer. His hand tightened in her hair and he buried his face in her neck. And then he drove himself into her over and over again. The climax ripped from him, and his back arched as he came with a forcefulness that stole his breath. Tess wasn't letting go. She screamed as she came again, and he felt the earth shake as he collapsed on top of her.

He didn't know how much time had passed. Seconds or hours. But his heart was still pounding and his breath still came in gasps. He tried rolling to the side, but it took some effort. He was too weak.

"Wow," she said, her voice hoarse. "I've always read that sex can be an earth-moving experience, but I always thought it was a figure of speech."

"Don't you see how the bed is tilted?" he asked. "We fucked right through the floor. I told you it needed to be replaced. We're lucky we didn't end up in slumber room one."

She froze against him, but he just pulled her tighter in his arms. "What should we do?"

"We should probably move very carefully and get the hell out of here." She was snuggled up warm against him, though, and he wasn't too inclined to ruin the moment.

"Why do I have a feeling you're not going anywhere?" she asked, narrowing her eyes at him.

He flipped her on the bed, making her squeak as a board creaked beneath them. "We just had a near-death experience. We've got to do something with all that adrenaline. Besides, I've been wanting to taste you again since the first time."

"Oh," she said as he kissed his way between her thighs. She moaned and her head dropped back as he suckled her clit. "I suppose we can be less vigorous this time."

"How much do you want to bet?" he asked.

CHAPTER SIXTEEN

Two days later, Tess was fully entrenched in a world she'd only seen on the big screen.

When Deacon had told her they could use her, she wasn't really sure she believed him. They'd shown her the control room underground, and then promptly sat her at a computer. According to Deacon, they'd been looking for communication between the four men—three now—who were coordinating the attack. They'd finally found it.

They'd done some of the work for her. The dialects shared common words. But there were large patches of blank space where they hadn't known what the words were. So for a full day and a good part of the night, she'd been translating the words and short phrases into English. The only problem was the words and phrases didn't make any sense and seemed to be in no discernible order.

"It's code," Dante said. "See here, the word *mat*, or 'mother' once translated, is used several times throughout each of these paragraphs. It's more than likely a substitute for *and* or *the*."

"Oh, cool," she said, seeing the pattern of several words now that she knew what to look for.

"It's a different form, but still similar to the coding used during World War II," Deacon said. "I doubt they were worried about the simplicity of the code. It was more than likely used as a secondary barrier of communication to the intended recipients. The first barrier is the hardest to break, and that's the language. None of these words," he said, pointing out several in the documents, "are words that are traditionally used in the Russian language. It's almost like a slang. It's as much of a difference as there is between Ukrainian and Russian. Only those deeply rooted in the Russian Mafiya would be able to translate the passages enough to decipher the code."

"I'll start running it through a deciphering program and see what we come up with," Dante said. "It shouldn't take too long. It looks like a fairly straightforward pattern."

"They're bouncing a false location through satellite," Colin said. He sat behind a large radar screen on the wall and used touch screen to zero in on the coordinates. "That's how we pulled their communication. They had it bouncing all over the place before we pinned it down. They're doing the same thing with location. Or at least trying to, but I chased it down. That tanker is more than fifty miles north of where they're supposed to be. They've hovering just on the edge of U.S. waters, ready to move when they're given the orders. If we'd HALO jumped with the coordinates we got from the satellite imaging, we'd have ended up in the middle of the Bering Sea. Even with neoprene suits we would've been fighting hypothermia by the time the Zodiac found us."

Tess hadn't realized the enormity of what they were planning to do until that moment. "There's no other way to get on that tanker?" she asked. She knew the worry was evident in her voice, but she didn't care.

"It's the only way to go in undetected," Deacon told her. "We're all experienced. We've done it plenty of times. Going in a safer way would put all of us in more danger. They'll be looking for visible threats. So we have to be invisible."

"Right," she said, remembering Deacon's explanation of what exactly a HALO jump was. "So you're going to jump from a plane at thirty thousand feet, in freezing temperatures, and you're going to free-fall for two and a half minutes until you're almost at your target. Then you're going to pull the chute at the last possible second and land on the tanker. Pardon my French, but that is fucking insane."

"You know that's not actually French, *oui*?" Colin said.

She growled at him, and his lips quirked in a smile as he went back to his computer.

"Insane," Deacon agreed. "But necessary. And fun."

"What am I supposed to do while you're jumping out of airplanes? And please don't tell me I'm not coming with you. You'll need someone there to collect your bodies if you miss the target."

"Damn, that's harsh," Elias said. "I like her."

"You'll stay with Dante," Deacon told her. "He's manning the sub."

"Sub?" she asked. "As in submarine."

"Yeah, you'll love it. Unless you get claustrophobic. Then you might not love it so much."

"Wow." She was trying to remember what it felt like to be a plain old mortician in plain old Last Stop, Texas. That seemed like a million years ago. "So all this equipment—the plane, the pilot, the submarine—they're just going to show up when and where you need them? No questions asked?"

"That's what The Shadow is for," Elias said. "Creepy motherfuckers. We've never actually seen them. Who knows how many there are or where they come from. We can only hope they never turn against us."

"Well, that's comforting," she said sarcastically, then turned to Dante. "When do we leave?"

"We'll all fly to Alaska day after tomorrow. You and I will head out to the sub hours before they leave for the jump. The sub is fast, but not quite as fast as the plane. We want to make sure we're there in plenty of time. We'll dock the sub as close to Russian waters as we can get, and then I'll take the Zodiac for the pick-up and bring them back. The submarine has advanced technology that will keep us from being detected from radar."

"Sounds good," Tess said. "If you're a deranged adrenaline junkie looking for a death wish."

"That pretty much sums up my SEAL team," Elias

said. "You're a quick study. You might survive this after all."

"Thanks," she said dryly.

***

DEACON WORKED TIRELESSLY, checking and double-checking plans, coordinates, and equipment. It was his job as team leader to make sure there were no mistakes. It was after midnight by the time he was satisfied, and when he looked up he noticed things had gotten quiet while he'd been preoccupied.

Elias and Dante had gone to their own homes to get a solid night's sleep before their early-morning wakeup call. He assumed Colin and Axel had done the same and adjourned upstairs. Levi sat at one of the computer screens poring over intel. He still wasn't approved for field missions, so he'd be staying behind. He was taking the night watch to handle any new intel that might come in while the rest of the team was sleeping.

And then there was Tess. Her head rested on the stack of papers she'd been painstakingly translating, and she was fast asleep. They had what they needed for the upcoming mission, but there were still missing pieces of the larger attack being planned. But for now she deserved the rest. Her hair was spread out over the table and her hands looked small and delicate.

He pushed back his chair and stretched stiff muscles that had been sitting still too long. He walked over to her and touched the tips of her hair with his fingers. Her hair glowed like fire, but was soft to the touch. He touched her back gently, expecting her to stir, but she didn't move.

Even when he picked her up in his arms, she only nuzzled into him and sighed. There were dark smudges beneath her thick lashes, and her face was pale, making the sprinkle of freckles across her nose more prominent.

He carried her upstairs and into the kitchen, and then up another set of stairs to the second floor. When he got to his door, he shifted her slightly so his thumb could be scanned to unlock the door. When he looked down, her green eyes were watchful and sleepy, focused solely on him.

"I didn't mean to wake you," he said softly.

"It's okay. I think I'd recognize your touch anywhere."

If it wouldn't have hurt his ego to admit it, he would've sworn his knees went weak with the way she looked at him.

"I was going to let you sleep," he said, pushing open the door and slipping inside the room. The lights were on low and the blinds were drawn.

"And now?" she asked curiously.

"And now I'm not," he said.

He was a simple man. The room was large and his space was clean. But it was a utilitarian space. The bed was large and the sheets and comforter were like a cloud of softness in simple neutrals. As in every home he'd ever had, he had no personal items or mementos. No photographs. It was just a room to sleep in. But he'd never had another woman in that bed, and that somehow seemed significant at the moment.

He let her down to her feet slowly, but kept her wrapped in his arms. And then he released her and tugged at the buttons of the soft dress shirts she favored.

"I need to put my hands on you," he rasped.

"Isn't that what you're doing?"

"Not nearly enough." He spread the shirt wide and let it fall from her shoulders. Her bra was white and plain—no frills—but it seduced him like nothing else ever had. He opened the button on her jeans and pushed them down over her hips and to the floor.

"The undressing part always seems sexier in the movies," she said. "I wish I was wearing something else."

"Believe me," he said, drinking in the sight of her long, lean body. "You're not standing where I'm standing. Nothing could be sexier."

He lifted her in his arms and carried her over to the bed. The lights over the bed were dimmed and cast her in a soft glow as he lay her down. Her hair fanned around her face like a flame, and her eyes were steady on his as he came down on top of her.

There was no hurry. No rush of hands. Only the simple need to savor and taste every inch of her. He never took his eyes off hers as he leaned in to kiss her—sweetly, softly—and his hands twined with hers. His mouth moved down to her neck, and he felt her pulse leap and quicken. And then he went farther still and took her cotton-covered breast in his mouth, dampening the fabric and feeling her nipple bead tautly.

She arched beneath him and her fingers tightened on his. And then she went limp and her grip fell from his as he continued to kiss his way down her body. He nipped at her hip and tugged at the elastic waist of the cotton that was all that was left between them, pulling it down so she was bared to him.

Need slammed into him, the scent of her enticing him. A barely restrained groan escaped her throat, and her nails dug into the sheets as his mouth found her and devoured. She tasted of liquid sunshine and nectar, and her legs wrapped around him so her heels pressed into his upper back. Her fingers tangled in his hair, and her hips writhed against his mouth. Her cry of release echoed in the room, and he tasted the rush of her pleasure as he savored every drop of her.

He no longer had patience. The need for her clawed inside of him and had to escape. He kicked off his shoes and tugged his shirt over his head. And tossed his jeans in a heap on the floor. His body was tense and his cock rock hard and aching.

He grabbed a condom from the nightstand and rolled it on. Then he knelt on the bed between her legs and came over her. She lay before him, panting, her body flushed and still yearning for more. Her lips were swollen, and he could see the marks from his beard across her skin. Her skin was so sensitive, and he ran two fingers down her neck and chest, causing her to shiver. He flicked the front clasp of her bra and she shrugged out of it, so she was completely naked. She shivered as he lowered himself and took a small nipple in his mouth.

"Please," she begged. "Hurry."

"I was in a hurry," he said, taking his time. "But I've

found I have a renewed sense of patience. I like seeing you writhe beneath me."

Her legs hooked around his hips, trying to pull him forward, but he held back, only the head of his cock brushing against the curls between her thighs.

"Just remember that turnabout's fair play," she panted. "As soon as I recover I'll have you begging for more."

He chuckled low and found her opening, wet and ready for him, and he pushed—just a little—so she was stretched around him but not fulfilled. A scream of frustration tore from her throat, and her green eyes blazed as she glared up at him.

"Deacon," she panted.

"Yes, baby?"

She leaned up and bit his bottom lip, surprising him, and then whispered, "Fuck me."

Any semblance of control was shattered at those two little words. He plunged inside of her, and they moved together as if there had only been the two of them since the dawn of time. Sighs mingled with gasps of pleasure, and he felt her tighten, felt the spasms start deep within her.

He gritted his teeth and their hands joined as she went molten around him. And then he felt his own release jerk from his body with no warning, so powerful it was as if his very soul had entered her.

They lay tangled together for what could've been minutes or hours, sweat cooling on their skin and their breaths evening out. He shifted their bodies and disposed of the condom, and then he gathered her close in his arms. He thought she might have drifted off to sleep, and he was about to move to pull the covers over them when she stretched languidly, her body rubbing against his. Damned if his cock didn't stir in response.

"What are you doing?" he asked as she halfway sat up and began sliding down his body. His erection was more than at half-mast at this point, and she laughed, the sound full of sorcery and seduction, as she noticed the effect her touch had on him.

"I told you turnabout was fair play," she said, kissing his hip.

His eyes rolled back in his head as she licked him in one long stroke, and he went from half-mast to full-mast in seconds.

"Fuck," he groaned as her mouth tortured him. "I believe you now."

"Too little, too late," she teased. And then she moved off the bed and left him wanting. She looked over her shoulder as she headed toward the bathroom. "You'll have to be patient with me. I've never swallowed."

She winked, and he watched her sweet ass disappear into the bathroom.

"Jesus," he said, taking a hard hold of his cock. He almost came then and there. "At least I'll die a happy man." And then he followed behind her.

CHAPTER SEVENTEEN

The darkness pressed in on him at thirty thousand feet. His skin was clammy with sweat beneath his specially designed flight suit. He kept his head pressed against the wall of the C-130 cargo plane and focused on breathing. He was closed inside a metal can at thirty thousand feet. It wasn't the fear of falling from the sky that had his balls in his throat. It was the ever-shrinking walls of the plane, the decrease in oxygen as they ascended higher, and the darkness that kept pressing in on him.

His only reprieve was to think of Tess. He'd been selfish to keep her up the hours before they'd left instead of letting her sleep, but he hadn't been able to get enough of her. He wanted to imprint himself on her memory, on her body, so that if anything happened to him she'd know how much he loved her. They'd made love for hours. And that's exactly what it had been.

Making love.

They'd only dozed for what seemed like minutes before it was time to get up and dress. Her eyes had been shadowed, and he could see the worry etched in her face, but she gathered her things in silence and nodded in thanks when he handed her an insulated cup of coffee.

Her eyes had grown large and round when they'd showed her the way to the underground tunnel and strapped everything to both of the ATVs, but still there was no talking. As they sped out of the tunnel, he kept his hands tight on the wheel, focusing on the end of it and not imagining the walls caving in on him—being buried alive in the rubble—again.

The chopper had been waiting for them, ready for takeoff, and he'd squeezed her hand in reassurance when she looked at the lake in its stillness—as if she'd never see it again. The ride had been short to the private airstrip where their plane waited. The sun was just peeking over the horizon when they made takeoff.

The jet was equipped with much of the same equipment HQ was, and their focus was on making sure the tanker didn't change course or that the Russians didn't try to confuse the satellite for the twelve-hour flight to Nome, Alaska. But the Russians seemed confident in their abilities of concealment, which was their mistake.

He was proud of her. He didn't think many civilians could handle the kind of pressure she was under at the moment—understanding how high the stakes were and thrown into a situation where she no longer had control. Where her mental and physical capacities would be tested, and her ability to trust would be her saving grace.

They landed on an abandoned stretch of land, nothing more than grass and gravel, just outside of Nome. It was the closest point of origin for traveling to the Bering Sea. Transport was waiting, two identical Humvees, set to take them to their destinations—Dante and Tess to the submarine, and he and the others to prepare for the HALO jump onto the tanker. If everything went according to plan, he'd see her again in another eight hours. He didn't want to begin to think about *not* seeing her again.

He kissed her good-bye—long and hard—and he knew he'd drawn looks from the others. He no longer cared if they thought he was just carrying out Eve's orders. Then he got in the Humvee with the others and focused on the job at hand. He had to. He couldn't afford to think of her when so much was at stake.

They suited up in the one-piece flight suits specifically designed for HALO jumps, which would protect them from the cold, and beneath they wore neoprene dive suits in case they had to spend time in the water. The footwear and gloves also protected them from the freezing temperatures.

Just after midnight, they loaded up in the C-130 cargo plane. Deacon sat across from Colin and Axel. Elias was to his left. They'd all begun breathing pure oxygen at takeoff, preparing their bodies for the dangerous HALO jump.

It was a cold and bumpy ride at thirty thousand feet, around twenty-five degrees below zero. Deacon let Elias run point on this leg of the journey because he'd been a SEAL and could do these jumps in his sleep. Experience of his kind was invaluable, and Deacon wasn't so ego-driven as the team leader that he didn't recognize the value of an asset.

They all carried explosives in the small, tightly strapped packs around their waists, a knife secured in their boots, and a pistol secured to their thighs via a healthy dose of duct tape. It was all they could carry in, and even those items had the chance of ripping free in the high-velocity free-fall.

There were dangers to HALO jumps, but it was the best way to get where they needed to go undetected. And where they needed to go was on that tanker. It was a blind jump, and it was the middle of the night. They wouldn't have a visual of where they were landing until it was time to deploy the chute. The last thing Deacon wanted was to end up in the water.

He breathed in the pure oxygen and exhaled slowly to get all the nitrogen flushed from his bloodstream. He had to be more careful because his pulse was already elevated from his claustrophobia. If any nitrogen was left in the bloodstream, it could lead to decompression sickness. Not something anyone wanted to deal with when approaching the enemy.

They all wore specially made goggles that could resist the cold from that altitude. Without them, their eyeballs could actually freeze. Deacon just prayed he didn't pass out on the way down. Many jumpers did, and the chute deployed on its own once they reached the right altitude.

They didn't speak, but they didn't have to. They knew the plan. They'd memorized every detail of the tanker from the blueprints. And they had a general idea of how many armed personnel were on board from the aerial satellite images.

Elias held up two fingers, signaling the two-minute mark, and everyone removed the pure oxygen tank and strapped on the regular oxygen mask securely to his face. The cargo hold of the plane slowly opened and the frigid wind whipped around them.

Elias had already gone through the scenarios. They were to stay in formation for a two-minute free-fall before opening their chutes. If all went well, they should go undetected by any radar the tanker might have, and it was unlikely any of the guards would see them as they bulleted from the sky.

Deacon took a couple of deep breaths and waited for the go signal. A red light blinked steadily alongside the cargo hold door, and then it turned green. Off they went, one by one, into the black of night.

The wind pressed against Deacon's chest with such force that it was hard to draw in a breath, even with the oxygen mask. The cold seeped into his bones and his vision dimmed as the velocity of the free-fall picked up speed. He watched his altimeter carefully and counted the seconds in his head. Two minutes was a long time to fall.

Just as the edges of blackness started to claim him, his altimeter displayed the right altitude and he pulled the ripcord on his parachute. It shot up behind him and he shook his head to clear his vision. The tanker was closing in fast, and he was still traveling at a high rate of speed.

He didn't focus on the others. That was a good way to end up in the Bering Sea. He looked straight ahead and touched down near the bulkhead. He immediately cut his parachute lines and rolled behind cover, gathering up the black parachute as he did. He reached into his boot and ripped off the tape securing his weapon, shoving it behind the small of his back. He would prefer not to use it unless absolutely necessary. There was no need alerting everyone they were there.

Only one of the eleven men on board mattered, and that was Jorgen Yevorovich. It would be even better if they could get him to talk before they killed him.

Deacon planted his explosives pack at the bulkhead and then darted from cover to cover. He caught sight of a guard dozing against the wall, and he came up behind him, snapping his neck before lowering him quietly to the ground. He caught sight of Axel from the other side of the tanker giving similar treatment to another guard.

Axel held up two fingers, indicating that was the second guard he'd killed, and then they each gave a thumbs-up, indicating their explosives had been placed and activated. It was time to clean up any other messes and get the hell out of there. All he needed to do now was find Yevorovich. And he had a feeling he knew just where to find him.

According to their intel, Yevorovich was fond of his vodka and nightly games of durak, a Russian card game. He was a man of comfort, and the last place he'd want to be was out in the cold, making sure the cargo was secure. In fact, from what they'd found out, he hadn't wanted to be on the tanker at all, but he'd been low man on the totem pole in their quartet and hadn't had a choice.

Deacon signaled to Axel, and they headed toward the communications room. Elias and Colin were tasked with heading belowdecks and planting their devices. They had seven minutes before the Zodiac would pick them up beneath where the life rafts hung from the side of the tanker.

Deacon smelled cigar smoke as he made his way up the stairs to the control room, and when he reached the top he heard voices. Axel squeezed his shoulder from right behind him, letting him know without words that he heard them as well.

Deacon crouched low and peered around the corner. What he knew about the game of durak was limited, but he did know there was a maximum of five players. He heard a second voice answer the first and then looked at his watch. Seconds mattered.

He signaled to Axel and they moved together— silent—and flanked the door. In theory they needed to ask Yevorovich some questions, but if there wasn't time it was understood that they'd kill him and hope for better luck with one of his remaining partners.

Deacon kicked the door in and opened fire, sweeping to the right as the four men sitting at the table scattered in all directions. He took down two in quick succession, and Axel made short work of the other two. Yevorovich hadn't moved from the table. He stared at Deacon out of cold blue eyes and clamped his teeth around his cigar.

"The Day of Destiny," Deacon said in Russian. "What are the targets?"

Yevorovich smiled and blew out a thick puff of smoke. But he stayed silent.

"Last chance," Deacon warned.

"I am prepared to die for my country. Are you prepared to die for yours?" Yevorovich asked.

Time's up. Deacon pulled the trigger and watched the man slump over. "I'm already dead."

They left the room and headed back down the stairs, moving swiftly toward the life rafts. Deacon caught sight of movement out of the corner of his eye, recognizing the way Elias moved. A SEAL's movements were distinct. Their training was so ingrained it was like breathing.

Deacon looked out and saw the Zodiac idle to a stop just as they reached the edge of the tanker.

"Where's Colin?" Deacon asked.

"We split off down below," Elias panted. "I took out two and started the charge for the explosives."

Deacon scanned the surface of the tanker, looking for any sign of Colin, but there was nothing but an eerily still calmness. Even the winds had stopped blowing. Dante tossed the rope from below and the weighted end made a slight clank as it hit the deck. Axel tied it off quickly and then hooked his foot around the rope and jumped over the edge, sliding down quickly into the waiting Zodiac.

Elias stared at Deacon and said, "We don't have time to look for him."

This was the job. To make the tough calls with logic when his emotions wanted something else. And logic said there was no purpose in risking the lives of several men for the life of one.

"I know," he said. "Go."

Elias nodded and hooked his foot around the rope before going over the edge and down to the Zodiac. Deacon ran his hands through his hair, his sense of panic mounting. He knew Tess was waiting for him in the submarine. She was probably terrified, watching from a distance, hoping he came back safe. Unless her feelings for him weren't what he thought they were. *Hoped* they were.

He had to make a decision. One of his brothers was missing, the other two were safe, and he was team leader.

"Shit," he said. "If I'm not back in two minutes get the hell out of here," he called down to Dante.

He got the affirmative and then he ran like hell back the way he had come. He didn't have to go far. Colin was heading toward him, his leg dragging behind him. There was a knife in his thigh, and Deacon was glad to see he'd left it in there in case his femoral artery had been severed. Smart man. Colin put his arm around Deacon's shoulder, and then Deacon took as much of his weight as he could and hauled ass back to the Zodiac.

The seconds were ticking down in his mind, and he knew they'd be cutting it close for their arrival back to the submarine. The sub was a safe distance away, and they didn't want to still be in the Zodiac when the blast went off. XTNC-50 could cover a fairly large radius under the right conditions. In an explosion that size, there was no way the Zodiac could outrun the chemical weapon if they were outside the protection of the submarine.

"What's the status?" Deacon asked him.

"It's pretty bad," Colin said. "Fucker was drunk and laying on the floor. Came up with a knife when I walked through the door."

"Drunks are always unpredictable. Can you hold on?"

"I can do what I have to," he said.

Deacon called down to Dante, and with Colin's help, he got him situated so he could hold the rope. He slid down and into the Zodiac, and then Deacon followed after him. As soon as he was inside, Dante accelerated, jostling Deacon before he had a chance to get settled.

Dante tossed a thermal blanket on top of Colin, and Elias pressed close to his side to keep him from getting thrown around.

"Is there full medical on the sub?" Deacon asked.

"Of course," Dante answered. "The Shadow never fails. But there's no doctor."

"There's Tess," Deacon said.

Colin laughed harshly and closed his eyes against the pain. "A mortician is just what I'll be needing," he said. "I'll bleed out. I'm fucked."

"She's got some medical training," Deacon told him. "She chose mortuary school when she decided medical school wasn't her cup of tea. She's the best hope you have right now. If we can get you hooked up and get blood into you, you have an even better shot."

"There's a stock of blood on board," Dante said. "We

can get him hooked up. You better hope she doesn't try to embalm you by mistake. I imagine it'd be quite painful on the living."

Colin was already white from blood loss, but he paled even more. *"Fous-toi."*

"No thanks," Dante said. "I've got a long holiday in the Virgin Islands and a lovely woman named Genevieve to take care of those needs. But I appreciate the offer."

Deacon knew what Dante was doing, keeping Colin alert and slightly agitated so his heart rate would stay up.

The water was choppy, and a spray of fine mist rained down on them, finding its way onto any skin left uncovered. They crossed into U.S. waters, but still had a ways to go to reach the submarine. It was a starless night—pitch-black—so even the water looked like ink beneath them. The handheld radar in Deacon's hand was their only guide. It was going to be close. Too close. Dante must've had the same feeling, because the Zodiac picked up speed.

It was so dark it was impossible to see the submarine until they were almost upon it. When they were alongside, Dante cut the engine and a panel in the sub opened up, just large enough for the Zodiac.

"This is going to be tricky to keep him stabilized," Elias said when they were inside and lights came on and the panel began to close.

As soon as the panel was closed, the water began to drain beneath the Zodiac, and Deacon felt his ears pop as the pressure changed. They all carefully lifted Colin and held him steady as the water drained. Once the green light lit indicating that the chamber was secure and there were no water leaks, the door hatches unlocked and there was Tess.

The look of relief on her face when she saw him was like coming home. He'd never had that before. She wore an oversized sweatshirt and jeans, and her mass of hair was piled up on her head. She'd never looked more beautiful.

She took one look at Colin and the knife protruding from his leg and never flinched. "How bad is it?"

"Pretty bad," Deacon said. "We've got to get him stabilized, and we've got to get submerged. We have less than five minutes until detonation. It won't do us any good to save Colin and die from the XTNC-50 gas."

"There's a backboard up in the triage room," Dante said.

"I'll get it," Tess said, already disappearing back inside the sub.

When she returned, they lay Colin on the backboard and the men each took a side to keep him as flat as possible. Dante split off from the group, and as they made their way to the triage room Deacon felt the sub begin to submerge.

"It'll be close," he said.

They moved Colin into the triage room and set the backboard on the operating table that was bolted to the floor. And then they waited as the seconds ticked by. No one spoke. No one moved. Metal creaked and groaned as the water pressed in around the sub. And then the concussion from the explosion rippled around them. The lights flickered, and as the submarine shifted subtly Deacon spread his legs to balance, catching hold of Tess as she lost her balance. After a few minutes, the soft rocking from the shock waves slowed.

"Does that mean we're not going to die?" Tess asked.

"Technically, we're all going to die," Elias said. "It's the nature of humans. But we probably won't die today, if that's what you're asking."

"Smart-ass," she said, blowing out a relieved breath. "If we're going to live, we should probably see about Colin's leg. I don't want to be the bearer of bad news, but he's passed out. He's lost a lot of blood."

"We're following your lead here," Deacon said. "What do you need?"

"Prayers. I've never actually worked on a breathing person before. But anatomy is anatomy, and you'd be surprised some of the things I've had to do to bodies to prepare them for burial. The good news is that I'm at least familiar with how to deal with arteries, considering that's the easiest way to embalm a person."

"Probably not something we should tell Colin when he wakes up," Deacon said. "Let's run this like an op. What supplies do we need?"

The medical bay wasn't a large space, but it was well equipped. Deacon had told her that it was The Shadow's job to anticipate and prepare for any situation, and it was obvious they were very good at their job. Whoever *they* were.

"Right," she said. "Like an op. Let's get an IV started

and a saline solution going. Someone check and see how many units of blood are in the refrigeration unit. I don't suppose anyone knows his blood type."

"Doesn't matter," Elias said. "We've got plenty of O pos in the fridge."

"What are you going to do?" Deacon asked her.

She blew out a breath, and the freckles on her face stood out in stark contrast against her pale skin. She was white as a sheet, but her voice was steady when she spoke.

"I'm not a doctor. If his femoral artery is severed when we pull that knife, he very well could bleed out and die."

"It's a risk we all knew going in," Deacon said. He spoke to her briskly, a bit harsh, knowing that taking her in his arms wasn't what she needed to get through this. "You're the best shot he has until we can get to land. We can have emergency personnel waiting for him there. We're lucky to have you with us. The rest of us have basic training, but we couldn't do anything of this level."

She looked over at Colin's pale, still form and took a deep breath. "It's best if I pretend he's already dead. There's a reason I chose not to go to medical school. It takes the pressure off of trying to save a life if that's already off the table."

"Okay," he said, raising his brows. This woman never failed to surprise him. "I guess that makes sense in a freakish kind of way."

She shot him an aggravated look, and he was pleased to see a little color seeping back into her face.

"I'm not sure I understood what I was getting into when I agreed to this. I don't understand this kind of life. I come from a place where the most exciting thing that happens is when someone forgets to pick their dog poop up off someone's lawn. Deacon . . . I don't know if I can do this."

His heart stuttered and his chest tightened in agony. "Not many people can. It's always your choice, Tess. Whatever you want to do. If you still want to leave Last Stop when we're finished here, I won't try to stop you."

She nodded and averted her eyes, having no idea how many pieces she'd just left his heart in.

CHAPTER EIGHTEEN

Tess was terrified.

But it wouldn't do anyone, especially Colin, any good if she hid like a coward in the bathroom. She wasn't a coward.

She'd had no idea the scope of what The Gravediggers did. For Deacon to live that kind of life for fifteen years was an unbelievable feat—the constant surges of adrenaline and danger, the skill, focus, and brilliance it took not only to be able to fight and win, but to strategize yourself and others out of complex situations when plans changed.

Waiting on the submarine had been the longest eight hours of her life, waiting to see if Deacon would appear back at the sub like he'd planned. When the doors had unlatched, she burst through, searching for him. She'd probably looked deranged, but the relief she'd felt when she'd seen him, looking like the devil's own nightmare, was the exact moment she realized she loved him.

The other realization was that this was only the first

of many times she'd have to watch him risk his life. She wasn't sure she had the strength to take that kind of punishment over and over again.

She went through the cabinets, pulling bandages and instruments, setting them out on a tray. The IV was ready to go in, and all that remained was for her to find her courage.

Axel wheeled a cart into the room. "We've got about fifteen units of blood and at least a three-hour journey back to the States."

"I can only think of one option," Tess said. "And it's going to depend on whether his femoral was severed or nicked. I'd actually prefer it to be severed. I don't have the skills to go in and repair a nicked artery. It's delicate work and requires a graph from another vein."

Tess put on a pair of gloves and turned on the bright overhead light so she could get a better look. And then she took a pair of scissors and cut off Colin's pant leg at the thigh. She handed the scissors over to Deacon.

"Go ahead and remove the rest of his clothing and let's get some warming blankets on him."

She was fortunate that the scientific part of mortuary work dealt with the veins. Femoral arteries were how the blood was removed from the body and the embalming solution inputted. She wasn't used to working with the smaller veins, but the principle was basically the same—the needle had to go inside for the solution to be delivered.

She slid the needle beneath the skin and felt the slight resistance as the vein was located. And then she hooked up the tubing to start the saline solution flow. When she looked back up Deacon and Axel had gotten the rest of Colin's clothes off and wrapped the warming blankets around him, leaving his leg exposed.

"You said you could only think of one option," Deacon said.

"Yes, and it's risky," she said. "But I can't think of another way. Or at least another way that I'm capable of being successful at. I once had to embalm a man who'd gotten caught under his tractor. He came to me in five pieces. Both legs, his head, and an arm had all been severed. I still had to embalm him and put all the pieces back together, but the embalming fluid travels through the veins, and theoretically, there should be one point of entry and one exit. With severed limbs and arteries, there are obviously multiple entry and exit points for the embalming solution to go in. So you have to somehow build a bridge and connect the pieces of the vein again, and still have it be functional so the solution can go through."

"So what does that mean?" Deacon asked.

"It means the only thing I can think of to do is build a bridge from the vein in the top part of his thigh to the vein in his calf with catheter tubing. We start the blood transfusion and get circulation going again, and that should buy us the time we need until we can get him to a hospital and someone who knows what the hell they're doing can take over."

"No time like the present," Axel said, putting on a pair of gloves for himself.

She'd seen the catheter tubing in a package on one of

the shelves and ripped open the paper, setting the thin coil of tubing on the tray with the bandages.

"What's the risk?" Deacon asked.

"I might not be able to get the catheter inserted in time. When the artery is severed the vein retreats into the body. It's going to take me a little time to hunt for it and pull it back out. He'll be bleeding the whole time, and it's a little different working on someone whose blood is still flowing."

Colin stirred on the table, and she looked up to see his dark eyes on her. His upper lip was beaded with sweat and he was pale.

He licked his lips once before speaking. "*Je besoin de medicaments*," he said in his native tongue, asking for painkillers.

"Pussy," said Elias. "Put a stick between your teeth like a real man."

Tess could see the worry in the other men's faces, but she thought Colin's lips twitched at the comment.

"There's a syringe of propofol in the cabinet," she said. "There's a good stock of drugs. Someone shoot him up."

"*Je t'aime*," Colin said.

"Hey now," Deacon said, injecting the propofol. "Don't poach."

"I'm not a damned rabbit," Tess said.

"No, you're an enchantress who bewitched me. But you're mine," Deacon whispered against her ear, then checked Colin's pulse. Colin's eyes closed almost immediately and his breathing was steady.

"He's out," she said. "Let's do this."

She hunted for the vein in his other arm to start the blood transfusion, and once she was finished she stood over the wicked-looking knife sticking out of his leg. Her hands wanted to shake, but she wouldn't let them. Once she took the knife out, things would have to happen very quickly.

"On three," she said. "One, two, three." She pulled the knife free and bandages were put in her hand to press against the wound. They were soaked through before she could grab her scalpel to cut him open.

"Keep them changed out and keep pressing down," she ordered Deacon. He grabbed a new set of bandages and took her place compressing the wound. She made a long, quick slice with the scalpel and went hunting for the femoral artery that had retracted into the upper thigh.

She found it with little hassle. Deacon exchanged bandages again, and Axel exchanged the empty pint of blood for a new one, and she very carefully inserted the thin tube of the catheter into the artery, clamping it off for the time being. She wasn't sure how far down the artery had retracted into the lower part of the leg, so she made a cut in his calf a couple of inches down from the knee.

She winced when she saw that it had traveled down a little farther, and she increased the size of the incision and dug around for the other end. Once she had it she connected the two ends of the catheter, and then she released the clamp.

Blood filled the tube and began to flow, and tiny black spots danced in front of her eyes as she let out a shaky breath.

"We've got six pints of blood left to get us to shore," Axel said. "Well done, mate," he said to Tess appreciatively.

Tess tried to respond, but found that her mouth had gone completely dry. She was covered in blood, and she looked down at her hands as if they belonged to a stranger. She looked at the incisions and the crude rig she'd made of Colin's leg. It was a messy job, but he was alive. Deacon had the forethought to clean him up a bit and give him a new compress at each incision. The blood was much slower to seep through.

"I'll take watch and call you if something happens," Elias said. "You look like you could use a stiff drink and a week's worth of sleep."

"And a shower," she said. "That's a must. I don't know how y'all deal with the constant back-and-forth of an extreme adrenaline rush, to the crash that comes after, and then back again for another rush. I'm exhausted." And she really was, a sort of bone-deep exhaustion that left her knees shaking and her head aching for a pillow.

Or for Deacon's strong warmth.

"Your body will adjust," Axel said.

"And there are ways to ride it out and get your body back on track," Elias said, smiling.

"What kind of ways?" she asked.

Elias and Axel chuckled and Deacon took her by the arm.

"I feel like I'm missing something, but I'm too tired to care. Show me the nearest shower and a bed."

CHAPTER NINETEEN

The living quarters on the submarine were like dorm rooms. Luxurious dorm rooms. She guessed that was the difference between being funded by the government and funded from an off-the-books account.

She'd staked out the rooms earlier when she and Dante first boarded the submarine. She'd been looking for a place she could crash for a few hours because Deacon hadn't let her sleep the night before, but lying in bed had been futile. Her worry for him outweighed her need for sleep.

Most of the rooms shared a bathroom and had single beds, but she'd found a larger room at the end of the hallway with a double bed and a private bathroom. It also had a sitting area and a desk.

"I, uh . . ." she said, the adrenaline crash making her brain slow. "I picked this room."

She opened the door for him and he looked around. The strain and exhaustion was evident in his own expression, but she could practically feel the energy pouring from his body.

"Good choice," he said. "Captain's quarters."

He pushed open the door, never letting go of her hand, and then the moment it closed behind them he lowered his mouth to hers and kissed her—*hard*. The minute his mouth touched hers, the exhaustion slipped away and was replaced with a need so fierce it took her breath away. She responded to him eagerly, his kiss seeming to replenish her strength as he probed and prodded with his tongue.

"That was the most incredible, terrifying thing I've ever experienced in my whole life," she breathed out when she broke away from him. "Any step of the way, one of you could've died. And all I could do was sit there and watch. And do nothing."

She bit his earlobe and he groaned. And then she tugged at the Velcro fastenings of his flight suit to the zipper beneath. Her fingers found the zipper and she pulled it down slowly, revealing the wetsuit underneath.

"I didn't realize getting you naked was going to be such a challenge," she observed.

"You're doing a good job. Don't be intimidated." He bent down to untie his boots and pull them off, and then he shrugged out of the flight suit so all he had on was the wetsuit.

It hugged him like a glove—*everywhere*. "That looks uncomfortable," she said, nodding to his obvious erection.

He barked out a laugh and turned around so she could pull down his zipper. "It's about to get a whole lot better. I need a shower. And I'm probably going to need help scrubbing my back."

"And your front too, I hope."

He peeled the neoprene suit from his arms and shoulders and let it hang at his waist. "You're falling behind," he said, pushing her toward the bathroom.

"Right," she said, breathless. "It's just that once you start taking your clothes off it's hard to think about anything else. Your body makes me crazy. I've never been lust crazy before, but when I see you naked I pretty much want to throw you on the ground like a she-wolf and have my way with you."

She kicked off her boots and yanked her shirt over her head.

"Here, let me help you with that," he said, unclasping her bra with a flick of two fingers.

"You're very talented," she said.

"I'll admit I've had some practice."

"Thank God," she panted.

Deacon was already completely naked by the time she got her clothes off, nudging her from behind. His hands came around her, cupping her breasts, and she pressed back against him, feeling his erection hard in the crease between her buttocks.

"Turn on the water before I forget and take you right here," he growled against her neck.

"That's not really a threat," she said, grasping for the handle of the shower.

The spray came on full blast, and she turned it to hot, until steam filled the small bathroom. The shower was larger than the others, but not by much. He reached around her to slide open the glass door and then nudged her inside.

The hot water felt amazing against her chilled skin, but she realized very quickly heat wasn't going to be a problem. She felt wild and wicked, the adrenaline from the past few hours making her feel recklessly alive, and before he could take control again she put her hand flat on his abs and pushed him back against the wall. And then she knelt in front of him.

"Tess," he groaned.

Her hands curled into the thick muscles of his thighs, and she stared up at him, his heavy shaft right in front of her face. She'd never actually done this before. But she'd read about it. And she suddenly found herself ravenous for the taste of him.

Her tongue peeked out, tasting the salty liquid at the tip, and his cock jerked in response.

"Mmm," she moaned. There was power here. And she liked it.

Her mouth surrounded him, and she felt the tension in her jaw as she widened her mouth to adjust to his size. She explored and tasted, and then she swallowed him deep, going as far down as she could before she had to come back up for air.

She looked up at him out of half-closed lids. One of his hands gripped the top of the shower door and the other was flat on the wall. His head was thrown back and his breath heaving in and out of his chest.

"Tess," he managed again, his voice coming out mangled and broken.

She wrapped her hand around the base of him and stroked as she sucked. She curled her tongue around the flared head every time she pulled back, and it seemed to drive him crazy, so she did it over and over again.

"So good," he moaned.

He grew harder and seemed to swell in her mouth, and she felt the tug of his hands in her hair as he pulled her back. She moaned in protest, but he lifted her to her feet.

"I need to be inside you when I come," he said, taking her mouth in a blistering kiss and pressing her against the wall.

She felt his hand slide between her thighs, his fingers stroking and probing as he made sure she was ready for him.

"So wet," he murmured against her neck. "So hot."

His hands clenched into her buttocks and he lifted her. She wrapped her legs around his waist, and her breath caught as she felt the bulbous head of his cock probing against her. There was no condom this time, and the knowledge passed between them as he looked deep into her eyes.

"I'm on the pill," she told him, her nails digging half-moons into his shoulders as he pushed in a little more. He was stretching her completely. And the feel of him, without the layer of latex between them, made her wild with need.

"I'm going to fill you," he whispered. "Every inch of you."

And then he slid the rest of the way inside of her and her breath caught on a scream. Her head fell back and stars exploded behind her closed eyelids. Her body convulsed out of her control. The orgasm pulsed deep in her womb and spread through her entire body. It was an out-of-body experience and all she could do was hold on.

She vaguely heard his shout and felt the pulsing release of him as he filled her completely, just like he had promised. And then she dropped her head on his shoulder and let the darkness take her.

CHAPTER TWENTY

Three weeks later, The Gravediggers were back in Last Stop and Sergey Egorov and Ivan Levkin were nowhere to be found. The coded messages had stopped, and there was no trace of the false identities they'd taken. The only other useful information Dante had been able to extract from the code was the month of September and several references to the Day of Destiny.

It *would* be in September. He could feel it in his gut. And their time was running out.

Colin was still in the hospital, but he was alive. An emergency team had been waiting for them when they'd returned to Alaska, and he'd been loaded up and flown off without a word. Eve had relayed in a briefing a week later that he could no longer fulfill the role of an active agent, and that he'd be reassigned to fulfill his contract. Deacon had no idea if he'd ever see Colin again or what Eve's plans were for him. That was the problem with Eve. No one knew. And her word was law.

Life had returned to somewhat normal since they'd come back to Last Stop. There'd been two funerals the

month of August, and it had mostly kept Tess preoccupied. She'd changed since their mission—it was impossible not to—and he noticed she watched things
differently now. There was no longer the small-town
naïveté.

Miller hadn't noticed Tess's brief absence from the
funeral home since she'd been holed up in her house on
a deadline, but the rest of the town noticed. By the time
they returned home, her voicemail was full and there
were notes stuck to the door asking if everything was all
right. They'd barely been gone three days.

Tess had also returned home to find that her mother
had come back, without Carl, and she'd opened the salon as if nothing were out of the ordinary. Theodora had
brought Tess back a snow globe from the casino and
given her a sweet hug before flitting away to do whatever
Theodora spent her time doing.

Tess had become more comfortable moving in and
out of the carriage house, though one of them still had to
let her into the restricted areas, and she couldn't be left
alone in classified areas. But she'd not slept a night out
of Deacon's bed. Though some of that had to do with the
fact that her suite was a construction zone.

Eve had been pleased with Tess's translations—as
much as Eve was pleased by anyone, and because there
were so many issues with the Russian Mafiya in power at
the moment, she'd had her listening to recordings from
surveillance equipment and translating them.

Deacon had given Tess a watch like the one he and
the others wore, and explained that if she was ever in

distress all she had to do was press the little button on the side and they'd all be alerted. Once she pushed the button, in case she was injured the watch would automatically begin to take her vitals and relay the information.

When her workday was through at the funeral home, she'd sit at one of the corner workstations at HQ for hours, headphones over her ears, typing furiously.

Deacon looked over from his own work area in time to see her stretch and take the headphones off. She stood and did a couple of yoga poses, as she did every hour or so, and it never failed to make his mouth water and his body ache for her.

She caught his stare and smiled, a secretive, Mona Lisa smile that made him wish they could escape upstairs. He wanted her alone. He just wanted her. Period. She was still dressed in her work clothes of black leggings and green blouse that made her eyes seem even more vibrant than usual. The weather was still miserably hot in early September, and the air conditioner was cranked high. She had her hair piled high on her head, and little tendrils had escaped at the nape of her neck.

She came toward him and he squeezed her hand, just a simple touch, but he'd come to treasure those small moments of connection between them.

"Any news?" she asked.

"Egorov and Levkin are here in the United States somewhere," he said, getting to his feet.

He was frustrated. They all were. Because it felt like the enemy was just within their grasp.

"They're together," he said. "Which is why there's been silence. They don't need to communicate through code any longer. They're talking directly to each other. But where the hell are they?"

He could feel the countdown looming closer, and the frustration of knowing they were skirting the edges but hadn't found what they were looking for was weighing on him heavily. The others stopped to look at him.

"They've put too much time and money into trying to direct all traffic into Texas," he insisted. "It's going to be here. My gut says it's here."

"Your gut is good enough for me, mate," Axel said.

Deacon appreciated the vote of confidence. "Pull up every major event in the city for the next few weeks," he told Axel. "Events where attendance numbers are in the thousands—concerts, sporting events, amusement parks, festivals.

"Dante, I want you to search satellite imagery. Let's see if we can locate a few potential hot spots. We'll be looking for locations with warehouses. Once they've de-livered the XTNC-50, they'll need room to equip it to whatever detonation device they're using. They'll want plenty of space. The more remote they are from civili-zation, the better. Use thermal imaging and satellite to watch traffic patterns. There's going to be a lot of in-and-out activity."

"If Egorov and Levkin are both here already," Axel said, "we should assume that they were able to bring in smaller quantities with them as backup. But they'll need the larger shipment to carry out plans of that large of a scale. They have an unending supply, as XTNC-50 was created by Russian scientists. We just need to figure out how it's crossing our borders."

"There are only so many modes of transportation," Elias offered. "Land, air, sea, and train. They've failed at land and sea. I'll cross-reference all the flight plans that have come through in the last few months and see if anything pops."

"How do we know they didn't succeed in getting it in before they bombed the stadium at the College World Series?" Tess asked.

"They don't have enough for an attack the size and scale they're hoping for," Deacon told her. "If they did, they wouldn't be trying so hard to bring more in. There's no doubt they have some in their supply. But the Day of Destiny is an attack nationwide. They need enough product to spread to multiple states and venues. They need a coordinated team."

They worked tirelessly for hours, sifting through mountains of data, and eliminating locations where Egorov and Levkin might be planning their master attack. It was some time after midnight when Eve Winter's face appeared on the screen.

"Status update," she said, her gaze zeroing in on Deacon.

"Still looking," he said. "We've narrowed it to three locations."

"Narrow it faster," she said shortly. "There's a United Nations summit scheduled for this weekend. We've just received intel that Putin plans to cancel his appearance, and that he's not sending any high-ranking government officials in his place. They're steering clear of the U.S."

"Not a good sign," Deacon murmured.

"Exactly. Focus on Egorov. Levkin is nothing more than a lackey. He'll be the sacrificial lamb. I doubt Egorov lets him live to see their plans come to fruition. Egorov isn't the kind of man who'd want to share the spotlight. If calculations are right, you have less than a week to hunt them down. I don't have to tell you what is at stake."

She finally turned to look at Tess. "Good to see you're settling in, Ms. Sherman."

"Thank you," Tess said simply, her voice neutral.

It was never a good sign when Eve's voice went from all-business to friendly. Deacon didn't think friendly was in her DNA.

"I'm glad our little experiment worked out. I've decided you might be more use in the D.C. office. We can arrange a transfer once this mission is complete."

"No, thank you," Tess said automatically, the ghost of a smirk hinting around that wicked, wicked mouth that seemed to have been created for the sole purpose of driving Deacon crazy.

Eve's smile was cold, and then she looked back at Deacon. "Didn't you tell her it's in her best interest to never tell me no?"

She didn't give him a chance to answer. The screen went black and the air was thick with unspoken words.

Tess's face was red with anger, and he shook his head when it looked like she was going to make a comment.

They were all on the same team, but things had a way of getting back to Eve. They all turned back to their work, Deacon trying to forget the threat that had lurked in Eve's voice.

"I think I've got something," Dante said a few minutes later. The three big screens on the wall flickered on, and multiple views of satellite imaging came on.

"This area didn't rank too high on my radar the past few weeks because it's a high-traffic construction zone. They've got bulldozers and dividers blocking the entire way around the area. But I just checked with city records and there's nothing scheduled for construction, and hasn't been for a couple of years."

"It sure looks like something is going on there," Axel said.

"What are we looking at?" Deacon asked.

Dante tapped a few keys so the image became a 360-digital view. "This is what used to be Texas Stadium. Just north of where we are now. When the Cowboys moved to the new stadium in Arlington several years ago, this one was set for demolition. Notice the industrial area that surrounds the empty space where the stadium once stood. There's an old train depot, and several large warehouses. That's where the thermal vision is lighting up the screen like Christmas. When I compare it to the thermal vision from a month ago, you'll see a noticeable increase in activity from the past few weeks."

Deacon whistled as he watched the time lapse of the satellite and heat sensors. "Like Christmas," he agreed. "That's a lot of semi trucks going inside the warehouses."

"But they're not coming out," Elias said. "They're outfitting them. There's got to be at least twelve of them."

"Thirteen that I counted," Dante corrected. "It's a good location now that I've started digging. The area has been in limbo since before the demolition. The developers don't really know what to do with it, so it's mostly forgotten about. The city itself is so busy no one is going to stop to check whether or not there's supposed to be construction. People just follow the detour signs and go on about their lives. Construction in this area is par for the course, so it's not like they're not used to it."

"Does satellite give us any visuals?" Deacon asked.

"I'm running a cross-comparison now with facial recognition. But this is the clincher." Dante used the keyboard to zoom in on the screen on the left. The men had looked like ants from a distance, but the closer they got the more he could see what Dante was talking about.

"Automatic weapons," Elias said. "Definitely something in those warehouses that is worth protecting."

Deacon stared at the screens and started running scenarios through his head. It would be an almost impossible mission.

"We're one man short." Axel read his mind.

"No you're not," Levi said, coming into the room. "I'm more than field ready. You all know it. I'm tired of being kept here like a prisoner on her orders. She might as well have let me die."

"You're right," Deacon said, not caring that Eve would probably be pissed.

He wasn't sure why exactly Eve was holding Levi back,

but it was almost as if it were some kind of punishment—the way she forced him into testing and recovery early, only to have him do grunt work when he was as well trained and operational as anyone on the team.

"We need to move in tonight," he said. "The way traffic has picked up on-site makes me think they're getting ready to roll out. They'll need time to drive to their destinations. What's happening this weekend?"

"The United Nations summit is the big one," Axel said. "But it's concentrated in New York. It's scheduled to start Sunday and finish up Monday. It's also the anniversary of 9/11. There are several large memorial services and concerts planned from state to state, and they're expecting attendance to be in the thousands. Most of them have been turned into fundraisers for families of fallen officers and members of the fire department, so they're all-day events."

"That has potential," Deacon commented. "And it seems like something a man with Egorov's ego might attempt. To wipe out the events of 9/11 with his own day of terror."

"It's also the start of the NFL season," Axel added. "Twenty-six teams playing around the country to sold-out stadiums."

"Twenty-six teams," Deacon said. "Thirteen stadiums. Thirteen trucks in those warehouses."

"If that's where they're going, they'll need to pull out within thirty-six hours," Elias said. "There are rules and regulations for when things from visiting teams have to be delivered to the stadiums."

"What's the projected casualty count?" Deacon asked.

Axel pulled up the data. "If they hit every major NFL stadium in America with sold-out crowds, you're looking at a potential casualty rate of close to a million people."

"Jesus," Elias said. "Catastrophic."

"Right, and it doesn't change the fact that there are still only five of us to stop all those trucks from leaving the warehouses."

"I guess I'm not completely understanding," Tess finally said. "The five of you are planning to invade these warehouses, with armed guards, and stop thirteen trucks from leaving the grounds that are supposedly all carrying a chemical weapon that kills almost instantly?"

"That pretty much covers it." Elias grinned. "Crazy, huh?"

"It's insane," she said incredulously.

"Five is all we need," Deacon told her. "A highly skilled five-man team can take down an entire army if it's done right."

"And what exactly is the right way to do it?" she asked.

The men all stared at her silently.

Tess nodded. "Yep. That's what I thought."

CHAPTER TWENTY-ONE

There was no relief from a Texas summer, not even at three in the morning. The heat was thick with humidity, and there was only a sliver of moon and a sprinkle of stars in the black sky. The lake was black and still, not a ripple since there wasn't a breeze.

It had taken twenty-four hours of planning and preparation. To make sure The Shadow knew of their equipment needs and the possible cleanup opportunities. They had four days until the world as they knew it would virtually end.

Deacon felt the vibrations of the stealth Black Hawk helicopter in the air before he heard the buzz of the rotor blades, and he watched as it touched down in the middle of the grassy field near the lake. He looked back toward the hidden entrance of the tunnel, thinking about Tess still curled up in bed, content as a cat. More than the memory of the way she looked, it was what she'd said as he'd leaned down to kiss her good-bye.

"I love you."

It was incredible how three little words could have

such an impact. He'd gone a lifetime without saying those words to a woman. His relationships had never lasted more than a few months. They usually ended whenever he had to go on the next assignment. He'd liked those women—respected them—and enjoyed them. But he'd never loved any one of them. Not like he did Tess. The sincerity of her words had left him speechless, and he'd only been able to hold onto her a little longer—kiss her a little deeper.

"Ah, that sight never gets old," Elias said, interrupting his thoughts.

"Up close and personal," he said. "Let's roll."

Their faces were streaked with black paint, and they wore leather gloves and balaclavas, along with helmets. They'd be rappelling from more than a hundred and fifty feet in the air.

They loaded up silently and hooked themselves into the rappelling gear, checking the nylon ropes and the attachments. They tested their comm units and gave the thumbs-up. Then it was go-time.

The helicopter went straight up, and Deacon's stomach dropped out from under him with a sense of adrenaline. It was always his favorite part of the ride. The doors were open, and the cool night air rushed in as they ascended higher and traveled across the city. A much better ascent than going up in the closed space of the cargo plane.

Egorov had kept nighttime lights to a minimum, hoping to keep his operation hidden, so when they arrived at the warehouses only the yellow glow of a few spotlights could be seen. They hovered high above the darkest building.

Deacon looked to Elias since he was in charge of all the ropes—the rappel master—and Elias tugged on each length of nylon, checking it one more time. Deacon tossed his deployment bag out the side of the helicopter and watched the rope fall to the roof of the closest warehouse. The others each did the same in turn.

Elias gave the nod and Deacon moved into position, sitting in the open doorway, his legs swinging out. When Elias gave the signal, he turned his body so his feet rested against the door frame and he faced the others. His left hand went to the small of his back where the brake was located. Axel mirrored him on the other side of the chopper.

On Elias's go signal, they both pushed off with their feet, and the rope slid through Deacon's hand as he sped to the ground. He saw the deployment bags from the others drop down next to his and knew they were only seconds behind him. He braked and slowed his descent when he was almost to the roof of the warehouse.

And then his feet touched down silently and he stood still, waiting for the rope to drop after him. He wound it up and put it in his deployment bag as the others landed also, and then a few seconds later, Elias dropped down next to them and the Black Hawk was gone. They removed their helmets and replaced them with black balaclavas.

They each had a target and an assignment, and they scattered off the roof and down to the ground, finding a place to stash their deployment bags. If they were lucky, Egorov or Levkin would be somewhere inside the warehouses, getting ready to send off their shipments. If they were *really* lucky, they'd both be inside.

Deacon waited in the shadows behind the warehouse he'd been assigned to. The noise had picked up from inside and there was plenty of movement. They were getting ready to deploy the trucks and head to their destinations. Deacon had his knife in his left hand and his right hand free. He moved behind several stacked crates, keeping to the shadows.

The warehouses were equipped with large doors on the front and backside. Big enough for a couple of eighteen-wheelers to drive in one side and out the other. The back door was closed, but there was a smaller, standard-size door that two men walked through.

They both wore jeans and T-shirts, and were probably somewhere in their early forties. They immediately lit up cigarettes and began to speak in Russian. Or at least one of them did. The other grunted on occasion and sucked down his cigarette as fast as he could, and then he lit up another.

Deacon caught Levkin's name and listened a little closer. He knew how to be still and wait for the right moment to strike. *Just a little closer.* The man who was sucking down cigarettes was nervous. He moved constantly as his friend talked, and if he backed up just a little more he'd be within reach.

Levkin was inside one of the warehouses. Apparently he was a real tyrant now that they were in the end game, and everyone was pissed their payments had been delayed. Egorov was supposed to have showed up that morning to pay them in cash, but he'd never come. And the men were getting restless. A lot was at stake.

The chain smoker had finished another cigarette, and Deacon could tell they were about to go back inside. They both moved toward the door and he came up behind them. He slid his knife neatly between the chain smoker's third and fourth ribs, pushing up as he did so to pierce the heart. It was the quietest and least messy way to kill someone. Deacon withdrew his knife and moved to the next one.

The other man had started to turn to see why his friend was on the ground, but it was too late. Deacon snapped his neck and then wiped his knife on the man's shirt, cleaning the blood off. He dragged both bodies behind the crates and then moved to the door. He needed to find Levkin.

There was a small window in the metal door, and Deacon peeked through it to see if he could get a head count. There were two eighteen-wheelers inside. One of the cabs was painted bright orange, and the trailer said "Broncos" down the side, with an image of the team logo. The other truck cab was painted navy and the trailer belonged to the Seattle Seahawks. Or at least they made a good impression of it.

The backs of the trailers were open, and he could see the equipment being loaded inside. Bags and bags of footballs, extra pads, sideline equipment. The preparation for this event had been months, if not years, in the making. They had everything they needed to get any explosives and XTNC-50 into the stadiums.

He counted six men inside the warehouse, and all of them were busy. No one even paid attention as he slipped through the door and kept to the perimeter so he could hide behind whatever cover he could find. He dropped whoever he came in contact with, making his way toward the two men talking at the front.

He recognized Ivan Levkin. He was a tall, thin man. Almost stork-like in appearance. His blond hair was fine and fell in wisps around a face that only a mother could love. He resembled a vulture—bony face, crooked nose, and prominent Adam's apple.

The comm in Deacon's ear buzzed as Elias came on and gave the all-clear for warehouse number one. It wasn't long after that Levi gave his all-clear. They indicated that they'd move together to the next warehouse and repeat the process.

Deacon didn't dare speak. He was completely focused on Levkin, who seemed beyond stressed.

"We don't have time for your tantrums, Josef," Levkin spat in Russian. "We must leave here. By this time tomorrow this place will be swarming with cops and God knows who else."

"I want my money. Egorov promised we'd be paid," Josef said, not budging.

"And you will be. After everything has been moved. Remember that if the plan is interrupted, you'll be getting no money at all."

"I don't trust you," he said. "Egorov either."

Levkin shrugged. "I don't really care. There are enough explosives and XTNC-50 in these warehouses to reduce the entire city to dust. It wasn't the goal, but it'll work in a pinch. Your family lives here, right?"

"Fuck you," Josef said. "Tell Egorov I'm not going down for him. If that money isn't in my hand before we leave, then you can find another driver. I'm not doing this for charity."

"Right, right," Levkin said, his smile cold. He pulled a weapon from the small of his back and fired point-blank at Josef.

It was one less man Deacon would have to kill.

"Who is going to drive your truck now?" Deacon called out in Russian. He was hidden behind the cab of the truck and well out of the way when Levkin turned and fired.

"Who is there?" he answered. "Is that you, Vasily?"

"I think Vasily is dead," Deacon said. "They all are."

Levkin turned in all directions, looking for the others. But there was no one. "Who are you?" he called out.

Deacon stepped out from behind the truck to face him, and to his surprise, Levkin broke out into a grin.

"Ahh, he said you would come," he said. "But I did not believe him. I thought his trap too trivial for one such as you. You are Deacon Tucker. You were CIA. I've read about you. Operation Quantum Leap was very impressive."

"Thank you," Deacon said, making sure nothing in his voice betrayed his anger. "It seems you know as much about me as I know about you."

"More, more, my friend. Much more. You see, Yevorovich's email that your team hacked into was set up specifically for those fishing to find out more about us. Instead of you finding out about Yevorovich, the tables were turned and we were able to find out all about you."

"I'm clear," Axel said in his comm unit.

"All clear," Dante said. "Heading to rendezvous point."

"How did you know we were coming for you?" Deacon asked.

"We've been linked into your satellite and communications systems. You are not the only ones who have top-notch technology."

"But it's not my men who are dead, and it's not my shipments that are going to be stuck here so they can be confiscated by Homeland Security."

Levkin took his eyes off Deacon to look around again, searching for his men and listening for the normal sounds coming from outside. There was nothing. Just silence.

"You're going to want to drop that weapon before my friend standing behind you breaks your wrist."

Levkin turned his head and saw Axel there, and then he turned back to face Deacon. "You cannot beat me. You cannot win against those who are willing to sacrifice it all."

Before Levkin could blink, Axel had snapped his wrist and the gun fell to the floor.

A voice buzzed in Deacon's comm again and said, "We've got a problem." He recognized Dante's upper-crust British accent.

He turned off the mute button in his comm unit and said, "What's wrong?"

"There are only twelve trucks here. The thirteenth is long gone."

Deacon looked at Levkin and said, "I'm going to give you one chance to tell me where the truck that's already left is going. And then I'm going to start putting bullets in you."

He pulled the Sig and pointed it at Levkin.

"Like I told you," Levkin said. "I'm ready to die for my country."

"Oh, I'm not going to let you die," he said. "I'm going to make sure you get the best hospital care you can possibly get to patch up all your wounds. And then I'm going to do it all over again."

"Go to hell," Levkin said.

"I'll give you one more chance. Where is the truck going?"

"Fuck you."

"Wrong answer," Deacon said and shot him in the knee.

Levkin howled and dropped to the ground. "I couldn't hear you the first time. Where did the truck go?" Deacon asked again. "If you give me the answer I want, I promise to give you death."

"Phila . . . Philadelphia," Levkin gasped out.

"See," Deacon said. "That wasn't so hard, was it?" He looked at Axel. "Let's wrap him up and put a bow around him for Eve. I'm sure she can get all kinds of information from him."

Levkin started laughing and rolled around on the floor, the high-pitched sound grating on Deacon's nerves. It was almost maniacal. Sometimes pain could do that to a person.

"Do you think we didn't plan for this?" Levkin snarled through gritted teeth. "Egorov is smarter than that. You'll never catch him. There are many chess pieces in play. There's nothing to do but watch the game. You've failed. In more ways than one."

TESS CHECKED THE clock for what had to be the hundredth time. It was close to five in the morning, and they still hadn't returned.

Deacon had kissed her good-bye and told her to get some sleep. Instead of kissing him passionately and giving him something to remember her by, she'd grabbed his shirt, given him a rough peck on the lips, and blurted out that she loved him. She had to be the biggest dork on the planet. He hadn't answered her. He'd only stared at her, and then he'd kissed her one last time.

It was impossible to go back to sleep after he'd left, so she got up and made a pot of coffee and turned on the TV. She'd listened to them play out the op over and over again. And she'd heard them lay out contingency plans in case one of them was killed or injured. They talked about death as casually as they talked about their favorite sports teams or the weather. They'd gotten so conditioned to it being a very real possibility that it was part of their daily lives.

She checked social media while she was waiting for the coffee to finish, and noticed that the only other person she knew online was Miller. Miller habitually kept weird hours, depending on when her writing was going well, and when it wasn't going well she could be found on social media.

Why are you awake and posting Kermit the Frog memes at three a.m.? Miller messaged her.

Tess smiled and replied, *Can't sleep. Making coffee and going to watch a movie.*

Good, I'm out of coffee. Why don't you bring some extra this way and we'll watch the movie together?

The book must be going well, she replied.

I don't want to talk about it. Bring chocolate if you've got any of that stashed somewhere. I ate all mine.

Tess laughed and dug out a package of Axel's stash of Tim Tams, and she grabbed a small bag of gourmet ground coffee from the freezer. She also grabbed a bottle of Tums because the worry was giving her heartburn. Loving Deacon wasn't going to be easy. There was no need to get ready or dress up. That was the good thing about having lifelong friends. She wore an old pair of gray sweats and a T-shirt, and her hair was piled in a knot on her head. She wasn't even going to bother to put on a bra. She was only going three blocks away.

She put everything in a bag and had reached to grab her keys from the hook when she caught movement out of the corner of her eye. Eve Winter stood just in front of the locked door that led to HQ. She had no idea how long Eve had been standing there or how she hadn't heard Eve slip through the door. But she was there, in the flesh, and Tess had never felt more outmatched in her life.

Intimidating didn't begin to describe her. Even at five in the morning she was dressed for serious business.

She wore a sleeveless black sheath dress that stopped just above her knees and a pair of wicked stilettos in a neutral color. Her legs were long, her nails manicured and painted crimson, and her lips slicked with lipstick of the same shade. Her hair was like black silk and hung to the middle of her back.

"Did I scare you?" she asked.

"No, of course not," Tess said. "I'm used to seeing strangers pop in unannounced. I'm actually just leaving."

Eve smiled and walked around the spacious kitchen, looking at the area as if she were a prospective buyer, her heels clicking on the tile.

"He's an excellent lover," she said. "Deacon, I mean."

Tess's blood chilled at the words.

"A well-oiled machine in his prime. Men like Deacon are trained for one thing. Don't you want to ask me what that one thing is?" Eve arched a brow like a teacher expecting an answer from a student.

"Not really," Tess said. "Like I mentioned, I was on my way out."

"You're stubborn. And you've got spine. I can see why he enjoyed this assignment more than the others."

The bottom dropped out of her stomach. It wasn't difficult to read between the lines and interpret what Eve was trying to tell her. It was clear Eve and Deacon had been lovers. Was she jealous? Were they still lovers? And the insinuation that Eve had ordered Deacon to sleep with her had been a debilitating blow. The slice had cut deep and she was bleeding, only she couldn't feel the cut yet because her body was numb.

"I'd told him you're an asset to us here because of your connection to the community in aiding our transition here. But I can see you're a woman who's ready to break free. It's hard being the steady one. The responsible one." Her nails drummed rhythmically on the granite countertop of the island. "It's hard being the one everyone always depends on. Everyone else gets to live their life as they choose and have adventures. To come and go as they please and sleep with whomever they choose. What's holding you back from doing the same? Fear?"

Tess's hand balled into a fist around her car keys and the metal bit into flesh. It seemed Eve knew every one of her secret thoughts. Knew exactly what buttons to push. She hated being manipulated. And worse, she hated that it was so effective.

"I'm exactly where I want to be," she said firmly. She could feel the blood rushing to her face and hated that she couldn't be calm and cool like Eve. That her emotions were too strong to contain. But she *really* hated Eve Winter, and there was nothing she could do to hold it back.

"Really?" Eve said. "My mistake. But are you experienced enough to be able to go on with your daily life, to see Deacon every day and not have it cut you to the bone when he moves on? You wear your heart on your sleeve. Men like Deacon don't have hearts. They only have love for the next mission. The next adrenaline rush. Though there are benefits to those adrenaline rushes, as I'm sure you know."

Her smile was smug and knowing, and a vision of Eve and Deacon, naked and wrapped together in an intimate embrace, flashed through her mind before she could stop it. Eve seemed like the type of woman he'd be attracted to. Beautiful and smart and polished. Not a small-town, blue-collar girl who didn't crave that same adrenaline rush.

"I just don't want you to get your heart broken," Eve went on. "You're useful to the team for now, and his interest lay in the fact that you're needed here for us to work effectively. But that'll change once this mission is complete, and he'll move on to the next mission. The next woman. There's always another woman. A man like Deacon is very . . . virile. They all are. It's learning how to contain and harness all that sexual energy that's the challenging part of my job.

"I've known of his fascination for you since he met you, and now that he's gotten a taste he'll be able to move on and become more effective. So I should really be thanking you. And as I told you earlier, I have use for you in another location. Your skills are useful, and you've proven to be trustworthy with our secrets. Your salary would be triple what it is now, and you'd finally have the opportunity to have your adventure and go off on your own. And it would make things easier on you. Putting that separation between you and Deacon while you're piecing together your broken heart."

"Wow," Tess said. "You are a piece of work. Really."

Eve arched a brow, her full lips moving into a sensual pout. "I won't make the offer twice."

"Thank God for that," Tess said. "If you're done, I'm still on my way out the door."

"Be careful, Ms. Sherman. I'm not someone you want to irritate."

"And I'm not someone you want to bully," she said, her anger past the point of no return. "Unless you want to deal with the mess of killing me and figuring out a way to keep the people in this town from noticing my disappearance. Because I can guarantee they'll notice and they'll have a lot of questions. Otherwise, I'm going to go on about my daily life and deal with my personal life how I see fit."

"You think I'd just make you disappear?" she asked. "That would be very reckless of me. It's so easy to have an accident in the home these days. Or for rumors to get started that you've been troubled and depressed recently. Everyone would be shocked by your decision to take your own life."

Tess felt the blood drain from her face, and her skin went cold and clammy with fear. She was dealing with forces that were more powerful than she could ever hope to be. She'd never be completely safe as long as she was involved with The Gravediggers.

"Make sure you clean up your brimstone residue before you leave," Tess said, and hurried out the kitchen door to her car.

Her hands shook as she hit the key fob, and they were still shaking as she drove the three blocks to Miller's house. She'd been stupid to think she could have anything permanent with Deacon. This was the world he came from. The world he lived in. And she had been naïve to think he was capable of having anything different.

CHAPTER TWENTY-TWO

Deacon had never been so terrified in his life.

He'd faced death dozens of times, sure—looked down the wrong end of a gun a time or two, been stabbed in the kidney with an ice pick, and he'd had an Italian double agent try to slit his throat while she'd ridden him to orgasm. But none of those incidents had inspired the deep, icy fear that had penetrated his being when he'd returned to the funeral home to find that Eve had taken up residence and Tess was nowhere to be found.

When they entered HQ from the tunnel, Eve was sitting at the head of the conference table, her legs crossed. She had a pint of ice cream in her hand and licked the back of the spoon like the damned cat who'd eaten the canary.

"Where's Tess?" he asked, his gaze narrowing on hers.

"Your kitten has claws," Eve said. She put the lid on the ice cream and set it aside. And then she leaned back in the chair and studied him.

"What did you do?" he asked.

"I told her the truth," she said. "You've always been big on wanting to know the truth, Deacon. Why shouldn't she get the same courtesy?"

"There are shades of the truth," he said. "Which ones did you choose to share with her?"

She smiled then and his brothers moved in beside him. He wasn't a hundred percent sure if it was to give him backup or to hold him back if he lost his shit.

"I just told her what she already knows. That you're an exceptional lover . . ."

"And how the hell would you know that?" he asked.

"You forget that you were on surveillance with that Italian agent. She certainly didn't have any complaints. A woman recognizes when another is faking. And she was enjoying every moment up until she tried to kill you."

"You explained that part to Tess?" he asked, already knowing the answer.

"She wouldn't let me finish my appraisal of you. She's got quite the temper."

"I know," he said. "It's one of the things I love most about her."

"Love?" she asked. "You think you're capable of love? After the things you've done? The things you've seen?"

"I'm the same man I've always been. I'll make sacrifices that no one else should have to make. And I'll do what's fucking right. Always. That's why you wanted me. And that's what you've gotten. Otherwise you would've let me die."

His heart was hammering in his throat, but he didn't let her see his anger. That wasn't the way to deal with

Eve. She shrugged and drummed her nails on the conference table, a habit of hers he always found irritating as hell.

"Where is she?" he asked again.

"I don't know," she answered. "She left."

"What else did you tell her?"

"Only that you were just following orders."

"That's fucking cold," Elias said, shaking his head.

"Is it?" she asked. "Is it cold to expect the best agents in the world to keep their dicks in their pants and do their jobs? To stay focused on saving lives. Do you think you would've put an end to this sooner if you'd been more concerned with finding their headquarters instead of fucking her bed through the floor?"

"You've got her suite of rooms under surveillance?" he asked, fury rising inside him.

"Of course I do," she said. "She knows about us. She knows classified information. It's my job to make sure our existence stays classified. I'm not going to let a nobody mortician from Nowhere, Texas, fuck that up. Think like the agent you used to be instead of the lovesick puppy you've become."

"I can do both, thanks. I've got five years, eleven months, and twenty-two days left on my contract," he said. "Tess is mine, and I love her. She knows the risks. But I'll ask her to be my wife if she'll have me."

"Damn," Dante said. "We really thought you were just following orders. Who knew you'd really fallen for her."

"I'd be pretty piss poor at my job if I couldn't make

you all think what I wanted you to think. But I'll not lie to Tess. Not about anything."

Eve smiled again. He'd never seen her lose her temper. She was always cool under pressure. And when she didn't get her way, she thought of different ways to get what she wanted. She wasn't a woman who liked to hear the word "no."

"Five years, eleven months, and twenty-two days is a long time," she said. "A lot can happen. A lot can change."

"That's true for any life," he said. "There are some people who know how to fight. How to stick when things are hard. And how to use the bad things in life to grow and become better." He thought of Tess and all she'd been through in her life. "Tess is that kind of person. If she'll have me, she'll be here for the long haul. I will always be better with her than I am without."

Eve uncrossed her legs and got to her feet. "It's your life," she said. "You know the rules. If you don't mind putting her life on the line, then by all means, marry her. You'll have to convince her to stay, of course. I think she's seriously considering the job offer I made to send her to D.C."

"Believe me," he said. "Tess is smart enough to see through you." At least he prayed to God she was. Eve was a masterful liar and manipulator.

"We'll see," she said. "Now, enough of this. I listened in on surveillance, but give me a full status update."

"According to Levkin," Axel said, "the Detroit Lions truck departed two days ago as an insurance policy, and it's headed to Philadelphia. That's where they're playing

THE DARKEST CORNER × 323

the opening game of the season. We've got him waiting for you in one of the holding rooms. We thought you might want to question him yourself."

"I do, thank you," she said.

"It's too late to stop the truck now," Elias said. "It's already confirmed as arriving at Lincoln Financial Field. Men dressed as advanced game day staff were there to greet the truck and unload it. They have credentials that are only issued every week by the league. Egorov and his men have *everything* they need to make their mission a success."

"When will you head to Philadelphia?"

"We leave in twelve hours," Deacon said.

"I'll have what you need from Levkin by the time you arrive," she said, walking toward the door that led to the containment rooms.

Deacon turned and headed toward his rooms, trying to keep out the emotion that wanted to spill to the surface. He'd spent thirty-six years of his life able to control his emotions. He couldn't let that change now. Not when so much was at stake.

"Don't let her fuck with your head," Elias said, coming up behind him. "You do what you have to do. We don't get chances like the one you've been given with Tess every day." Elias slapped him on the back and then said, "I'm heading home for a few hours' sleep."

Deacon nodded and hurried the rest of the way to his rooms before anyone else could give him advice. He only knew one thing. Tess had left. He needed to find her. He needed to know she was safe and whether or not she still loved him. She'd told him she did just hours before. He had to believe she hadn't changed her mind.

———

TESS HADN'T BEEN good company.

Miller had known immediately something was wrong when she'd shown up pale-faced and white-knuckled, bearing the bag of chocolate cookies and coffee. But she hadn't pressured her for answers after Tess had told her everything was fine.

They'd watched movies until the sky turned dark gray with the first inkling of daylight, Tess all the while checking her watch over and over again, wondering when Deacon would be back home. *If* he'd make it back home.

Then she'd given Miller a hug and driven the three blocks back to the funeral home. It had been tempting to climb the stairs to the third floor and sleep in her own room, no matter the mess that was inside. But she wasn't a coward. And she knew the longer she waited and wondered, the worse it would be.

The last thing she wanted to do was run into Eve again, so when she opened the door to the carriage house and stepped into the kitchen, she breathed out a huge sigh of relief to see that the other woman wasn't there.

She had no idea whether or not Deacon had returned, but either way, she had to face things head-on, so she went up the stairs to the rooms they shared. She used her thumb on the fingerprint pad and waited as it scanned her and unlocked the door. He'd had her programmed in once she'd moved her day-to-day things there.

The door snicked open and she pushed it wide. The room was empty. Her palms were sweaty and she relaxed as she put her purse away. She'd shower and try to get some sleep. It would do no good to worry herself into exhaustion.

She sat down on the bed to kick off her shoes and undress, but fatigue came over her and she lay back on the bed for a few minutes to rest her eyes. The next time she opened them was when she heard the familiar sound of the lock opening on the door and felt the presence of someone else in the room.

She turned her head and drank in the sight of him. She was still sleepy and disoriented, but her brain was new enough to see that he was whole and uninjured. Though he looked like hell. His black face paint was smeared from sweat and his hair was damp. He looked like a savage.

"Hey," he said softly, his gaze taking in every inch of her. He looked surprised and relieved to see her.

"Hey, yourself," she said. And then every word Eve had poisoned her mind with came back like a flood.

They stared at each other in silence for a few moments before Deacon came toward her. He picked up the chair that sat against the wall and moved it in front of her on the bed.

"I'm filthy," he said. "I don't want to get the bed dirty."

"I need to talk to you," she said, coming to a sitting position to face him. She probably looked like hell, but there wasn't anything she could do about it at the moment.

"I thought you might," he said, his voice sober. "I ran into Eve downstairs. She mentioned you have quite a temper."

She tried to smile, but she wasn't a miracle worker. "I need to ask you something," she said. "And I need the truth."

"Before you do, I want to tell you something."

She swallowed and thought this might be the end. His face was so serious, his expression almost sad.

"Okay," she agreed. "Go ahead and tell me."

"Actually, I want to tell you two things." He reached out and took one of her hands and squeezed it gently. "The first is that I won't lie to you. If you have something to ask me, you'll get the truth. I promise you that."

"What's the second thing?" she asked.

"I love you."

Her mouth dropped open and she tried to remember to breathe, but it wasn't coming as easily as it usually did. It wasn't what she'd been expecting.

"You . . . you do?" she asked. And then she burst into tears.

Before she knew it, she'd been scooped up into his arms and was sitting on his lap. Her head was tucked into his shoulder, and she didn't care one bit how ridiculous she must look or that he might be smearing black face paint all over her.

"I'm sorry," she said, sniffling. "You just surprised me."

"I can see that," he said, and she could feel his smile

on the top of her head. "I'm sorry I didn't tell you sooner. That you couldn't tell how much I love you. You're like my oxygen, Tess. I can't breathe without you.

"For two years I've been living as if I were already dead. But loving you has given me a hope I've never had before. You're my light in the darkness. Don't you see that?"

She saw the sincerity in his eyes and she trembled as she stroked his shoulder. "I didn't believe her," she said. "Eve, I mean. Not really. Though she got in her fair share of darts. She knew exactly what to say to hit me where I'm weakest."

"It's her specialty," he said. "I told her you were too smart to be fooled by her half-truths."

"I have to know though," she said and swallowed again. "Did she order you to seduce me?"

"Yes," he said without hesitation. "A few weeks ago. But I'd already decided a long time ago that I was going to pursue you with full force once you were ready. It just so happened you being ready and her orders coincided."

"Okay," she said. "I just had to ask. I would've wondered forever if we hadn't cleared the air. I let her get to me. Even as I was standing there telling myself not to let it happen, she succeeded. I don't care what she says. I love you too. I know the consequences of this life and what it means. We can do this. What I don't want to do is live without you. I'd also prefer to not have to ever speak to her again. All I can think of when I see her is how damned perfect the two of you must have been together. She's the most beautiful woman I've ever seen.

It still baffles me you'd pick me when you've had something like that. I've never really felt jealousy before. But when I look at her I want to claw her eyes out."

"First of all, she's not the most beautiful woman. She's got a heart of ice, and the soul she once had has long since been bargained for in her line of work. I picked you because you're everything I see that's beautiful in this world. I'd stopped seeing those things before I met you. You're the kindest, most sincere person I know. You give selflessly and you know how to love, even when you've told yourself it's not worth it. You never give up."

Her tears had started to fall again and she swiped at her eyes.

"If you saw yourself as I see you, you'd know Eve Winter can't hold a candle to your beauty. You light up the room." His hand touched the ends of her hair. "The soft warmth of fire in your hair and your sorceress eyes. Your beauty bewitches me. It's you who makes my head turn and you who captivates me. Only you."

She nodded because she couldn't find the words to say anything. How could she even come close to saying the right thing after such beautiful words?

"And second of all," he continued. "Eve and I have never been lovers. I'm not and have never been a monk. I've had lovers in the past, and there have been missions where I've done what I needed to do to get the job done."

"You don't have to explain," she said.

"I don't ever want you to have doubt or feel that jealousy. She's not worth the emotions it drains from you. The only reason Eve knows what kind of lover I am is because on one of those missions where I did what I had to do, she was watching through the surveillance we'd set up. That's her only basis for what she told you."

Tess was surprised at the relief she felt. She'd known Deacon had had lovers in the past, just as she had. His past was his past. But there'd been something that hadn't settled well at the thought that he'd chosen Eve as a lover. She couldn't have blamed him, because Eve was gorgeous. But she'd hoped his taste had been more discerning. It pleased her immensely that it had been.

"I need a shower," he said, standing to his feet with her still in his arms.

"I was just thinking that," she said. "We do really good work in the shower."

CHAPTER TWENTY-THREE

Twelve hours later the team was in Philadelphia and they'd set up a mobile headquarters in connecting suites at the Ritz-Carlton. Tess had been through the emotional ringer the last twenty-four hours, and it had shown in the drawn expression on her face and the shadows under her eyes. But when she'd looked at Deacon that morning, they shone bright with the love she had for him.

It had already been decided that Tess would stay at HQ and watch events unfold on the monitors. Much like the rest of the world. She wasn't happy about staying behind, but Deacon wasn't willing to risk her if something went wrong and they failed to stop the attack. If they hadn't found the trucks ready to depart at the warehouse, they never would've been able to save everyone.

By early Sunday morning before they left, Eve had called. It had taken her longer than the twelve hours she'd promised them the night before. But none of them mentioned that to her. The good news was she had the information. And just in time too, because kickoff was only hours away.

"I told you Levkin was the weak link," she said coldly, though Deacon could see the frustration in her eyes. Levkin must've been a harder nut to crack than she'd estimated. "I have full confidence the information he gave me is the truth. It took longer because he was resistant to the truth serum." She looked at Levi as she said it, as if it were somehow his fault since the serum had been created by the Mossad.

"The Russians have been torturing their own soldiers for years to prepare them to withstand serums such as that," Levi said. "Sometimes it works and sometimes it doesn't. Their methods aren't as effective as my own country's."

"I'd say ineffective," she said.

Deacon had never seen Eve question a suspect, but he'd never seen her not get the answers she was looking for.

"Give us the play-by-play," Deacon said. "We're running out of time."

"Kickoff is at noon," she said. "At eleven-thirty, Lieutenant Joshua Sykes, with the 101st Airborne, should be landing on the field. The only problem is we can't find Lieutenant Sykes."

"How long has he been missing?" Elias asked.

"The last time he was seen was at dinner last night with a few friends," she answered. "They said he left early to go back to the hotel and get a good night's sleep before he had to parachute onto the field today. He went toward South Street and disappeared. We're keeping this quiet for now. His friends think he got up early and is preparing for the jump."

"Is that his normal pattern of behavior?" Dante asked.

"Apparently," she said. "We have every reason to believe that the initial detonation will be attached to whoever is taking Sykes's place to parachute onto the field. According to Levkin, Egorov will be making his last mission a big one. And Levkin wasn't happy about it. They both wanted the glory that would come to them and their families after their sacrifice."

Deacon felt Tess's hand slip into his, her presence reassuring him that everything would be okay. It *had* to be okay.

"Your mission is simple," Eve said. "To take out Egorov before he touches ground and save the lives of everyone in that stadium. This is why we do what we do. We can't fail. The problem is that you're going to be on live television, and no one can know what the hell you're doing or how much danger they're in. I've told you all before that this is a job no one can tell you thank you for."

"We've never done what we do for the thank-yous," Axel said.

Eve stared at him, her eyes bleak. "Neither have I," she said. "The Shadow has provided everything you need on the fourth level of the parking garage at Fifteenth and Sansom."

DEACON TRUSTED ELIAS with his life, and the life of every person in that stadium. He had to. There was no turning back. No second-guessing. And there was no other way.

There was no one more qualified to take a sniper shot at a moving target than the ex-SEAL. The stadium was filled to bursting, crowded with excited fans wearing a mix of black and gold and powder-blue. The decibel level of the crowd made it difficult to hear through their comm units. Even during the pre-game entertainment, the home crowd was riled up with the possibility of a potential win.

The noonday sun was blistering and the air stale with the heat rising from the stands. The crowd was pressed in together as close as they could be, and even the aisles were thick with people as they jostled to get to their seats with drinks that slopped over the tops and popcorn that littered the concrete stairs.

Deacon, Dante, and Levi stood at the end zone, dressed as EMTs, and Axel sat behind the wheel of the ambulance behind them, ready to take off at the first sight of injury. It was the only way they'd been able to think of to be where they needed to be. There was no potential for a second shot if Elias missed. The turn of events would flow too quickly for any of them to react and take Egorov out if Elias's bullet didn't find its home.

Elias had slipped his rifle into the stadium un-detected, and he had a limited amount of time to scout the best location from which to take the shot based on the information they knew about which end zone Egorov would be coming in from.

"I'm in place," Elias said through the comms.

"Ladies and gentlemen," the announcer said over the loudspeaker. "Please rise for our national anthem."

At the fifty-yard line, a full orchestra in black tuxedos and sequin dresses sat poised and ready to play. And with his hands in the air, the maestro waved his baton and music filled the stadium. They'd put tiny microphones on all the stringed instruments so they were amplified through the loudspeakers.

"And the rockets' red glare . . ."

From one end of the stadium red fireworks shot straight into the sky. Deacon breathed a sigh of relief. The fireworks were crucial to their mission.

"The bombs bursting in air . . ."

People's attention was starting to waver from the flag and fireworks as they noticed the giant American flag parachute making its way toward the field. Deacon's breath caught as Egorov masterfully maneuvered the chute where he wanted it to go.

"And the home . . . of the . . . brave."

Fireworks exploded at the other end of the field as Egorov entered the field. And then Deacon saw it happen. He saw Egorov's body jerk as it was hit with the force of the bullet, straight through his side.

Deacon and the others ran onto the field before Egorov's feet hit the ground. His landing was hard, and the crowd gasped as they watched the parachuter's knees buckle and his body crumple to the ground. The fireworks boomed a continual blast, and they were able to shield the body and assess the situation.

Blood bloomed at his side, and Deacon used his body to block the area from the crowd and the news cameras he knew would be on them in moments.

"He's dead," Levi confirmed, feeling the pulse in his neck. "Nice shot."

"Thank you," Elias said. "I'll meet you at the rendezvous point."

Dante went to get the stretcher, and Axel had already gotten out of the ambulance and was waiting with the back doors open so he could help Dante get it out. They lifted Egorov and set him neatly on the stretcher, covering him with one of the thick blankets they used for people in shock.

The blood was more than noticeable now, and Deacon noticed some had gotten on his clothes. They rushed the gurney back to the ambulance and got Egorov loaded inside just as the first news camera made it to them.

They all noticed the black bag strapped to Egorov. And they all noticed how close the bullet had come to going through the bomb instead of flesh and bone.

"Hell of a shot." Axel let out a low whistle through his teeth.

The comm unit in Deacon's ear crackled and he heard the sweet sound of Tess's voice. "That was insane!" she said. "I watched the whole thing on national television and I still have no idea what happened. If I hadn't heard you say that he was dead I never would've had a clue."

"Marry me, Tess," Deacon said. He'd had no idea he was going to say the words. They'd just popped out. But now that he'd said them, he desperately wanted to know the answer to the question.

"I'm sorry, what?" she asked, clearly stunned.

"He said 'Will you marry me?'" Elias said from wherever the hell he was.

"Yes, I believe that's what he said," Dante agreed.

"Y'all shut up," Tess said. "You're ruining my moment."

"Don't mind us," Axel said. "We're just along for the ride."

Deacon didn't let Tess hear his laughter, afraid she'd take it the wrong way. He didn't want to get her temper riled at a moment like this.

"I asked you to marry me," he repeated. "What do you say?"

"Wow," she said.

"Oh, for fuck's sake, Tess," Elias said. "Just give the man an answer. We're all on pins and needles here."

This time it was her laughter he heard over the comm units. "I'd hate to leave you in such suspense. I'll marry you, Deacon Tucker. God help you, I'll marry you."

CHAPTER TWENTY-FOUR

Six months later . . .

Tess walked the long hallway of the second floor, peeking in the finished rooms and wondering if she'd made the right decision.

These weren't the rooms that she'd known since she'd lived there. These were the rooms of a home. The renovations had been finished only the week before, and the top two floors were now as spectacular as the bottom. She saw the swish of a black tail as the cat slunk inside the bedroom at the far end of the hall, but she turned and went up the stairs to her suite of rooms.

The memories there were strong, especially of her and Deacon—as he'd demolished her bathroom, teased her unmercifully, or stripped her bare and made love to her until the sun peeked through the big glass windows.

Her life had been irrevocably changed. She'd seen and done things she could never unsee or undo. She knew the truth. She'd be lying if she said there wasn't fear or doubt. Fear for his life. For hers. For the family they'd make one day.

The only thing that mattered was that Deacon was her home. Wherever that may be.

"Deep thoughts," came a gravelly voice from the doorway.

She turned and smiled at him and held out her hand. His expression was solemn, but he took her hand and squeezed it once.

"They did a good job on the renovations," she said. "Much sturdier," she said, bouncing up and down lightly on the new floor.

It was a good space. The floors had been replaced with gleaming oak, and the wallpaper had been stripped. The walls were a soft ivory, and the ornamental ceiling had been restored to its full glory. The windows let in lots of light, and with the light paint and floors, the room was open and airy and comfortable. The king-size bed sat intimidatingly against the far wall, the duvet soft and white, the pillows mounded up at the headboard. The bathroom and sitting room were equally beautiful and spacious. And she smiled as she saw one of Deacon's T-shirts draped over the chair in the corner. It was still theirs. Only theirs.

"What do you want to do?" she asked.

"I want to marry you," he said. "We've waited long enough. You've won that bet at the Clip n' Curl a hundred times by now."

"I've already told you I'd marry you," she said, looking at the ring on her finger. "Set a date and find a preacher. I'll be there."

"You've been planning this wedding for the last six months," he grumbled. "You made me buy a suit."

Tess rolled her eyes. Men. "Then maybe you should just wait until Saturday and show up at the church on time. It'll be here before you know it."

"Smart-ass," he said, smacking her behind.

"Do you want to leave?" she asked, seriously now. "Do you believe we'll be safe?"

"I don't know," he said, pulling her down to sit on the bed next to him. "I've learned from experience to never take anyone at their word. It's too dangerous. Would I risk leaving if I felt it was the right thing to do? I don't know that either. I worry about your safety. I wouldn't forgive myself if anything ever happened to you."

"So our options are to stay, to make this our home and continue doing the work you've done all these years. To use the funeral home as a front for everything else. Or we can pack our things and start over. New names and backgrounds. A new country. We'll be together and be able to live a life free of the dangers of covert life. But we'll always be looking over our shoulders."

"That pretty much sums it up," he said, his smile wry. "Do you regret loving me?"

"Not ever," Tess said firmly. "I'd do it all again. Deacon, don't try to second-guess yourself or do what you think would be safest. I know you love what you do. It's been your life. It's important. And you're good at it."

His lips twitched and he squeezed her hand. "I want to stay here," he said.

"I know," she said. "This is our home. We'll never

have a normal life, but we can make the best of an abnormal life. We have each other."

"Always," he said. "And plenty of room for children on the second floor."

Her smile was radiant. "You want children? That's the first time you've ever said so."

"Yes. I especially want to make children," he said, rolling her to her back and kissing her senseless. "As long as we never leave them alone with your mother."

"She seems very happy and mostly stable for the moment."

"That's because you moved her into one of those retirement villages. She's got no choice but to be happy and mostly stable. She can cut hair at the little salon on-site and she's got plenty of new people to charm and steal stuff from. It seems like a match made in heaven to me."

"And best of all, she's a thirty-minute drive from here," Tess said, no longer feeling guilty for having peace.

"I promise I'll be at the church on time," he said, nuzzling her ear and working his hand beneath her shirt. He stripped her quickly and settled between her thighs, nudging at her silky folds. "I especially promise not to be late for the honeymoon."

He pushed into her, and her ankles pressed into the small of his back. It never took long for the first orgasm to build.

"Ohmigod, yes!" she cried out and clung to him.

"I'm glad you stopped telling me no," he said into her ear. "Yes is so much better." And then he followed after her into oblivion.

Keep reading for a sneak peek excerpt
from the next mysterious, riveting
installment in the Gravediggers series

Gone to Dust

Available Summer 2017
from Pocket Books!

CHAPTER ONE

She'd captured his heart.

This woman of noble birth—a queen—who'd traveled across vast lands to bring him gifts—to seek his wisdom and knowledge. But it was she who was wise, and her intelligence and cunning enticed him. Never had he met a match such as she. Her presence was greater than any gift she'd laid at his feet.

"You're quiet, my Lord," she said.

He lay on a pile of furs, his chest bare, and a soft breeze stirred the air and cooled his overheated skin. The thin linen sheet couldn't hide his desire as she walked through the shadows of his chambers and came to stand before him, bathed in the soft glow of lantern light.

Her beauty stole his breath—her skin dark and smooth—her eyes black as the rare diamonds she'd presented to his kingdom. The white silk of her robes was tied at each shoulder and plunged deeply—displaying the fullness of her bosom—the material so thin he could see the jeweled adornments covering her nipples.

The silk was slit up each side so every step she took gave him a glimpse of the heaven he knew was hidden beneath. Her hair was her glory, rich and full, and she'd unpinned the crown of curls so it flowed almost to her feet.

"You leave on the morrow," he said, his heart pierced with sorrow.

His body was rigid and stiff with pride. He was king. And he would beg for no woman to stay. But he wanted to.

"I am queen," she said, her smile sad. "My kingdom needs me. My people need me."

"I need you," he rasped, his hand knotted in a fist at his side.

"And you shall have me," she said, moving toward him.

She released the ties at her shoulders and the white silk slithered down the length of her body, leaving her bared before him. His phallus throbbed and his chest burned with desire. She was exquisite. Never had he wanted another woman as he'd wanted her.

The days had turned to weeks, and the weeks to months since her arrival in his lands. But never had she offered herself. The desire had burned between them, the flames fanning hotter and higher as time passed, but he'd respected her wishes to remain chaste in her own bed, though he could have taken her, as was his right as king. And now she honored him by giving him her body.

"You are more beautiful than all the treasures in my

kingdom," he said, his gaze lingering on her full breasts, the lantern light reflecting off the diamond adornments that sent fractals of light glittering across the floor.

"I am your greatest treasure. Long will you remember me. Long will you love me."

He knew the words she spoke were truth. She knelt next to the bed and bowed her head, submitting herself to him. And then she said two words that made him rage at the injustice their positions had wrought.

"My king," she whispered.

"As you are my queen," he said, voice hoarse with sorrow and desire. "We could rule together, combine our lands."

She looked up at him, knowledge and wisdom in her eyes, and his hand moved to her cheek, stroking it softly. "Do you forget the lands between us?" she asked. "That which is ruled by another?"

"I do not forget," he said with a sigh. "And I know you are right. Those are lands not ours to take. To conquer would bring wars that we cannot fathom."

"Then tonight we will give our bodies to each other. And when dawn comes and I take my leave, you shall know you are well loved."

She took his hand and kissed it softly, and then she joined him on the bed, sliding the sheet from his body and moving over him, so she was poised to take him into her. Their hands clasped and their gazes met, and he knew this would be a spiritual experience, that they would truly meld—mind, body, and soul—with their union.

His jaw clenched and sweat beaded on his skin as her heat enveloped him. And then her head fell back with a moan as she sank down on him. The world spun away as pleasure unlike he'd ever known surrounded him.

His vision dimmed and the incessant chime of a doorbell chimed in his ears.

"A doorbell?" Miller Darling said, shaking herself out of the scene she'd been writing. "What the hell?"

She narrowed her eyes and tried to put herself back into the world she'd created, but a familiar, atonal chime echoed through the house. She snarled and her head snapped up at the interruption. She was going to kill someone. No jury would convict her. The sign on the front door clearly said *Do Not Disturb*.

She hit save on her keyboard and headed out of her second-story office, stubbing her toe on a box of books she didn't remember putting directly in the walkway. The pain was fleeting. Her anger was too great.

Her footsteps pounded heavy against the stairs as she raced toward the front door and the unsuspecting victim who continued to ring the bell.

The click of the deadbolt seemed unusually loud as she unlocked it with indignant righteousness and jerked the door open, only to have it catch on the chain. She closed it again and undid the chain, muttering under her breath at the wasted opportunity to make a real impact on the intruder.

Miller stared into the startled eyes of the UPS man, ready to flay him alive. He was tall, thin, and pale, his sandy hair thinning on top, and his cheeks were red from the blistery wind and cold. He held a package and an electronic clipboard in his hands.

She was pretty sure she growled at him. The last week of a deadline was the *wrong* time to disobey the instructions on the door.

"Geez, lady," he said, eyes wide. He took a step back and beads of sweat broke out over his upper lip. "Are you sick or something?"

"Or something," she said, eyes narrowed.

She wasn't sure when she'd showered last, but she was pretty sure she'd been wearing the same clothes for at least three days. Maybe longer. Her gray sweats had coffee stains on them and what might have been a smear of jelly from a PB&J she'd slapped together—minus the peanut butter because she hadn't had time to go to the store.

She wasn't wearing a bra, but it was hardly noticeable beneath the fuzzy red bathrobe her best friend Tess had gotten her for Christmas about a dozen years before. There was a small package of Kleenex in one of the pockets of the robe and a mega-size box of Milk Duds in the other.

"The sign says *Do Not Disturb*," she said.

"You've got to sign for the package." He shrugged as if he hadn't just ruined her entire day, and then he held out the package and clipboard for her to sign.

She ignored the gesture and took a step forward. He took another step back. "I'm not sure you understand what I'm saying. I don't care if you're delivering gold bullion or the electric pencil sharpener I ordered three months ago and never received. The sign says *Do Not Disturb*. Do you know how long it's going to take me to get back in the mood?"

His eyebrows rose and his mouth opened and closed a couple of times. "No?" he said, phrasing it like a question. He was starting to look scared. Good.

"That's right. You don't know," she said. "Lovemaking like that can't just be performed on a whim. It takes preparation and the right frame of mind. I had the candles lit and the music playing, and she was about to ride him like a stallion. You've set me back hours at least. How would you like it if someone kept ringing the doorbell right before you were about to have an orgasm?"

He swallowed hard and dropped his clipboard. "I . . . I wouldn't." He bent down to pick it up and then shoved it and the box at her once more. "I'm sorry for interrupting. But you're the last house on my route. I've got to get it delivered and signed for so I can go home."

She sighed and scribbled her name in the little box and then took the package. "Next time do us both a favor and sign it for me and put it on the rocking chair. I won't tell anyone if you don't. And I also won't want to kill you, which is what I want to do now."

"I appreciate your restraint," he said, swallowing again. "Sorry about that. I guess I'll uh . . . let you get back to . . ." He gestured with his hand, and she realized what he thought she'd been doing and what she'd actually been doing were two very different things.

"I'm a writer," she said by way of explanation.

"Right," he said, looking skeptical.

She ran her fingers through the rat's nest on her head and two pencils fell on the porch. Her shoulder slumped in defeat and she turned back into the house, leaving the pencils on the ground and dead-bolting the door behind her. The UPS man was still standing there. He was probably reevaluating his career choices.

There was no point trying to get back to work. The moment was broken and the mood was gone. Besides, she'd had the opportunity to smell herself and feel the rumble in her stomach. A shower was in order, followed by whatever she could find to eat in her kitchen. Writing wasn't a pretty profession. When she was in the trenches of a story she often forgot to tend to day-to-day life. Sometimes, the story took hold of her and wouldn't let go, and that's where she'd been the last several days.

She tossed the package on her entryway table on top of the mail that had been accumulating for the past week. Her housekeeper, Julia, came in every Tuesday and Friday, but she knew better than to knock on her office door and disturb her, so she put the mail on the table and cleaned around her office. She also made sure Miller didn't leave the coffeepot or stove on and burn the house down.

The mail was the least of her worries. The bills were all done automatically online, so she assumed anything in the stack wasn't urgent. She caught her reflection in the mirror as she headed back up the stairs and had to do a double-take because she thought a stranger was following behind her.

"Yikes," she said, grimacing.

She looked bad, even by her usual definition of deadline-crazy. She needed desperately to get her roots done and have her color touched up. It was rare she kept it the same color for a long stretch of time, and it was currently black with bright blue highlights. She looked like a cross between the Cookie Monster and Don King.

Her face was pale and there were dark circles under her eyes. She couldn't remember the last time she'd been out in the sun or to the gym. And Lord, her eyebrows needed a pair of tweezers.

Since work was over for the moment, she decided to do damage control and transition back to human again. When she was writing, she could stay cooped up and alone for days without noticing, but eventually she'd feel the loss of human interaction. She was a people person. Watching them and being around their energy always filled her with ideas and creativity. And maybe that was just what she needed to get back into the groove of things and not leave her poor characters on the verge of orgasm. She'd been there. It wasn't a fun place to be.

Maybe that's what she needed to get back in the mood. It had been weeks since Elias Cole had left her high and dry, and her pity party had lasted long enough. Sex was sex. It was a natural human function, and she could always call up an old boyfriend or two and see if someone would be willing to scratch her itch.

It didn't matter that the only person who came to mind was Elias. She knew her own ego well enough to understand that the reason she couldn't get him out of her head was probably because they'd never done the naked tango. Fine. He'd changed his mind and it was time for her to move on.

She hurried the rest of the way up the stairs, her mind on him instead of the work she was abandoning, despite the mental pep talk she'd just given herself. The majority of her adult life had been spent writing the romances women dreamed about, but Miller was more practical than that. The kind of love she wrote about—that soul-deep connection to another person—wasn't something she expected to find for herself. It wasn't something she *wanted* to find. That depth of love could be devastating, and it wasn't worth taking the chance. She much preferred for her relationships to be fun while they lasted, for the sex to be great, and to part as friends in the end. She'd never had her heart broken, and she had no plans to.

Her parents had loved each other with the same focused obsession that they'd loved the treasures they'd sought their entire married life. From her earliest memories, the stories of King Solomon and the Queen of Sheba were part of their daily conversations. Her bedtime stories had been filled with tales of adventure and temples of treasure. And of the love of two people who spent their earthly lives knowing they could never be together.

It had broken her heart as a child to think of what it must have felt like to know a part of their soul had been missing. Her father had always told her that's how he'd feel if he had to go through life without her mother, and Miller had decided as a young child to never subject herself to that kind of heartbreak.

Her parents had spent their marriage traveling the world, searching for the lost temple and piecing together a history that the greatest books in the world hadn't achieved. And it was her older brother who'd been burdened with the responsibility of taking care of her. He was four years older, and probably the last thing he wanted to do was babysit his younger sister, but that's exactly what he'd done. He'd been her only stability as a child, an adult long before he should've been, and they'd always been close. He'd never resented the fact he'd been stuck home with her when he'd wanted to be hunting treasure alongside their parents.

After a few weeks, her parents would come back full of excitement and stories of their adventures. And more often than not they'd have some trinket that had supposedly been housed in the temple where King Solomon kept his treasures. She had a box full of them in her office. It was sad to think her best memories of her parents all rested in that box.

Her brother had eventually left home and joined the military, much like her father had at his age, but the obsession with a three-thousand-year-old king and the queen who would never be his must've been hereditary, because Justin had taken up the search, and it had only intensified after their parents were killed when their small plane went down.

Their obsession with each other and the love of two people in history had led to their death. And she hadn't seen her brother in close to ten years, though he sent letters like clockwork. All she knew was that kind of love and obsession had left her without her parents and a cynicism she worked hard to keep out of her books.

Miller had a good life, and normalcy was very important to her—at least as normal as one could be when making stuff up was how she made her living. To say she was a control freak was probably an understatement, but she liked knowing she was responsible for her own happiness and achievements. Her work fulfilled her. And the occasional relationship satisfied her.

It wasn't often she found a man she was intrigued enough by to invite to her bed. She was damned picky actually. She wrote romance novels for crying out loud. So what if she wanted great conversation, a smoking hot body, and great sex? She'd never seen the point in settling. And since she didn't believe in the happily-ever-afters she wrote about, she figured her chances with a man like Elias Cole were a done deal. He hadn't seemed like the kind of man who was interested in happily-ever-afters either. He'd all but ravished her on her front porch and then calmly walked away, leaving her more sexually frustrated than she'd ever been in her life. But the past was the past. It was time to let it go.

She shivered as she walked into her bedroom and she turned up the thermostat on her way to the bathroom. Her bedroom was tidy—the king-size bed neatly made and all her clothes folded and put away. She hadn't felt the mattress beneath her in days. She'd been taking catnaps, crashing on the couch in her office when she needed to recharge.

Miller loved color, and the bedroom reflected that.

The bed was like a white cloud, but pillows in cobalt, teal, and turquoise added vibrancy, along with a crocheted throw using all the colors at the foot of the bed. The large canvas on the wall was an abstract ocean scene using thick layers of paint, her bedside lamps were blown glass in the same bright blue, and the cozy chair in the corner was yellow with thick blue stripes.

It was her favorite room in the house, and that was saying something because she loved all of her house. But this was *her* room, and she'd never invited another man to share it with her. Except that night when Elias had taken her home and made her lose her mind with his kisses. He would've been the first to see her private sanctum. And she didn't want to analyze too closely why she'd chosen him, when she'd never had any desire for another man to step foot there.

Most people in the small town of Last Stop, Texas, considered her eccentric, and many of them had much more creative names for her. She hated to not live up to people's expectations, so when the Gothic home on the corner of Elm Street and Devil's Hill went on the market, she snapped it up in a heartbeat. And she got it for a steal too because no one wanted to touch it.

It was the house that had scared the bejesus out of every kid in Last Stop for the last century. It was the house that sat dark and looming, so people made it a point to always walk on the *other* side of the street instead of passing directly in front of it. It was the house with the creaking gate and the overgrown rosebushes, and it looked spectacular at Halloween. She never passed up the opportunity to help solidify her reputation by adding a little graveyard in front or sticking a voice box in the bushes that let out horrible moans. The house was rumored to have been haunted by Captain Bartholomew T. Payne and his wife, Annabelle, after old Bart had decided he'd rather see his wife dead than leave him for another man.

Miller had always been fascinated by the story, even though she'd yet to feel the presence of the original owners of the house. She rarely had visitors other than her friend Tess or her cleaning lady, so the outside was rather deceiving. Even with fresh paint and repairs done to the sagging porch and leaking roof, it still gave off a menacing presence.

She loved every square inch of it, and she would *never* move. The house fit her personality like a glove, and she cackled every time she peeked out her office window to see kids scurrying across the street and staring at the house in wide-eyed horror. It was the little things in life that brought joy.

She sighed as she passed the bed. The soft sheets were looking a little too enticing. She couldn't afford a comfortable sleep. Not until the book was done. If she got in that bed it might be a week before she woke up. It was important she keep her energy high, so she'd shower and dress, and then she'd go find some company—and if she was lucky, a sexual pick-me-up—before sitting back down at her desk and getting back to work.

She stripped out of her clothes and considered throwing them in the trash instead of subjecting Julia to laundering them. Julia was a single mom to five boys. She not only cleaned Miller's house, but a few other houses as well. Then she cleaned the schools on Saturday, and the church on Sunday evening. Miller could only hope that the laundry of five boys was worse than that of a writer, though she wouldn't have bet money on it.

The pipes creaked as she turned on the water in the claw-foot tub, and while she waited for it to heat up she found an extra box of hair color under the sink so she could tackle her roots. By the time she'd gotten the color on and her head wrapped in plastic, the water was hot. She lit the candles on the windowsill and dimmed the lights, and then she tossed a bath bomb in the water and hoped the smell of roses was strong enough to overpower the smell of deadline.

An hour later, her skin was pruny, her roots were dyed, and she smelled a whole lot better. She blow-dried her hair, moisturized her face, and put on double the concealer she normally would because she could've slept in the bags under her eyes.

By the time she got out of the tub, she was exhausted. And the sexual pick-me-up she'd considered didn't have any appeal at all. Her mind was still stuck on Elias Cole.

"Ridiculous man," she muttered.

Instead of a night out on the town, she decided to drop by and visit Tess to convince her to have a girl's night. Those didn't happen that often anymore since Tess's marriage to Deacon Tucker. They were still in that honeymoon phase of their marriage where if they weren't working, they were rolling around naked on whatever surface was available.

Miller was only a teensy bit jealous.

She put on black leggings, a sports bra, and an oversized gray shirt that warned people if they annoyed her they might end up in one of her novels. People always laughed, but she'd been known to kill off the occasional annoyance in one of her books. Comfort was the name of the game for the evening's activities. She'd give her brain a quick break, and then get back to business.

Miller hopped on the bed and struck a quick pose propped against a mound of pillows, and then she held up the latest release of one of her good friends. She took a selfie with the book and then uploaded it to Facebook, pimping her friend. The great thing about social media was no one would know she'd worked ninety-plus hours in the last few days, eaten nothing but carbs and chocolate, and drunk an unhealthy amount of coffee. She wouldn't change things for the world, though she needed to hit the gym very soon so her behind wasn't as wide as her chair. When it came to her readers, she'd continue to put on double layers of concealer so they'd see the fun and glamorous life they wanted her to live.

She stuck her head into the massive master closet and dug out a pair of black ballet slippers. Organizing her closet was on her to-do list, but she hadn't had time to get around to it. Along with the thousand other things on the list. She grabbed up her dirty clothes and robe, embarrassed to leave them for Julia to find.

Her stomach rumbled again and she bounded down

the stairs, making a stop at the laundry room and dumping the clothes in the washer. She hummed as she measured the soap and turned on the hot water, and then she added a little extra soap just to be safe.

The pile of mail on the entryway table caught her attention and she scooped it up, taking it with her to the kitchen. Unlike her friend Tess, Miller used her kitchen for actual cooking, so everything about it was functional, from the hidden cabinets where she kept her small appliances, to the wine refrigerator in the big butcher-block island, and the pot filler over the stove.

She dumped the mail on the island and then opened the refrigerator. A bottle of ketchup and a cold pack she sometimes used on her eyes were the only things on the shelves. It'd been a while since she'd had a real meal, and even longer since she'd been to the grocery store.

She closed the refrigerator door and saw the note beneath the magnet in Julia's handwriting.

You need everything. This is no way for a grown woman to live. You'll get scurvy. Make me a list and I'll get what you need when I come on Tuesday.

"I could be dead of starvation by Tuesday," she said.

At least she didn't have to go to the grocery store. The only things worse than going to the grocery store were visiting the gynecologist or getting bad book reviews.

She went through the mail quickly, discarding most of it as junk. Then she turned to the package. It was a plain brown box, no bigger than the length of her hand, from her wrist to the tip of her fingers, and just as wide.

There were several layers of brown tape around the box, so she grabbed a knife from the block on the counter.

Her name was written in neat block letters and a PO box was given as the return address, but there was no name at the top. She slid the knife under the layers of tape and lifted the flaps. A small envelope lay on top, and she recognized her brother's handwriting immediately. He'd been sending her letters just like this one from the time he'd left home. He'd never trusted email. But he'd also never sent her a package before. Her days of collecting the trinkets of Solomon and Sheba had ended when her parents had died.

She pulled out the envelope and set it on the counter, and then emptied out the rest of the contents of the box. Something weighty and wrapped in tissue paper fell into her hand, but it was the clank of metal hitting the counter that grabbed her attention.

She picked up the heavy ring with the large purple stone. Within the stone was the carved insignia of the king she'd been told stories about her whole life. King Solomon and the Queen of Sheba had been her family's obsession.

And despite her resentment of the tales and adventures that had broken her small family, the obsession had become hers. Because now she was writing their story, hoping that putting it on the page once and for all would finally give her freedom.

It was her brother's ring, given to him by her father, as it had been given to him by his father. There was nothing in this world that would've made Justin send her his ring. It had been passed down from father to son for more generations than she could count. And if Justin never had a son it would go to her son, though she had no plans of having children. The ring was priceless. And it was always to be worn by the living male heir. Which meant for Justin to not be wearing it was more awful than she could imagine.

Cold fear clutched at her belly and her hands shook as she took the tissue paper in her hand and slowly unwrapped it. When she got to the contents inside, her mind couldn't process what she was looking at.

She dropped the package and took a step back, her hands clammy and bile rising in the back of her throat. In the middle of the tissue paper was a human finger. She had a sinking feeling she knew why her brother no longer wore his ring.